Betty Villeminot is the author and co-author of numerous books and films about Australia. In 1956, together with Jacques Villeminot and with the encouragement of Professor AP Elkin, she had the opportunity to spend a number of months with Aboriginal people of the desert who had been only lightly touched by Western civilisation. This first encounter, followed by others, completely changed her perception of the world in which she lived.

Andrew Riemer lives in Sydney. His books include *Inside Outside*, *Sandstone Gothic* (a memoir of academic life) and *Hughes*, a study of the career of the art critic Robert Hughes. His translation of Anouar Benmalek's *L'Enfant du peuple ancien* (*The Child of an Ancient People*) was published in 2003. He is the chief book reviewer of *The Sydney Morning Herald*.

Alcheringa

ALCHERINGA

The Eternal Dreamtime

Betty Villeminot

translated from the French
by Andrew Riemer

D
S
Duffy & Snellgrove
Sydney

Published by Duffy & Snellgrove in 2004
PO Box 177 Potts Point NSW 1335 Australia
info@duffyandsnellgrove.com.au

First published in 1997 by Albin Michel as
Alcheringa, Le Temps du Rêve éternel

Distributed by Pan Macmillan

Cover design by Alex Snellgrove
Cover photograph by permission of
the National Library of Australia
Typeset by Cooper Graphics

Printed by Griffin Press

ISBN 1 876631 94 5

visit our website: www.duffyandsnellgrove.com.au

Foreword

I was about to turn fifty and was headed for Cambodia when Andrew Riemer approached me with a request that I write a preface for his English translation of Betty Villeminot's novel *Alcheringa: The Eternal Dream-time*. With the manuscript in my backpack, I was contemplating the fascination that French explorers had for the Mekong River and Angkor Wat during the nineteenth century. It was French explorers who brought the grandeur and mystery of Angkor Wat back to the attention of Europe. They were captivated by the Mekong not just for its majestic passage through the flatlands of Indochina but also because they were seeking a route into southern China which might offer big trade possibilities. When Betty Villeminot came to Australia two centuries later she did not find any Angkor Wat but she was equally fascinated by the grandeur and mystery of the local population's religious sensibilities. She did not expect to find any new trade route but she too was possessed by the landscape she encountered.

It is a bold undertaking to place before Australian readers the translation of such a novel in these times. When Helen Garner was turning fifty, she observed that there was the special problem of embarrassment for writers wanting to explore the spiritual depths, regardless of whether this was being attempted across cultural divides or not. Garner observed, 'People are embarrassed about religion, they're embarrassed about God, they're embarrassed by religious imagery and angels and ideas of redemption and salvation. The people I'm thinking of want materialism and realism, and if that's not what you've written this time, they'll bloody well distort your book till that's what they get out of it – anything rather than read what you're actually trying to say.'[1] Such readers would be very frustrated with this novel because there is no way it can be rendered from a materialist or realist perspective.

Villeminot's central character, Nari, is an Aboriginal man who ends up in police custody. In fact, he ends up swinging by a noose of his own creation in his dark cell, but not before he takes us on a mystical journey connecting us to the world of his ancestors and giving us his people's perspective on the strange new encounters with the white man. It is a brave undertaking for any writer who is not Aboriginal. Perhaps only a foreigner would dare. There are some tasks that can be performed only by visitors or which can be undertaken with greater forgiveness and forbearance offered to visitors. The novel is refreshing in that it is the white men and the very few white women who do not have names and faces. They are the ones who all look the same. They are the ones with underdeveloped characters in the script. The reader is introduced to a vast array of Aboriginal actors with names, faces and discrete character. Each has their own way of relating the fresh assault of white contact to the activity and presence of the Ancestor spirits. Villeminot is able to evince fecund descriptions of the vegetation in the harshest environments without grounding the narrative in any identifiable part of Australia. The story line is all too familiar. It is the frontier in all its aspects: explorers meet Aborigines, cattlemen poison waterholes,

---

1 Helen Garner, 'On Turning Fifty' in *True Stories*, Text Publishing, Melbourne, 1996, p. 141

land grabbers infect blankets with smallpox, farmhands take Aboriginal women, missionaries come doing harm while thinking they are doing good, and Afghan Camel riders come being neither white nor Aboriginal. In the present, the prison guards are almost parodies of themselves. But this time, this is only the beginning of the story. The real story is the Aboriginal interpretation and proactive response to these triggers in the storyline.

It is the all too familiar story-line that gives Villeminot the licence to explore the spiritual dimensions of those who are radically grounded and uprooted at the same time. Being a foreigner, she cannot be dismissed as a land rights advocate disguised in novelist dress. She can be forgiven for making the amoral whites simply part of the background for the action of the novel which is the psychological and spiritual search for meaning beyond a present. This search is disrupted by foreign actors who have no moral sense of what they are doing and therefore no openness to dialogue even if there were no language barrier. The parts of this novel that work well are those that bring the past and the spiritual perspective to life in the present as an Aboriginal community wrestles with the real and material challenges thrown up by wholesale dispossession, rape and murder. Passive presence in the new post-colonial order cannot lead them again to transcendence. In the slightly moralising tone of the last chapter, 'To achieve that, they would need to participate physically, with their bodies, dancing to the appropriate rhythms. They would need songs, with the cadence and sonority inherited from the Knowledge of the beginning of Time. These alone have the power of allowing human beings to escape the evils of the temporal world'.

Nari leads us down a past spiritual path that permitted such an escape. He leads himself into a future only at the end of a noose. Villeminot is so respectful of what she has uncovered of that past path that she, as the other, leads us to the space in the prison cell where it is only for Nari and his kin to show us the way back to a future where we are not merely rational beings limited by our individualism and material circumstances.

The descendants of the creators of Angkor Wat have suffered dreadfully in recent generations recovering from the scourge of the Khmer Rouge. Angkor Wat stands as material proof to them and the foreigners that they carry within them this capacity for transcendence. Without an Angkor Wat, Nari and his kin have their dance, their song, their story, and their ritual. Like Angkor Wat, these need recognition and repair. This French writer has roughly mapped the territory of recovery in this novel, taking us beyond the real, material white world, straining to reflect faithfully something of the spiritual, transcendent, black world, rendering more comprehensible and wasteful the option of the self-made noose as the only way into the new world where the song, the dance and the initiation into the group bring escape from the malicious temporal world. This translation is welcome because it renders the work accessible to those whose ancestors enacted and experienced the shattering of the eternal dreamtime. Without religious sensibility on both sides, Nari and his guards will be resigned to the noose being the one sure action providing access to this eternal dreamtime.

Fr Frank Brennan SJ AO

Preface

In all likelihood, this book found its origins several decades ago in the Central Australian desert. At the time, I spent several months there with Aborigines who had experienced almost no contact with outside influences. Once I had gained their trust and after I was accepted by the group, I was able to observe ceremonies in which I saw women weeping with extreme emotion and the men's faces transfigured by the effects of a transcendental faith; I watched dancing of a surprising emotional impact, admired sacred designs which revealed disconcertingly modern symbols. I witnessed the manifestation of paranormal forces, the existence of which have also been vouched for by Australian anthropologists.

Since that time, I have been convinced that these proud desert-dwellers, who led a nomadic or semi-nomadic life, were in no sense trapped in the past but had simply evolved differently from settled people.

Some little time ago, the West began to accept the notion, no matter how ancient, that humankind had been presented with several evolutionary choices, which it exploited at the prompting of one or another of the brain's functions.

Settled people, by embarking on a relentless struggle against the environment in order to make it conform to their needs – with well-known consequences – would have exploited the positivist imagination, suppressing the mystical aspects of their mental make-up. In doing that, they would have severed their links with the cosmos, and, through lack of opportunity, strayed from true spirituality. Such a suggestion raises, in turn, the ancient debate over the nature of revealed religions: do they represent progress or a regression of spirituality?

Unlike settled people, the first Australians would have allowed the positivist imagination to lie fallow in order to cultivate the mythic to its limits, developing a sensorial intelligence influencing the 'soul', poetic creativity, rendering them receptive to what is transmitted by other forms of life as well as by mineral matter and the stars. Out of this emerged the remarkable richness of their myths and legends, comparable to those of ancient Greece. Anthropologists have gone as far as to say that this civilisation allowed for the emergence of individuals who, according to the level of their initiation or of their imaginative capacities, think that they have entered into a dimension infinitely superior to that of individuals constricted by the ego; individuals fully able to answer Jung's question: what is the world, and what am I?

Such an outcome would have been possible thanks to the growing maturity of the human psyche – little tarnished in this instance by material worries and swathed by the waves of unspoilt nature – and would have led, as well, to the emergence of intuitive knowledge. It is, without doubt, such an intelligence that acted as a guide for Aborigines in their observations and comprehension of the intricate rules governing all living things and allowed them to elaborate the structures of an extremely intricate sociocultural system. It was necessary, consequently, to wait for the development of information technology and its analytical resources to grasp the entirety of its construction; it seems, therefore, that only a mode or reasoning close to that of modern mathematics could have created it.

Doubtless, such a social organisation would not have improved human nature, but it would have obliged people, in an unfailing manner, to respect the ethical imperatives of their society. My investigations into this field brought me face-to-face with the notion that here was the creation of a great civilisation and not that of 'subhumans' as the early colonists called these people and as too many white Australians still think of them. Later visits confirmed this impression.

I then witnessed their despair and the destruction of their way of life. Accordingly, an unexpected urge drove me to write this book in order to add my contribution, no matter how tiny, to a better understanding of these Australians who had undergone a unique experience in isolation from the rest of the world; for me, a migloo from elsewhere, but in command of observations culled in the course of time, and of those of some noteworthy anthropologists, to attempt to shatter the negative image which still clings to Aboriginal civilisation.

I quickly realised that only the story of the transformation of my central character into a 'True Man' then into a 'Man of High Degree' – Medicine Man – could allow the remarkable man he had become to be comprehended. For that end, it was necessary to describe the different stages of this lengthy transformation, that is to say his experience of a number of initiatory trials.

Other nomadic people have been familiar with similar trials in the past, despite some variations, and some of these cannot but bring to mind those endured by certain great initiates of world-wide fame, such as Buddha or Jesus, to name but two.

Even though all these ceremonies have been described in numerous studies readily available in Australia and Europe, and even though some investigators are of the opinion that their true secrets have never been revealed, I hesitated for many long years over publishing my manuscript, out of respect for Aborigines. Then, all of a sudden, I grew convinced that this book might be of some benefit for them, even if only in the long term. That is why *Alcheringa* came into the world.

Nevertheless, I invite Australians of Aboriginal descent to consider these matters or to seek the advice of their leaders – the Men of High Degree – before starting to read this novel.

1

Early afternoon. The dry, parched air of the red desert of Australia seeps through the roof of a lock-up, filling the interior with even greater heat. Nothing stirs, except that, now and then, a fly buzzes around. It rouses Nari, a black man with a white beard, who is stretched out, with his arms crossed, on the floor of a prison in the back of beyond.

Nari opens his eyes, looks wearily at the walls around him, raises his head and, in a harsh voice, utters a few indistinct sounds. Then, yearning to sink once more into the oblivion of sleep, he lets his head crash violently against the beaten earth.

But images rise from the deepest recesses of his being, stirred up by the turbulence of these last days. Fragmentary images of his adolescence, of his childhood; even more remote images, mingling myth and reality. Then his memories fall into place, clear and precise.

'No!' the man murmurs. 'No more memories!'

With a final effort of defiance, he turns his head from right to left, makes his body grow stiff. Protracted moaning escapes his lips. But, too feeble to continue struggling and stifling a last sigh, he lets his muscles relax. Memories wash over him. Staring vacantly at the beam above him, he allows visions of his people's life to unfurl in front of his mind's eyes. Visions of a Dreamtime he had believed to be eternal.

I am about ten year's old. For several weeks now, I have been walking in the desert with my mother, my father and his blood relations. These are my other fathers, my other mothers and their children, who are my brothers and sisters. As our fancy prompts us, as we are making for one of our sacred High Places, where the Great Assembly, the yearly reunion of our people, is about to be held. There will be many boys and girls of my own age; the prospect fills me with excitement.

In the evening, lying close to the fire we have lit for the night, I am unable to go to sleep. I am gazing at the flames from which Tumenti, our Man of High Degree, has just driven out the manus, the powerful dingo-spirits who are most partial to the flesh of the little children they capture whenever one of them strays too far from the glow of the fire.

My naked body is curled up in the sand, which still retains some of its heat. I snuggle up against the warm bodies of my relatives and our four dogs. I watch as the shadows spread out over the endless plain. I listen to the total silence, the superb silence of the desert. Above me the Southern Cross and so many other stars, the entire Milky Way, sparkle with a pure white light. I am at peace.

'Look. Bahloo, the Man Moon is plump again. Once more, he has eaten too much,' Batalja, one of my elderly fathers, whispers to me.

'Do you think he will die again?'

'Without question. In time he will grow thin again, then he will disappear, killed by his own greed!'

'So the night will stay dark forever?'

'No, no! The Man Moon is not like human beings; he has not lost the skill to return to life in the same body. A little time after his death, you will see that a tiny piece of his skeleton is going to appear. It will shine on us with its faint light. Night after night, that little bone will grow and, as it grows, its light will become brighter. Until the Man Moon returns to life. To illuminate our nights with his cold light. He is a splendid Ancestor. Too greedy, but he keeps good faith. Do you know that before the birth of Okerka, the Woman Sun, he alone shone down on us human beings?'

'Yes, I know. Tell me about the stars now.'

'The stars, our Ancestors who have climbed into the sky. They seem pretty close to us this evening.'

'Why don't they come down to see us?'

'Oh! It's been a great while now since travelling between sky and earth came to an end! It's a long story. A solemn story which we will teach you later on.'

'When? Tell me when?'

'After the beginning of your instruction into manhood, which will lead you out of the condition of a small animal. Just for now, listen to this fine story yet again. Once up a time, during the Night of Time, the men of the Maludaianini people were always looking for ways to seize women belonging to others. You know that that's forbidden. There were bloody combats. And those combats did not cease, as should have happened, with the first injury or the first death.'

'A violation of one of our Great Ancestors' laws!'

'A grave violation, certainly! Because they were guilty of such sacrilege, the Maludaianini were banished to the sky; there their men became the stars of the Milky Way and their women the nearby stars. At the same instant, a terrible prohibition was imposed on earthly beings: they lost every possibility of travelling between the sky and the earth.'

'Before that time, could you walk on the stars?'

'Yes. You could. For a long time before this calamity,' my elderly father went on. 'You cannot imagine for how a long time, some of our Sacred Heroes were sent on quests into the sky. Therefore they could not return to earth. Those that had accomplished great feats worthy of commemoration are still sparkling there, transformed into stars. Look at the brightest star just above your head. Do you see it? That's our Ancestor the Grey Falcon, and those other, smaller stars around him, those are his lubras. All of them are our friends.'

'Would I be able to speak with the people in the sky one day?'

'You will be able to speak with all those who dwell in the beyond. Later on.'

'But, all the same, I am big enough already.'

Batalja chuckled silently.

'Yes, yes! Great is your body composed of flesh and blood, sprung from the entrails of Waela, our splendid True Woman. But the seeds lurking in your head are still quite small. It will be necessary for us, the True Men, those of us who are endowed with Knowledge, to make them sprout, then spread, so that the other part of you might be born. Those things are invisible, impalpable. It will take a long time. For the moment you are incomplete; you are still in your cocoon, not yet a butterfly! Go to sleep now.'

Dear Batalja! He was always so patient with me!

I forget about the Ancestors soon enough. I hear the cry of the curlew calling its nestlings, which had been driven high into the sky by burning scrub, the legend says. I turn this way and that. Waela, my favourite mother, the one who bore me in her belly, fed me with her milk, who thought the world of me, places a calming hand on my thigh.

The old black man is relishing the last of the images to have struck the eyes of the child he used to be before sleep closed them that night: he sees once more the shape of a dingo at the top of a mound, outlined against the white light of the Man Moon. The wild dog moves forward, agile and silent, soon to merge into the starry blue of the night. This is his personal Dreaming, because they both share the same Great Ancestor. The Man Dingo, one of the Giants of the Dreamtime. Each of them is obliged to help and respect the other. Remembering the calming, comforting sense the sight of his 'brother' brought him on that evening so long ago, the prisoner sighs with yearning, turns on his left side and continues living in the past once again.

'Yes, that's it,' he murmurs with a sigh. 'With a few little twists of my body I sink a little deeper in the soft and fragrant sand. Waela has put a kangaroo skin on top of me. Soon, I am overcome by a sense of well-being, all the more welcome because of the cold all around me, suddenly much more biting. I can at rest at last, deliciously content.'

The mornings of those days! Mullyangah, the morning star winks at us, bidding us farewell. The gugurgaga breaks into song to encourage the day that is about to be born. On the horizon, a faint golden glow announces that Okerka, the Woman Sun, daughter of the Thunder, is leaving the land of the dead, where she has dwelt throughout the night. Soon, swathed in the gift of the magnificent red cape she received there, she rises slowly above the immense, dark plain still cloaked in darkness. Plants shine with the hoar-frost that fell from the sky, as the numberless little clumps of sparkling ice, with which the seven Makara sisters adorn themselves, begin to melt with the first rays of sunlight. These sisters, I was told, are young women of extraordinary beauty, with wonderful golden hair cascading over their bodies; I love looking at the seven stars they form in the sky. I try to imagine what their faces are like.

I love the dawn. It makes me want to imitate the song of the morning bird, but Waela insists that if I were to wake the others while I'm having fun doing that, a nasty tooth would sprout above one of my incisors. So I stay mum.

A few gruff words uttered by the grown-ups, who are still stretched out on the ground, break the silence. In the distance, in front of us, the red sand is set alight by Okerka's fire. The icy, crystalline air grows milder. It is charged, now and then, with the scent of plants and then with vapours rising from the bed of a salt lake. I relish breathing them in. In silence, parents and their children observe the return of day. They are grateful to the Woman Sun for keeping faith with them.

My favourite mother stands up and, with a slow pace, makes for a tuft of spiky desert bush. She gathers a handful of dry twigs to revive the embers of the night fire. Tumenti slowly intones the words with which, this time, he drives away the evil spirits of daybreak. Now I feel calm, I am able to get up.

The smell of the burning wood and its joyful crackling enhance my liveliness and high spirits. I place some fat white grubs in the hot ashes, and I move them around slowly with a stick. They are cooked in a trice, and then it's time for the pleasure of tasting them. Around me, none of the grown-ups or children says anything; their hands travel back and forth between fire and mouths.

Then our little group begins to break up the camp, wanting to start travelling before the great heat of the middle of the day. The men set out first, one behind the other, each holding at arm's length, parallel to the ground, a long spear in its shooting stick. Each of my mothers puts her digging stick in a piti, then, with one hand, picks up the wooden platter and places it on her head.

In no way hampered by her burden, her back straight, Nganamana, Tumenti's elderly wife, grasps the end of the largest clump of smouldering wood with her toes; she will take care to keep it alive until our next stopping place. Then, still with the one foot, she covers the fire, for safety's sake, with a thick layer of sand.

Niumta, the other old woman of our group, waits for her, the expression on her face as sad as ever: she cannot get over the death of her son, Guningbal, even though he left us so long ago. Then both of them make for the tall, burnished shapes of their sisters etched against the orange light of early morning. Erect on their long, slender legs, one arm curled up against the head, the other swinging, the women move with the slow but tireless pace of the wanderers of the desert. They separate at times, prompted by a whim, by the need to gather food, confident of catching up with the group again by reading the traces left behind by the footsteps of those in a greater hurry. I run ahead of them with the four other piccaninnies and, laughing all the time, we are soon scattered.

I get bored with the game, so I go over to one of my fathers, he who fed me with his semen when I was still inside my mother's belly. Just then, a smoke signal rises in the east. I love those tall, dense grey plumes that turn the emptiness of the endless sky into a promise of hope, a message to come. Tumenti interprets the signals: my mother's people are telling us that they have three evening camps to go before reaching the ceremonial grounds. At the thought of seeing them again so soon, I whoop with joy, in the same breath as my playfellows Mau and Wongu. We leap up and down, we laugh, we raise our arms to the sky. I call out, for the ears of the youngest and prettiest of my mothers:

'Soon Kamal will be able to sleep with her lover!'

Kamal, who is furious, tells me to make myself scarce and hurls a volley of insults at me. Strictly speaking, her love affair is a secret because it transgresses the stringent marriage laws of our people, and all of our group pretends to know nothing about it; so no one reacts to my provocative remark. Only Nganamana mutters in her low, gruff voice:

'That silly girl will never learn how to soften her anger with a little good humour. What terrible manners! Pah, young people!' she sighs.

I run off with my mates, singing:

'She has lost her tem-per; she has lost her tem-per!'

Then, having got away from the grown-ups, we inspect the little girls with whom we will be imitating the adults' love games this evening.

How much did my thoughts turn to Natati that evening, the prettiest and liveliest of them all! Natati and her way of speaking in a funny little accent!

In little groups of two or three, we start walking again. A grey falcon swoops almost vertically down on us. Its shape is clear-cut, but hardly have we noticed its snowy breast feathers before it is already plummeting like a stone on the prey it spotted from high, all the while calling out its solemn 'cluck, cluck'. As if to greet us. The presence of our Dreaming overhead reveals itself to be a good omen. Adults and children watch the bird of prey as it disappears and, each in their own way, make happy comments about this meeting.

The clatter of chains startles the old man. Then the heavy silence of the stifling day descends over the prison once more. Voices from the past surge again, for him alone.

That of the kind Waela, behind whom he is walking, grumbling.

'Come on Nari, buck up! Go and ask old Nganamana to read the landscape for you. Her stories will make you forget how tired you are. You wouldn't want to be like the people of the north who always live in the one place because their land is so poor that they are forced to grow their food: they plant, they harvest, they plant again. They don't have time to praise their Sacred Heroes. They don't have the time to enjoy all the leisure we are lucky to have!'

Calmly, we make our way in the scalding air of the endless desert, which has now become absolutely flat. Then, as the shadows accompanying us stretch out over the sand, and when the immense flat expanse of the mineral world stretching in front of us is covered by the golden sheath of Okerka's cape, the purple, shimmering, other-worldly image of the mountain range, where our sacred site lies concealed, abruptly cuts off the horizon. Late tomorrow, we will arrive there.

A substantial waterhole gives life to clumps of palm trees and some low scrub. The sight of all that greenery fills us with joy, because wallabies and kangaroos like to come there to rest; lizards and snakes abound; at dusk the rock python arrives to spy on the wallaby, the small kangaroo, which is often preceded by a solitary emu.

Other groups have arrived before us. They have

found places on either side of the site, so marking the division of our people into two moieties, Sparrowhawks and Grey Falcons. Wiltjas, simple humpies made out of branches, have already been erected and fires have been lit. And the sounds of happy conversations reach us.

I am a little anxious about meeting all my relatives. Because for each strand of relationship there is an appropriate manner of behaviour and way of speaking. Will I be able to remember them?

The women arrive with their pitis piled with the various kinds of seed, fruit, berries or eggs they found during the day. Mangala, the almost-dead, is mightily proud of the bee honey she collected from the trunk of a tree with a reddish sap, but her smile fades when she catches sight of Nganamana arriving with a large quantity of ant honey.

Two of my mothers go off a little way to dig yams up with their sticks. I see Lamanga, helped by another of the women, digging in the ground at a spot to which the tracks of a monitor lizard had led them; in a few moments, they force the animal out of its lair and, as it rushes out, stun it with a blow to the head.

Laughing, I am running around with my friends among this throng of relatives.

We rush past a group of men who are discussing something, squatting on their heels around the embers of a fire at a little distance from the rest of the group. Not far from them, Tumenti takes a large piece of a plug of wild tobacco, ground with ash, from a cleft in the rock-face; he had hidden the tobacco there on a previous journey. He goes back to his friends to share it with them before sitting down in his turn. He catches sight of us and shoos us away with his hands. We guess that they are making up teams of hunters who will set out to kill large game for the feasts to come.

I already know that at sunset they hope to spear a solitary emu, after making it drowsy with a sleep-inducing powder sprinkled over its usual watering place. I also know that the Wise Men of the two moieties of our people are going to meet to discuss how to go about these preparations. Other teams will be formed. Some will go in search of ochre, indispensable for the ceremony to be held in a secret place; others will make for a creek to gather the leaves of a cycas palm, necessary for the preparation of brews and certain sacred ceremonial objects.

A little later, the last group of my father's relatives arrives. I only have eyes for Natati. Natati, whom I will never marry because, like me, she belongs to the Grey Falcons.

As I am walking beside her, I remind myself what Kokalja, whose personal Dreaming is the dingo, the same as mine, told me. We are Dreaming-brothers, the most important relationship. He studied for a long time, much longer than my father Djingili, who is not very bright. At last he is going to gain the right to get married. He cannot marry Kamal, whom he loves, for even if the Dreaming of the moiety of their people allows it, one of their personal Dreamings, their sexual Dreaming, forbids it.

Once upon a time, he told me, people got married without rules or regulations, without bothering about their respective Dreamings, mingling two sometimes incompatible Memories of Alcheringa Time! 'You cannot understand this yet, before you have received Instruction,' he told me. 'But understand that that lack of care, extended over the span of time, caused them to grow most aggressive, very ugly, physically and morally; they wallowed in irresponsibility. To save our people, one of our Great Heroes created strict marriage laws. And it turned out that our unions came to constitute a single great family. That is why you have many mothers and fathers who indulge you and console you whenever necessary.'

My playfellows' shouts bring me back to reality. Each recounts the amorous secrets of relatives whom he had surprised by spying on them. And I laugh along with them when one of them tells us about the forbidden adventures of an old man with one of our pretty young mothers. Because of these amusements, which they are unable to control, the grown-ups are wary of us, as much as they are grateful to us, for they know well enough how to worm secrets out of us whenever the need arises.

We gambol around the camp, we stop in front of a large clump of sundew, the flesh-eating plant of the desert. We watch how insects are attracted by the sparkling liquid seeping out of the end of each filament, and how they get stuck, as soon as they land, to the small round leaves covered with green hooks. As soon as they start struggling to escape, they make those hairs close over them, and they disappear, eaten alive by the juices the plant begins to excrete straight away. That is what our mothers told us.

Bored soon enough by the spectacle, we run off to set free a female kangaroo one of our fathers brought here in a net, in order to replenish the game in this region. When we come back, we gorge ourselves on the little transparent balls, as sticky as they are tasty, of a parasitic plant growing on a tree.

Tumenti, walking by, calls out to us to make sure that we don't make ourselves sick. And whispers to me, for my ears alone:

'Don't forget to observe everyone carefully so that you can learn how to recognise their character. One day, that may be of benefit for you.'

That I should observe others closely seems to be my grandfather's obsession! Waela says that he has great ambition for me.

Exhausted by our games, we decide to go back to our elderly mother Nganamana to ask her to tell us a story. We come upon little Inoa, who is in tears as he is gazing intently at the sand, searching for the footprints of one of his parents. We would like to help him, but he finds them before we do, and goes off, all cock-a-hoop, placing his little feet where the people he is looking for passed by.

Nganamana begins to tell us a story about fire.

'Once upon a time,' she says, 'a woman called Karakaruk possessed fire. Because, in the old days, women possessed Knowledge.'

'Women possessed Knowledge? What kind of a story is that?'

'I am telling you the truth. They even knew all the secrets of our ceremonies, the ritual objects, the songs and the sacred words. One day, it was a very, very long time ago, our mothers generously allowed the men to get hold of these secrets for they had realised that their fathers, their brothers and their husbands would never be content as long as they felt that they were useless. And it must be said that at that time men did not amount to much. That's why the women said: "Let's share our secrets with them. What does it matter, since we have Knowledge. We will always remain the ones to give spirits human shape." There, that's what happened. Later on, the men will explain all of this to you at greater length. Let me go on with my story. Karakaruk, she wasn't generous. She kept the fire for herself, not at all concerned for her kin, who were often cold and got sick from eating raw food. But Wang, the Man Crow, hatched a plot to get it away from her. He knew that the woman Karakaruk was very fond of ants' eggs. So Wang created a large number of snakes, which he hid beneath an anthill. Then he invited Karakaruk to come over to dig up the eggs she liked so much. As she was digging, Karakaruk found the snakes. Wang told her to kill them quickly with her firestick. And sure enough, Wang grabbed it from her.

'You see, my little ones, selfishness and greed make people stupid.'

'Pah!' we cried. 'Your story isn't very funny at all!'

And ran off to join the other children.

Okerka, the Woman Sun, is approaching the land of the dead. As she makes her way through the sky, she drapes flimsy veils over the rocky outcrop, turning the softest ochres into the deepest red, before abruptly casting the dark blue herald of the night over the world.

I gaze at the immensity of the sky, which is adorning itself with ornaments for the night. All around me, the red glow of the many fires dances joyfully and makes the darkness less painful to endure. Families visit one another. News are passed from one fire to the next; they are discussed at great length.

And now the joyous sound of the tjirmukmuk breaks out, the game in which adults relieve the tension of their daily lives by vigorously throwing all kinds of things, food, whatever comes to hand, at the faces of others; they speak to one another in a mocking tone, using coarse words, words entirely forbidden by the rules of courtesy and politeness in everyday life! I am shocked to hear Waela uttering a crude remark about Ngargala's sexual exploits to her face: but everyone laughs, I realise that I must do likewise. I hear Djingili making indecent suggestions to his mother-in-law, with whom he is in love and to whom, in ordinary circumstances, he should not address a single word.

Lovers pair off and, adroitly, vanish into the infinite darkness of the night. The desert, rich in invisible and silent life, echoes for a long time with the sounds of human beings who, tomorrow, after this fugitive time of licence, having abandoned their inhibitions in this way, will accept without rancour or complaint the burdensome duties of their everyday life.

Why is it that I retain such a clear memory of that period of my life, the old prisoner wonders, seeing that from the time I was born I lived in the same protected world, knew the same joys, the same mocking words that are the sole punishment reserved for children? I took part in many another devout wandering over the land because, throughout each year, we made our way from one sacred place to another, as our beliefs demanded.

Now a large piece of quartz surges in his memory and revives old recollections.

We are playing, tracing stories in the sand. Around us, men and women are busy making preparations for the ceremony. Using the same gestures as their parents, their grandparents, their great-grandparents, the very actions that have been theirs since the beginning of Time. Or very little different. Some are fashioning everyday objects; others, hidden from sight, are making sacred objects for the ceremony. Their trust in the rites to come, which are intended to preserve the world here below in the image of the parallel world of the Dreamtime, is unconditional. And the game of tjirmukmuk has cleansed them of the petty little harassments of their daily life. They find themselves once more in a state of perfect accord between trust and understanding. The wave of happiness mounts as the preparations draw near to completion. The site is filled with the sounds of extraordinarily joyful voices, much more so than usual, increasing the exuberant noise the children are making.

All of a sudden, Tumenti cries out, his voice filled with surprise of an entirely unprecedented kind. Standing opposite one the Sparrowhawks, he is looking at a lump of quartz the man is holding in his hands. Quartz of an unusual colour, it strikes me. Their lively discussion attracts other adults. We go over to watch. Slithering between their legs, I manage to get close to the long, strangely coloured piece of stone. One after the other, men and women pick it up respectfully, and then let go of it, fear etched on the faces. I did not think that quartz could be such a pronounced and transparently green colour. I see that it is perfectly round. One of its ends is smooth and flat, the other, ending in a narrow elongation, hardly thicker than a thumb, is pierced with an opening. Tumenti leans down to gather some of the red sand in the palm of his hand, then allows it to sprinkle through the aperture. We see it trickling down, almost to the bottom of the hollow stone. Tumenti repeats the operation until the stone is almost filled with sand. The perfection of the shape of the cavity matches that of the outside.

'With such a rigorous symmetry, this can only be a shell,' Tumenti says.

Everyone around him agrees. An unknown kind of shell? It is hard to believe that no one had ever seen one like it or heard tell about it! Has it really come from one of the tribes of the east, close to the sea? Had it been sent down by those who dwell in the sky? Or is it an evil object, abandoned there out of malice or for revenge? Slowly, the men and women drift away, not knowing what to think. Mashubi, one of the Sparrowhawks' Men of High Degree, goes over to Tumenti, near whom the owner of the strange shell is standing. The latter explains that he got it from one of his trading partners among the people of the east in exchange for an armband. That person is related to him by marriage, though belonging to a different people, whose sacred sites extend as far as the seashore.

'What do you think?' Mashubi asks Tumenti.

Lost in thought, Tumenti pours out the sand, strokes the 'shell', which is smoother than a woman's skin, murmurs an incantation intended to neutralise potential evil influences, and whispers:

'Bah, I don't know what to make of this! Better exchange it as soon as we reach our next bartering place on the path of the Woman Kangaroo. It is never good to keep a possession too long, but this one perhaps even less so,' he mutters, handing it back to its owner.

That was my first encounter with a bottle, the first stage in the long tale of my downfall.

2

Nari, the old black man, is startled when the gaoler comes into his cell to put a can on the bench. The guard glances at the prisoner, telling him to get up and eat his dingo stew.

His eyes staring, the old man doesn't move a muscle.

'Don't want it? All right, leave it. And keel over!'

The prisoner shudders, makes his body grow stiff, then waits. How could he eat the flesh of a dingo, the flesh of his Dreaming-brother? The violation of one of the strictest prohibitions! As unthinkable as eating human flesh! Besides, how could he swallow anything, trapped as he is between these walls where he can hardly breathe! Hunger does not make him suffer. Is he not a Great Initiate? Mastering the needs of his body no longer holds any secrets for him.

The gaoler shrugs, turns to leave, fastens a large padlock and goes to sit down with the other prison guard.

'What's up with these apes? The old man hasn't had any grub for more than three days! And the other one for even longer! Really! Why don't we just kill them like we did before? Why drag before a court people who aren't really people? When you say something to them, they don't understand you, or no more than animals do!'

'Isn't it a bit dangerous to be so categorical?' his colleague replies. 'Certainly, the bishop insists that they have no concept of ownership, and that clearly puts them at some distance from human beings who have, generally speaking, a much too developed sense of it.'

'What's that supposed to mean?'

'That they have no personal possessions, that, setting aside our rifles and axes, they want nothing, that they keep nothing of whatever white people give them.'

'All right then. For me that's proof enough that they are beasts!'

'Perhaps you're right. The two experts who spent time among them claim that none of their beliefs could belong to a religion. But I too, after what happened to me, have no religion. I am no less of a man, for all that!'

'Yeah, you're a man, but not like those who came on shore with me as convicts! You have a peculiar way of talking. Where do you come from? What are you doing here?'

'I was accused of a murder I hadn't committed. My sentence was commuted to transportation.'

'It's true enough that they shove you in prison for a crust of stolen bread! To make money for themselves!'

'Maybe. In my case, I rotted in prison, surrounded by rats, until they sent me here, to the other side of the earth, to the end of the world.'

'To the end of the world? You mean hell! It's true, you're no longer on the earth in this godforsaken hole! Have you looked at the countryside? Here or at the coast, it's always the same. Nothing looks the way it does at home. Trees that aren't green, with upside-down leaves, turned at an angle so that they give you no shade. Rivers without water, or ones that have too much water, but only once a year if all goes well! And daylight that's snuffed out like a candle in the wind, seasons back to front! If you can talk about seasons seeing that leaves never fall, that it gets cold only at night! This is hell, I'm telling you. Not to mention the animals. No rabbits, no hares. Not a stag or a doe. And what about those fucking kangaroos, where did they come from with those back legs that are too long and the front ones too short! I've heard that they don't carry their young like animals do at home! That their kids are born in pockets under their bellies! All that's enough to scare the life out of you. I tell you, I'm scared stiff! When I think of what I've had to put up with to get here! I dreamt of going ashore straight into prison in a nice enough country! Chained for so long in the hold of that blasted ship where everyone carked it! For this!'

'We all went through that before reaching this continent. You and I, we've survived the trial, then we were set free, we should be content. It's true that in this country there's only ugliness and deformity. I too am sometimes filled with dread when I find myself all alone among these unknown trees and plants, surrounded by colours I've never seen. I have the feeling that I am on another planet. However, I want to stay here because, as a zoologist, these unfamiliar animals fascinate me.'

'Zoologist?'

'Yes, someone that studies animals, how they are constructed, their behaviour. No scientist had the least notion of the existence of so strange a fauna as of this land. Sometimes I think I'm dreaming, that I've landed on a Noah's ark at the beginning of the world!'

'Right. I don't understand everything you're saying. Your scientists, if they knew nothing about these animals, do you think they would have known that these people, like our prisoners, are not quite human, not quite animals? Blackfellas ugly enough to scare the daylights out of you, loafers, not even able to do a little work for a few pennies. There are no people created by God around here!'

'Perhaps so. Perhaps God has entrusted us with the task of civilising them. As for me, I say again that it isn't these poor wretches that interest me, it's the animal life of the continent. I wonder whether there aren't fossils to be found, like the platypus which was discovered around 1800; something that stirred up such a dispute in the London scientific world when they received a stuffed specimen. They thought the taxidermist had played a joke on them. I've just had a letter from one of my former colleagues telling me about the storm that broke out because of a telegram sent from here by some scientists to the meeting of the British Association for the Advancement of Science in Montreal. By the way what year is it? 1888 or 1889? I've lost all sense of time. That telegram announced that the echidna lays its eggs and suckles its young in a pouch that doesn't appear until the moment the animal gives birth. It took a century to discover that link in the chain of evolution! At the prospect of having to revise their systems of classification, which they thought were definitive, the experts almost went mad! So you see how much interest the animals of a place you call hell provoke in Europe! That's why, once I was set free, I arranged to come to this remote place. I'm certain that I am also going to discover—'

Abruptly, the man falls silent: head tilted back, mouth open, his companion has just set about snoring mightily.

'Poor fellow, he really can't stand the heat!'

In the cell, the smell of the soup has stirred up the flies which, by their dozens, are swarming to feed, buzzing noisily. On his own again, the old black man sighs with relief. He turns on his back once more, stretches his limbs. With his long, slender fingers, he wipes the blood seeping from the wound on his neck. A wound made by the iron neck brace which chained him to other blacks for many days. Touching the warm, sticky liquid takes him back to the past.

So he has become a pubescent boy again, sensible enough for the Wise Men to being to transform slowly the invisible body, still in its larval state, dormant in his brain. A second gestation, aided by the men this time, a gestation much longer and more painful for him than what took place in his mother's belly. This masculine gestation should succeed in awakening the memory of the Ancestor of the Eternal Dreamtime he had once been, which still slumbers in the innermost depth of his being. Memories which only the True Men, the wise ones, have the power the bring to life again. For that end, over the course of many years, they impart true Knowledge to young boys, imposing numerous moral and physical trials on them. With the sacred songs they engrave on their minds, with the physical and moral suffering they impose on them to force them into greater self-knowledge and into accepting themselves for what they are, they help them to climb back, once more, to the time where they will discover, with greater or lesser acuity, a little of the Knowledge of what they were at the beginning, a shard of the memory of the world. For to know is to remember again.

The prisoner remembers. He has just sat down with Wongu and Mau, not far from the old Nganamana, who is busy grinding wattle seeds. He is holding a round, milky pebble in his hand, which glows softly like the light of Bahloo, the Man Moon. He rolls it in his palm to see how it catches the rays of sunlight. A little boy crawls towards him on all fours, with hand stretched out to this wonderful discovery. With a rapid movement, Nari snatches it from his reach, then, just as brusquely, holds it out to him: an arrakuda could have come down to punish him for not knowing how to give spontaneously. Then, to console himself for his loss, he acts like a grown-up:

'I'm giving it to you, that way you won't be jealous of me. As for me, I won't be afraid of losing it, and that way everyone will be happy. Now, go and give it to Wongu. Off you go!'

Babbling away, the baby goes to give it to a grown-up. Nari smiles in a snide way, glancing at Nganamana, who sees and understand it all: he has denied her the pleasure of telling him yet again that keeping things for yourself only brings trouble, irritation or bad luck! That we must pass things around.

He forgets about the pebble quickly enough to dream once more about Julumggul the python, one of the most important Ancestors of the Dreamtime.

For some time now, his mothers have been constantly telling him that the snake has noticed his foreskin and is looking for an opportunity to eat it. This morning, that worries him more than usual. He tries to imagine the trial in store for him. He pictures Julumggul in numerous ways. He is afraid but also impatient for him to arrive, because he does not want to be left with an overlong penis, that would be ridiculous.

Wongu's laughter cuts short his reverie. He goes over to his friends, who are tracing stories on the ground. He thinks up a new adventure about three hunters setting out to chase a giant kangaroo of the kind that used to exist once upon a time.

All of a sudden, the children stop playing and, as one, turn in the direction of an unusual noise. Several of their fathers, spear in hand, bodies covered in ritual designs, have just rushed into the camp. Instinctively the little boys know that they are looking for them to take them to Julumggul! Without waiting for confirmation, Wongu stands up and runs off to look for the women's support.

Just as unsure of what will happen to him, Nari does the same.

He bumps against the first of the mothers he runs into, old Nganamana. He clings to her belly, burying his head between her long, warm, comforting breasts. He wants to stay there! Just as he remembers doing the first time he was really frightened!

The men go over to them: rather brutally, they separate them from their accomplices and hold them by the shoulder, pressing them against their bodies, which are covered in symbols the boys had never seen! Symbols of an unknown potency! They shudder when their skin comes into contact with these paintings that give the men a most disturbing smell.

Alerted by their cries of fear, the women, who had carried them in their wombs, run after them, each armed with a shield and a spear, with which they menace the abductors. Women bearing arms! This unnatural, unthinkable fact increases the young adolescents' panic! Surging from everywhere, other women, also armed, mingle with the first group. All the women form a circle around the men, who nevertheless do not let go of their captives. The drawn-out, sorrowful sobbing of the old women, who have stayed crouching by the fire, the sharp yelps of despair from their mothers and sisters, mixed with the babies' cries, increase the young boys' terror! All the more, because, through their tears, they can see the women striking their skulls with stones, as they do when there is a funeral. Who has died? Or rather, who is about to die? An idea is born in their minds, as searing as lightning: each of them is sure to be led to the land of those who have vanished!

Indifferent to their state mind, the men hold onto them with one hand while waving the other around to chase the mothers away. In this heightened atmosphere, the young boys' terror reaches fever pitch. They begin to shake.

Suddenly, the circle of women breaks up. All walk away slowly, as if indifferent. Even their favourite mothers turn away without looking back. Then their despair is boundless! Their mothers are abandoning them! Can it be possible? For the first time in his life, each of the boys feels all alone in the world, as if he had been thrown into a nest of venomous snakes! Their shivering increases, to subside soon enough when their kidnappers speak to them affectionately.

There follows a long time spent in the bachelors' camp, far removed from where the families are camping, each of them under the protection of an educator appointed to instruct him.

The old man is still able to hear the joyful voice of Ibala, his young uncle, who has become his master, as he utters the words he himself will speak much later on to other children.

'So there you are! You have just left the world of women, the world of little children. The end of your indulged childhood! Playing with little girls! Here you are now embarking on the path of study and trials which will make you rediscover the memory of who you once were during the Eternal Dreamtime; studies which will make you into a whole being, worthy to enter the world of the True Men. A long and difficult path! But have no fear, your stay here will not be filled with hardship. Not the least in the world!'

In the suffocating heat of the prison, the old man smiles as he remembers how reassured he felt. And how proud he was of having set foot in the world of men!

He hears the kindly voice continuing:

'Look, in a few days the paperbarks will be in flower. That signals that the geese are about to start migrating, because this flowering tells them that the water lily tubers in the billabongs of the north are coming to maturity. It signifies too that the bee is about to produce the most fragrant honey and the time for harvesting it is drawing near. It is necessary for you to know that we rely on the immutable cycle of the multiple forms of life. That of the stars which influences the fecundity of animals and plants, of plants which play a part in the lives of birds and insects, enticing them by flowering in a certain region or, by contrast, in another.

'You understand how important it is to know the precise characteristics of every kind of plant and every kind of animal in order to make use of them while also taking care to preserve them. Their only means of maintaining their generosity towards us, so that our life as endless wanderers may be perpetuated. A life composed of long enriching journeys and ample leisure.'

It is true, the old man thinks, it was at that time that I began to sense that I was a part of the Great Whole, it was at that time that I developed my powers of observation without which, Ibala told me, our land, so much loved, so generous, would have seemed to me a huge emptiness.

The voice from the past continues:

'As you know, you are composed of two bodies, one visible, the other invisible, the latter still slumbering. At this first stage of your formation, it is the former you must learn to know fully, in order to be able to exploit all its potentialities. Believe me, that will only come about through strenuous training of the faculties of all of your senses, a training to make all your muscles resistant but also, and above all, through the development of your power over your own self. Learning to safeguard, whatever the circumstances, a moral sense as hard as flint.'

The old man goes on hearing Ibala's voice and silently repeats those words which remain so sweet in his memory:

'To travel the long path which will make a complete man of you and make you enter into the world of the True Men, that of the wise ones, you will rise step by step on the difficult rungs leading to Knowledge. Without Knowledge, our life would be nothing but painful frustration, even more trying than all the trials you are about to endure. Instruction is the same for us all, but we do not all achieve it with the same success. Some, despite their good intentions, do not reach the last stage of their formation. Others, on the contrary, complete it with ease. In the course of their years of study, they will shed their animal carapace which, until then, prevented their human nature from emerging in all its glory.

'Some wish, at times, to continue in their search for Knowledge. After long years of solitude, of meditation, they climb even further into the Memory of Time, they become therefore men of great skill and are admitted into the company of the Men of High Degree. Like your grandfather Tumenti, they become outstanding thinkers endowed with exceptional powers.

'At your age, the word Knowledge does not signify very much. Understand well enough, though, that without it your life would resemble that of an animal that only knows how to drink, eat, sleep, propagate its kind and enjoy its life! Remember that well.'

The memory of Ibala's serious face makes the old man smile tenderly. He sees again his instructor falling silent for a long while, throwing a dry root onto the little fire, next to which they were squatting on their heels, before continuing:

'Listen carefully because you will need to remember this story word for word. Like all the other sacred and profane tales!

'Once upon a time the land was covered in kwatye alia, salt water. Little by little it was enticed to the north by people who always wanted to own it and to keep it for themselves. They succeeded at last and, ever since then, the salty water has remained with them.

'During the Eternal Dreamtime, at the time of Alcheringa, there was only one form of life on earth. A life without motion, represented by a huge, transparent embryonic mass made up of an amalgam of unfinished creatures, folded in on themselves, the inapertwas. And each of these potential beings belonged to one kind of animal or plant life.

'The fate of humanity was engraved on this primordial matter. All of it! The past, the present and the future of the world was all there, recorded. Remember this, it is most important. When he considered it necessary, He who came from nothing, existing only for his own sake, what we call the Supreme Being, changed the shape of that mass. He fashioned a body out of it, arms, hands, legs, a head; on one side of the head he made two openings for the eyes; he fashioned the nose and dug his fingers into it to make the nostrils appear. He made a slit for the mouth and a hole for the anus. That's how the inapertwas were transformed into beings capable of standing upright.

'Each man, each woman remains attached to the kind of animal or plant life from which he or she emerged: that animal becomes their Dreaming. So within every human being, within animals, plants and minerals, the stars and the air, and within water, the Supreme Being, the sacred Energy of Life, spreads its divine essence, causing all forms of Life to merge into one immense family. But, alas, he was summoned to return to the world above, and he did not have time to finish his work. So mankind was born imperfect.

'Rich in the primordial Knowledge from which they emerged, inspired by the divine essence with which they were impregnated, the Great Ancestors, gigantic creatures, neither human nor animal, set out to create the world as it is today. As you know already, all over the immense plain which was at that time our land, they created river-beds, hills and every feature of the landscape. They laid down laws intended to link all of mankind by means of highly intricate systems of kinship, which overlap with one another, rising here to bound up again there, involving all the members of a people in a veritable tumult of mutual obligations, linking them one to another from birth to death; they cast, likewise, similar links between different peoples. Accordingly, from the north to the south, from east to west, all the kinships that were created in this fashion were woven into a kind of vast spider's web, the strands of which guide us and protect us for ever. Then, before vanishing, before the Alcheringa Time came to an end, at the moment when mankind appeared in its actual shape, they said to them: "This is your land. We have created it for you. You will dwell here and it will be your duty to preserve it in the image of the parallel world, the World of the Dreamtime. You will never leave it for you are its Guardians. You are the Guardians of our Creation".'

Ibala threw another root on the embers and continued:

'Now, this fabled past which our sacred tales recount is not, as you might imagine, lost forever. It has become a parallel world, inaccessible in ordinary time, but which, for a few moments, during certain sacred ceremonies, through the power born from song and dance, from ritual rhythms and sacred representation, by means of all those powers that transcend our physical forces, we can make live again; in that fashion we rise again into the Time of Beginning. For, tucked away in one of the deepest recesses of our being, we possess all of the primordial Knowledge. That's why, during rites, all the events of the Dreamtime are reproduced. For the space of an instant, we become once more the one who created himself by himself. For the space of that instant we are the Great Ancestor allied to the Sacred Energy, to the Supreme Being, do you understand?'

The old man smiles again, for he recalls that he had not understood very much. It took him many a long year to learn that story by heart, then to understand it and finally, having become a spiritual guide in his turn, to recite and explain it to other young men.

'You young boys,' the voice from the past goes on, 'you don't remember anything. It's in the course of rituals over long years, in the course of discovering sacred objects and sites, in the course of a long training, long reflection, long periods of meditation that, little by little, and step by step, you will go back again in Time, that you will learn again what it was that you yourselves perhaps created. For, know this, to learn is to go back to the past. These are the physical and moral trials, the isolation, and the meditation that provoke the jolt necessary to make this process unfold. I, a bachelor, your appointed master, even though I have not yet reached the end of the long journey in my formation as a True Man, my formation as Guardian of Creation, have started to remember. That is why I can help you to begin the search for the exemplary model that you were at first.'

The old man recalls how, all of a sudden, he felt more comfortable in his own skin, how much he desired to learn, impatient to recover the Memory, to know which Great Ancestor lay hidden in his small body! What feats he had formerly achieved! In short, what kind of a man he would become when the Wise Men succeeded in making the little seeds locked in his brain sprout, as his elderly father had told him!

He sees himself sitting again at the side of his guide, reciting once more the story of the great disaster which, for a time, made the flowers, and with them the honey of his land, disappear. There are only a few more words to be uttered, and, this time, it will be without fault, without hesitation, with clear intonation.

In an inaudible voice, the old man recites the words accompanying the memory of the day that became for him a landmark in his history:

'Men and Women wept because they had been deprived in this way of their favourite nectar, wept to see their land deprived of its scented splendours. Then, a Hero was courageous enough to clamber up to the summit of Mount Uboo. He slid into the magic circle he found up there. That circle carried him far into the sky, into another world where he met strangers. He asked these strangers to contrive to make our earth flourish once more with abundant rain.

'The men of the other world agreed. They promised that our land would never again be deprived of such beauty. That with this recovered beauty the bees and their nectar would return.'

'Good, but you changed one word in the final part. Start from the beginning.'

At that moment Mauwulan, Wongu's teacher, comes up to them, bursting with excitement, accompanied by one of his trading partners from the far east.

'This is some news that reached me by way of my kinship extending far into the east. One morning, my brother from another people told me, as a group of men were making towards the ocean to fish there, they noticed a winged monster not far from the shore, cradled by the swell. Without trying to find out much about it, overwhelmed by panic, they made their way back to the inland to tell their women to run off, far into the bush, and hide their children.

'Then, mastering their fear, they returned to the endless water and approached the apparition in silence, creeping from shrub to shrub, from dune to dune, dragging their spears flat on the sand.

'When they were certain that they could not be seen, they observed the scene calmly.

'The bird, taller than a eucalypt, more bulky than the largest baobab, had many wings raised vertically to the sky. Beneath the whitish wings, they could make out a huge body that seemed to be made of gigantic scales.

'All along, having inspected it carefully, the men thought that what they had taken for an animal could have been a tree that had risen out of the sea during the night. Prudently, they decided to move further away and to return later to find out what became of it.

'The next morning, the apparition had vanished. After lengthy discussions, after having considered the possibility that the apparition might have been a floating island drifting further south in the course of the night, they returned to their original idea that it was a huge bird, the size of those of the Dreamtime. They walked for many days, travelling to question all the Men of High Degree and the almost-dead among their people. But no one had ever seen anything like it.

'Since then, they have been afraid. They daren't go fishing. They wonder what this bird of the Dreamtime, returning to the world of the living for an instant, might be. They cannot understand its meaning. And, likewise, my own people are asking a thousand questions. They are afraid.'

The old man hears himself asking, in a voice about to break:

'Why will something happen to us?'

'Why? You are asking why!'

For once Ibala lost his self-control.

'Do you not know that if something changes without regard for the parallel world only disaster can follow? The least alteration could unleash a series of disasters, which would mean that, sooner or later, everything would disappear, everything would return to chaos, as it was before the coming to earth of those to whom we owe everything! It is up to us, the Guardians of Creation, to ensure that such a catastrophe will not come. Nari,' he finishes in a calmer voice, 'think before you speak.'

Ashamed, without saying a word, the child drops his head.

During the long night of wakefulness, the winged monster is the only thing to enliven the conversations in the bachelors' camp. The young masters seek in vain for an explanation of this strange apparition. Throughout Time immemorial, the Men of High Degree, their assistants, every Guardian of Creation were able to keep the world intact as it had been created. What could have happened now? Their pupils sense their apprehensiveness. An apprehensiveness which, in the course of their discussions, turns into fear. From that day on, their isolation was harder to endure.

'Yes,' the old man murmurs, 'I remember.'

Sleep eludes him, he ceaselessly conjures in his imagination a new form of that fantastic animal. He examines the starry sky, fearing that the monster might suddenly crash down over the small fire lit for the night.

He searches through his memory for the legends he can recall; sometimes he fancies that it has to do with the Man Brolga coming back to earth; the giant Brolga, half man, half bird, the creator of the moon. Perhaps he was going to create a second star to illuminate the night. But no! It could not be that because birds, formerly superior to men, had lost Knowledge, and along with it their pre-eminence over the other forms of life. It had abandoned them a long time ago. Then it floated between earth and the sky, diffuse matter, impossible to seize. Later, attracted as if by a lover, it cast itself into the bodies of human beings. Now, Ibala says, men must never be unworthy of that infusion, lest, like the birds, perhaps like other forms of life before them, humankind become once again just an insignificant portion of the long strand linking all living things.

No! It could not have been the Brolga.

Was it not, perhaps, the Supreme Being, returning to earth to make human beings perfect? Perhaps he is about to breathe Knowledge into the minds of young boys, perhaps adolescents will no longer have to endure the tribulations necessary for its acquisition! And he fell asleep at last, at the hour when the gugurgaga sends its first peal of laughter into the brisk early morning air.

How could I have imagined, the old man thinks, that other monsters were to follow the first! That out of their belly our invaders would sally forth! For that which had terrified us to such an extent, had kept me awake, was the first sailing ship to be noticed on the east coast. With it the world would in effect change, and the chaos foreseen by Ibala inexorably arrive.

3

In the prison, the two night warders settle down to their work.

'Devil of a country. You die of heat during the day and perish from cold at night! What the fuck are we doing here? Why did they build a settlement here? Nothing will grow, and not even a sheep could survive, with all these stones everywhere, all this red sand – it should be yellow, anyway – all these spiky bushes. And nothing to drink!'

'In fact, the water transport should be arriving soon. Mind you, it's no use being impatient with those Afghans and their camels! They are still a few days away. They have to make a couple of stops, they claim, to water their animals. Real loafers those wogs! Only think about taking things easy! And fuck the English who need water!'

'Me, I don't think of myself as English any more. I was often starving to death in England! Here we're going to build a country where there's much more justice.'

'Dream on! You'd do better to be thinking about the arrival of the caravan. I hope the fleet's brought enough beer for six months. And mail. It's been almost a year since we've had any.'

'I'm not expecting any. You know that the blacks have gobbled up Johnny's cat?'

'What a filthy mob they are! Even lazier than the Afghans!'

'They seem to be sorcerers. I know there are some

people that are scared stiff of them because of that! In England it was much the same, there were lads that could make cattle keel over. And witches everywhere too, even in towns.'

'I don't know whether it's some kind of sorcery, but the blacks around here reckon that one day our station will be drowned by that river of theirs. What river? It's been more than a year since I've seen a drop of water in that river they keep talking about. It's not their sorcerers, moreover, who're going to fill it and make it break its banks!'

'Perhaps. They frighten me. Like their country. Did you know that some blokes from the south turned up here for a couple of days to bore for water? They found a fool's source, a boiling spring. Salty. Undrinkable. So, no water! And no women. A devil of a country! I hear that a mob of fillies will be arriving soon, at long last.'

'You need a woman? One of the blacks hanging around here offered to lend me his for a bit of tobacco! They walk upright, proud as devils, but they lack any sense of morality. Savages, what?'

'Yeah, they're weird zebras. To get back to women, it's true that I need one! But an Abo's woman – I'll have to wait for the urge to get stronger!'

'My word, he seems happy with his lubra, that young fellow who can think about nothing but animals. He says she's nice. I think she makes him happy. Have you seen her eyes? Huge, and blacker and brighter than jet; but deeper, softer, calmer. They make me uneasy! They all have the same eyes as that prisoner who's eaten nothing for I don't know how long. How can he sleep with a woman whose eyes make you uneasy?'

'It's no surprise that he can. He's only interested in animals and in those people, they're more like animals than humans!'

Indifferent to the darkness, to the cold, to his gaolers' talk, the old black man remains wholly immersed in the past.

He has now reached the climax of his first initiation rites. A time so rich in events – which, the better to test the young boys' bodies and minds, take place during the torrid heat of the dry season.

More than the piercing of his nostrils, than the tearing out of a nail or the pulling out of his right incisor, more than the long days of teasing, during which, in order to prove his mastery over himself, he had to remain stock-still while the others jeered at him, it is the period of total isolation that commands his attention.

Abandoned in a distant, unknown place, a disturbing place therefore, left with the parting injunction that he must not utter even a single word, a hard testing of his moral fibre. He hears each of the words one of his fathers whispered in his ear:

'On leaving the world of women, you've lost the life women gave you. So now you are dead. The dead do not speak. We forbid you to speak, from now on, even a solitary word, although you will be on your own.'

The hardship of obeying this command, when lost in the vastness of the place, ears constantly alert to catch a familiar sound! In vain. The great temptation of uttering a sound, one sole sound, to find out if he is still alive. Keeping faith because of the fear of reprisals. And each day, with a little more certainty, the sense that he is dead increases.

Suddenly, the prisoner experiences again the intolerable heat of a particularly memorable day. He is sitting with his initiators around a large fire.

'Fix your gaze on the flames, Nari. No, do not look

away. You must look at the flames without flinching.'

The old man relives the scene with intensity; the young boy who has just been reborn within him cries out in anguish:

'I'm melting away, my body is covered in sweat; I think that I've reached the limit of my strength. I'm going to go blind! I must keep staring more and more intently at the dazzling glow while my whole body wants to draw away from the blaze. But I must stay here, I must not shift my gaze. I must not. The Great Ancestor slumbering within me will give me strength. And I am still resisting. Then, at the moment when I am about to faint, someone pulls me from behind while two of the men extinguish the flames.'

Then my masters lead me to the hot coals and force me to walk with them over the glowing embers. I must not cry out because I still do not have the privilege of uttering a sound.

'The secret of fire will be revealed to you later on. Never forget the harm it has done you.'

How could I forget!

Despite the pain, I am happy. I have just won a victory over suffering. I now know how much my body's capacity to endure surpasses what I believed it was capable of, how my determination to resist weakness has helped me overcome what I thought were my limitations. Something new has just been born in me. Will these be the first inklings of the return of my memory of the Dreamtime?

What revelations were imposed on him in that fashion! What shocks he had to confront! How many victories over his self had he achieved! The old man remembers another trial.

He is carried, stretched out, in the arms of several of his fathers, who are holding him parallel to the ground. They sing as they are carrying him feet first, their faces turned to the sky. Abruptly, he feels himself hurled above their heads. So high that he is hard put not to cry out in surprise as much as in alarm. No sooner have they caught him than they hurl him up again. Once, twice, ten times. Are they trying to send him into the beyond?

He falls into their arms once more, and his whole body grows tense, ready for a new despatch. But nothing happens.

'We have just introduced you to the invisible world, to prepare the way to the Dreamtime.'

A wave of relief, then of great joy overwhelms him.

The prisoner rapidly skips over certain periods of his adolescence. His mind dwells on the day when, disguised as a newborn, curled up in the hollow of a giant shield, he is surrounded by a multitude of torches, their tall flickering flames distorting the faces around him.

'You are in the belly of the Men,' one of the masters of the ceremony whispers to him.

A flint tool in his hand, one of his maternal grandfathers crouches over his pubis. The young boy he has become for the instant masters an upsurge of fear by biting a little more strongly on the small bundle of twigs Ibala has poked between his teeth. A sharp pain runs through his member. Blood flows between his legs, strangely warm and viscous.

'Scream!'

He lets out a long, piercing cry which is immediately followed by the chanting of the men and the unsettling sound of the didgeridoo.

Here he is stretched out on the ground on his stomach, on top of a heap of hot ashes. His maternal grandfather bends down to whisper to him:

'You are about to emerge from the body of the Men, just as you emerged from your mother's body. You have screamed in the way you screamed when you left her entrails. And the blood you have lost is the blood of your rebirth. In cutting your foreskin, your wondubu, your maternal grandfather, has snatched you from the world ruled by women, just as you were separated from your mother's belly when your umbilical cord was severed. You have just entered the world of men. From this instant on, little by little, they are going to transform you into a new being. As your mother transformed the spirit that entered her body into a creature of flesh and blood. Rest now. Prepare your body and mind for the Great Communion which will make you unconditionally accepted by the Guardians of Creation. The trial of blood.'

When he has not yet mastered his fear, they make him stretch out on the ground, tough not without difficulty. Two of his fathers are standing over him, their legs apart. He sees them driving long spikes under their sex. Straight away, blood flows, large drops, warm and soft, falling on his body. Before he is able to recover from his surprise, the dry rhythmic sound of struck sticks rings out; a stirring chant rises, accompanied by the sombre, hollow sound of the didgeridoo, resonating right inside his belly.

With a rapidity and strength that amaze him, the two men raise and lower their feet in rhythm. Above him, legs, thighs, erect sexes leap, mingle, and vanish like lightning in front of his eyes; his lips, his eyes, his thighs are smeared with drops of blood. Eventually, the two dancers stop. But two others have already replaced them; and the chanting and dancing continue above his body. And the fluid of Life splashes over him more freely. For what seems to him an eternity!

'Swallow calmly,' his father says, handing him a small receptacle. 'This is our blood. It bears fragments of the memory of each of the Great Ancestors of our people, whom we represent, fragments of the sacred Energy of Life, the stream of Knowledge in which the visible world is bathed. Drink, so that our memories may mingle, so that we may ascend together towards Alcheringa Time, so that we may become for an instant the Beings we once were, and that for a moment the past, the present and the future may flow into one another. Drink, for it is in our blood that the new being which you will become will have its birth.'

The warm blood trickles down his throat. Soon his stomach is in revolt. But he dare not vomit! He must not, because that would bring about the death of his mother, his sisters and his father, the last of whom is whispering to him. To avoid such a calamity, he keeps his head and chest straight. The young boy swallows back the bile surging inside him, tries to breathe between two bouts of retching. Blood trickles down his chin, his trunk, his thighs. He sees the men drinking after him, sprinkling themselves with blood, splashing and tipping what remains into his mouth. He is in a trance, ready to faint. Finally his father puts the dish down. He is aware of the thick liquid filling his stomach, which seems to churn around with the smallest movement. The stale taste lingering in his mouth makes his gorge rise anew. His body is going to reject this fluid, no matter how sacred it might be! With one last effort of will, he stops himself from vomiting.

In the afternoon, he drinks, time and again, the blood of the Great Ancestors. And the next day, it goes on! As soon as he is able to get his breath back, someone pours, once, a second time and once again, warm, thick blood over his body. Slowly, the sacred fluid coagulates, wrapping his whole body in a second black skin: the Men's placenta. By dusk he feels thoroughly exhausted. His father leans over him and murmurs:

'We are leaving you; remember everything you have been taught; concentrate with all your might; meditate for a long time and perhaps you will begin to remember.'

Here he is now, alone in an unknown place, his body covered with a black crust, so nauseated, so terrified! His fatigue has, nevertheless, conquered his fear. He falls asleep.

The next day, he no longer belongs to the tangible world. He cannot return yet to the world of the living, for the gestation of his yowie, his invisible body, is far from finished. Throughout the rest of the dry season and for a great part of the wet, he is going to live, successively, in the sacred places impregnated with the Knowledge of various Ancestors. He will be taught the customs, then the mystery of things. When his memory will have succeeded at last in registering perfectly the many legends, numerous myths and sacred stories it had carried there, he will have to learn and relearn the secret language, the language of signs, the code of certain words and the meaning of numerous symbols.

Yes, the old man thinks. It is during that time that my austere way of life slowly transforms me into a somewhat less futile creature, that I become more and more aware of the important role I will play later on, more and more aware of the sacred nature I am in the process of acquiring. How impatient I am, then, to reach my goal! Each day, my desire to learn grows more ardent.

It is at that period that a strange dream is sent to me. Yes.

In my dream I am Wyungara, the Great Hero with the magnificent physique. I am so handsome, adroit and courageous that the two wives of old Nebel beseech me to become their new husband. I agree, and all three of us go away. But in the evening, the wronged husband contrives to set fire to the humpy where we are sleeping. We just manage to escape the flames; we take flight in the dark, making for the lake. Our footsteps resound mightily because we are giant creatures. In order to be sure to escape from my enemy, I decide to climb into another world. With my barbed spear, I hurl a rope high into the sky. I can hear my wives following behind me. The ground amplifies the sound of their steps, a harsh, clanging sound, unknown down here. They catch up with me. We climb the rope as far as the sky. At last we are safe. There we turn ourselves into three stars.

Nevertheless, the sound of footsteps goes on echoing in my mind, approaching, so loudly that I wake up, still greatly moved. I stretch my limbs. In the silence of the desert around me, the noise increases, muffled, rhythmic. It seems still to be drawing nearer. I have never heard anything like it. My imagination is on fire. Is it a being from the Dreamtime, huge, neither man nor animal, that is coming, as it used to happen in the old days?

Reality brings me back to myself. What horrifying trial must I now endure? Ear to the sand, I listen to the noise reverberating in the ground, louder and louder, coming nearer and nearer. I feel the dry air stirring above me. I lie flat on the ground, unable to make the least movement. A strange smell invades my nostrils. And at the same time, the thrumming stops. The smell becomes more pronounced, absolutely unfamiliar. A smell from the world beyond, I am convinced. I dare not lift my face, which I've buried in the sand. All my limbs are shaking. But nothing happens. I risk taking a sidelong glance, but very quickly close my eyes again. To open them once more.

By the wan light of the moon, I see an incredible creature standing in front of me. I shut my eyes, thinking that I am still dreaming. I bite my fist before taking another look. But the same image strikes my eyes once more: an enormous beast, with hide redder than the red kangaroo's, a creature larger than the largest of the kangaroos; with a long and bloated body, a body supported on four huge paws, each ending in a peculiarly large and elongated horn. A tail no less strange, which sways right and left, seizes my attention; beneath the trunk, two large bags, from which hang two huge teats, entrance me for an instant. Then an enormous head leans down towards me. I see two large nostrils; warm breath spreads over my whole body. I fight back the desire to flee, thinking that this is without doubt another test of my courage and self-control, from which I must emerge victorious. I manage to sit up.

The animal gazes at me, softly and reassuringly, with its huge eyes surrounded by long lashes. It lifts its tail and drops a clump of steaming dung, the likes of which I have never seen! The peculiar smell grows stronger. The beast stays still, standing near me, apparently waiting for something. Suddenly, it lifts its head and from its jaw, which has a very thick tongue inside it, there emerges a deep, lugubrious sound, which goes on for a long time, in the way that the wind in a storm sometimes goes on and on; a sound that resembles the kind of sounds human beings make, a little like a sigh!

A spirit, a spirit starting to speak to me! Panic overwhelms me this time. I leap to my feet, letting out a howl. The animal turns tail, disappearing behind a clump of bushes. My fathers and brothers, who have probably been hiding not far from me, rush to my side. Unable to speak, I point with my arm at the foliage. They run over there, stop, raise their spears only to lower them straight away, unable to decide what to do. I see the animal making off with the strange gait of its four feet; and the ground, once more, sends out the weird sound I heard in my dream.

The men come back to me. Ibala takes me in his arms. The others speak about the apparition, making the most unlikely suggestions, discussing it for a good part of the night.

None of them could have guessed that we had just met our worst enemy: a cow, the first of the millions of heads of cattle which were to spread out over our land to deplete our waterholes, to rob the kangaroos of their food, and, in a word, to bring famine amongst us.

4

The silence of a clear night, sparkling with all its jewels, shrouds the little prison in the back of beyond. The calm is shattered, for an instant, by a short bark, by a drunkard, who is returning home late and swearing at the top of his voice, or by a distant woman's laughter.

One of the guards takes the bunch of keys from the wall and goes to look at the prisoners.

'Better go and have a look, there might be another one of them dead by now. I don't like sleeping under the same roof as the dead.'

Nari's stillness troubles him. He stares at the man's body. Not a muscle moves. He prods one of the old black man's legs with his boot, pushes against an arm with somewhat greater force. The man opens his eyes, gazes absently at him.

Relieved, the guard leaves him, secures the padlock, and returns to his companion. Exhausted by a particularly torrid day, both fall asleep and, soon enough, start dreaming of a country which has been transformed, by their memories, into an England filled with beauty.

Unaware of the life around him, Nari continues reliving the past. He is walking along the path to the sacred place of Talrana. That is where the ceremony of the propagation of the kangaroos must be held.

As he is walking, he recalls the skill his instructors implanted in him over a span of time; the High Places forbidden to women and children; some of the secrets and the sacred objects attached to each of these places; the meaning of certain symbols. He does all this in the hope that these revelations, these successive jolts, would trigger in his memory the slow rebirth of the Dreamtime.

They taught him patiently, over the long years, about the traces of the innumerable paths left behind by the footsteps of the Creators of their land. Down the years, the traces of these paths, which cross one another, interlacing from the north to the south, from the east to the west, merging at times with the paths of strangers, have engraved themselves on his memory, becoming a part of his body, in the way that carvings become parts of a rock face.

Then, in the same indelible manner, the lengthy chants which the Creators invented to guide men along each of the paths came to be fixed in his mind. Since then, throughout each wandering, these songs, which the land makes ring out in his people's hearts in rhythm with each of their steps, have been describing every feature of the landscape, each waterhole where glorious deeds occurred; they are true memory threads linking sacred sites. And these sites of worship shine with the virtue and the strength of mind of those who created them. In the flat immensity of the red desert, where the horizon always flees farther and farther away, they form a vast constellation of the world below. In the image of the world in the sky.

Then other sacred songs, inexhaustible sources of contemplation, became familiar to him, also fixing themselves, word for word, in his mind, in as definitive a way as the paths of song.

Nari, the prisoner, is walking in the sun. The rhythm of his steps makes him forget the vagaries of earthly life. Now he is at one with minerals, with plants, with all the living things around him. He has become the Path, rich with all its lives, the Path traversed by something intangible, invisible.

In the evening, his group camps beside a permanent waterhole in a rocky outcrop worn away by time. Plants have taken root almost at the top of the red rock-face, a few steps above the men.

An overhanging ledge, long and wide, allows each family to find a place to build a fire. At the far left of this natural windbreak, a passage between two cliffs leads to a vast cave, often used in the course of journeys in winter. This evening everyone stays outside, facing the immense flatness of this region, where a few shrivelled wattles are swaying to and fro, and also a few tufts of spinifex grass. The men are protected from the violence of the wind. The uproar of its gusts reaches them, muted.

Suddenly, a veritable whirlwind breaks out. In the distance, a mighty churning, a willy-willy, tears a shrub out of the ground and sends it flying upwards in a cloud of vermilion dust. Above the plain, the sky has grown as black as charcoal; not far from the shelter, a white-gum is twisting dangerously. The muffled sound of thunder, the most powerful being there is, creator of the Woman Sun, rings out, draws nearer, rolls, swells, colossal, disturbing, to fade abruptly into the distance.

The spectacle of the brief storm has increased the sense of gentle tranquillity the men are experiencing. The changing light of evening illuminates the large faces of the Ancestors, ochre, red and white, depicted on the walls of the shelter. The play of the sun's russet rays makes them move for an instant, truly alive. They protect the group. And the handprints on the rock, traced by blowing red ochre over fingers, remind everyone that since the dawn of Time, by means of this simple action, their people came to be impregnated with the virtue locked within the protective mineral.

Yes, the old man remembers. That was the day I finished making a boomerang. After passing the wood over the hot coals, I reduced the angle of the curve by exerting pressure at both ends. I've always loved working with wood; the skill of my hands has always brought me great pleasure.

As I am working, I watch Kamal, who is sitting not far from me with a group of women. She has long ago forgotten Kokalja, her first love. For the moment she is playing with her little girl, who has not yet learnt to walk. The child has a yam clasped tightly in her fingers. Singing a simple rhyme, Kamal takes the chubby little hand and holds it against her breast, then points it towards one of her relatives, then another.

'You give it to me, you give it to her, or to her, you give it to all of us!'

Calling out 'Well done', she makes the little fist open; the tuber falls on one of the women's knees.

'Diktali knows how to give! Diktali's such a pretty little girl!'

The baby is passed from arm to arm; she plays with a breast, puts out her hand to grasp a lock of hair, peals with laughter. My relatives smile as they look at her chubby little body, magnificently copper in colour, with a sweetly expressive little face. From time to time they exchange whispered comments. The serenity of the setting sun envelops us all.

My gaze lingers on Natati, who has been for a little while now the wife of one of the Elders; both of them are visiting our group. She notices that she is being watched and raises her large soft eyes to me. We forget the people around us. But her husband has grown suspicious. He stands up abruptly and calls out to me to stop fooling around. And here I am in front of him, trying to make excuses for myself.

Voices are raised; gestures become more and more expressive, with the intention of persuading others. More men are attracted by the noise of the argument; they take one side or another. Young men of my age find this an excuse to put on a show of defiance against the Elders, these old men who are married to young and pretty women and oblige these youths, by the authority their age confers on them, to marry children, sometimes even babies, altogether useless for sex – ridiculously conservative people who refuse to countenance change in any respect whatever!

Tension mounts, fighting soon breaks out. Holding their boomerangs at arm's length, the most aggressive are already striking their skulls with the cutting edge; others, the more restrained, are simply threatening to hurl their spears, while still others have already sent theirs into the air, aimed at thighs.

Women run around, chanting a sad song consisting of three tones. They surround the enraged men, and, staring them in the face, circle around them, thrusting their pubis in and out, in an erotic dance intended to incite them, to draw them into the game of love, and make them forget the dispute. Foaming at the mouth, their sex erect, the men ignore them. Soon, a cloud of red dust rises from the ground, stirred up by feet which come and go, tramp and stamp on the ground in rage, as does the kangaroo when aroused. Dust clings to the bodies of the combatants, which are shining with sweat, to their hair, between their eyes.

I fall. My thigh is pierced. Blood flows. Immediately, the combat ceases. Also the women's dance.

To show how distraught they are, the women weep, strike their skulls with stones, wound their scalps, start bleeding in their turn; the evening air carries away their prolonged sobbing; the echo brings it back, amplified. Then, satisfied with their demonstration, grumbling, moaning, the women go back to their small fire to take up their work again; and, calmly, they discuss the battle, leaving the men to tend the wounded.

Tumenti is summoned. He has stayed away from the group until now, at a little distance from the camp, absorbed (as is his wont) in his meditation. He leans over my thigh, looks at it, seems to be thinking things over; then, with a swift and precise gesture, he pushes on the end of the spear-shaft until the tip emerges from the other side of my flesh. I know how to overcome pain. I do not budge. Our Man of High Degree pauses, then, solemnly intoning the appropriate incantation, cuts off the protruding portion of the shaft; finally, having got his foothold, he seizes the head of the spear with both hands and, with a jerk, pulls out the portion of the shaft which has remained in my flesh. The wound bleeds freely. To stop the bleeding, he applies a paste made from earth and pieces of crushed leaves and roots, pressing firmly for a good while, then, to avoid infection, he puts some medicinal leaves over the wound, fixing them in place with a thread he winds around my thigh. He takes a few pain-killing leaves out of a small basketwork sack he wears around his neck, holds them out to me, signalling that I should chew them and, without a word, returns to his meditation.

I get up with difficulty, and limp over to the nearest fire to lie down next to it. I look at my friends.

Forgetting, as I have also done, their resentment against the older men, they show off their wounds with pride, without the least feeling of ill will. How could they wish each other harm, they, the future Wise Men, future reincarnations of the sacred beings? Their ill humour a thing of the past, they can only respect one another, because they have endured the same trials. They help each other, even though their hearts are not in it, because that is what the law demands. And that helps them to be reconciled to that august precedent.

'Oh! Oh!' they exclaim in sad accents, while demonstrating their regret by mimicking distress.

A little later, young and old are seated around the red embers of a smouldering branch. A plug of green tobacco is passed around. Life continues as if nothing had happened. Waiting for the punishment of those responsible for the battle.

And, in fact, the following morning the most influential of the Wise Men make for a little clearing at some distance from the camp. They squat on their heels, taking great care to place their bodies around the perfect circle traced on the ground, the symbol of the Rainbow Serpent. This placement of the men and the propitiatory chant they intone as soon as they have taken up their positions are conducive to calm, to reflection and to the silent exchange of thoughts.

Having prepared himself in this way, each man speaks his mind. When they reach an agreement, they return to the camp to deliver their verdict: the one responsible for the combat must set out on his own to hunt and kill a kangaroo for the benefit of all those who claimed to have been offended.

The black prisoner can still hear Tumenti whispering, for his benefit alone:

'A mild enough punishment for a young man of your calibre, who is unable to control his tongue and his anger. Bah! Young people!'

Yes! Mild, oh how mild a punishment: the truth of which only the future will teach me!

The image of the gaoler's face he glimpses leaning over him penetrates his consciousness at last. It interrupts the flow of the prisoner's memories of the time when he is making his way along the path of the Woman Goanna.

There is an exceptional drought, and several underground waterholes have dried up. Gauera, Tumenti's young wife, has difficulty keeping pace with the rest because of her large belly. Her fellow wives set out in search of a frog, a kind that survives drought by burying itself in the ground with a reserve of water in a bladder under its neck. The women inspect the surface of the sand. Soon enough, they detect the presence of one of these frogs, and swiftly drive it out of the ground. Gauera grabs it.

'Thank you,' she says to the frog, 'for saving my life and giving me your water. I know well enough that without it you could not endure years of drought. Thank you.'

Gauera pierces the bladder, lifts her arm to allow the water to trickle down her throat, and puts the frog back in its hiding-place, taking care to cover it with sand. Then, with a more lively step, she rejoins her companions.

This is Jimbin country, the underground realm of baby spirits. A world of joy and laughter, a world where cares are unknown. Sometimes little creatures rise to the surface, but only the Men of High Degree can see and hear them.

Even though it is late in the day, as the rays of the sun lengthen the shadows cast on the sand, a young woman is slowly walking up and down in this place, hoping that one of those invisible babies would enter her belly and give life to the foetus every woman carries inside her. There, nourished by her husband's sperm, it will regain its human form.

Dispersed as their fancy took them until this time, the members of the group are now walking purposefully, one behind the other, in a hurry to reach the next stopping place, where they will find saturated kurrajong roots.

Nari can see himself again walking in the front, a good way behind Tumenti, the others far behind them. Suddenly, his elderly father stops, rooted to the spot. And now he is trembling from head to foot, not answering the questions the others are calling out to him.

I am so afraid, the old man remembers. I rush towards him, he is still frozen in that unusual attitude, as if turned to stone! I go up to him and look at his face, which is streaming with large drops of sweat. I notice that his eyes are popping out of their sockets. I follow his gaze. And I see what he sees!

Straight away, I start shaking in turn, I am sweating, and I can feel urine trickling down my legs. Without being able to do anything about it. Ngargala, who has joined us, cuts short the question he was asking and is shaking in his turn: I can hear him urinating, too, without the least wish to do so. We are there, standing side by side, immobile, unable to react in any way, horrified and fascinated at the same time by what we can see.

A spear's throw in front of us, something, oh how strange a thing, is coming nearer. You would think that it is human. But with some kind of puffy skin around its body. A thick skin, that seems torn, hanging in strips! The colour of the creature's face resembles the petals of certain red-flowering plants. No trace of any sex below the waist. Its hair looks as if it's made out of the dead grass of the desert, the colour of straw. A monster.

Tumenti is the first to master his blind panic. His limbs stop shaking, they resume their normal posture. Following his example, I make an immense effort to come to my senses. With a deep sigh, Ngargala spits out the name of a Hero, a name so illustrious that you should, in principle, only pronounce it in a hushed voice! Soon, profound consternation replaces panic. The thing that looks like a man seems not to have noticed us. The creature stops in front of a heap of stones, takes its head between its two hands and hurls itself brutally to the ground. We continue watching it, to convince ourselves that all this is real. Then, with one movement, we turn our backs on it and run back to the group, which is still far behind us.

At first no one will believe us. Everyone stares at us in disbelief, torn between laughter and terror. We have to repeat our incredible tale. Our faces, our tone of voice finally persuade them. Straight away, with an abrupt movement, the women, who had just put the youngest of the children down on the sand, grab them under their arms, heaving them on their hips once more and, leaning forward in order to move faster, run off to hide in the scrub of a hollow a few paces away.

After a lengthy discussion, broken by long silences of reflection and indecision, Wongiman and Mandji, two of our Wise Men, set off towards the apparition, guided by Tumenti. They tell us to stay where we are and to wait for them.

We see them making a long detour to get downwind of the creature and to approach it from behind, without letting themselves be seen or heard. They move forward without making the least noise, the way hunters sneak up on their prey. Now and then they crouch, instinctively, behind a small sandhill, or lie flat to the ground behind a tuft of thorny scrub. They must have got near enough to be able to see, because they have stopped.

Not long afterwards, they are on their way back, obviously very shocked. We return to the women and there, protected from the monster's gaze, settle down to consider what should be done.

'It's true! You could take it for a man with a red face,' Mandji says. 'But what a smell of death! How ugly it is!'

'A red face?' repeat those that haven't seen it.

'I, who have looked at it for the second time, saw clearly the skin flapping around its body. This could be the fragile bark of an unknown kind of tree used to obscure its lack of a sexual organ.'

'No sex, no feet! So this is not a man, not even a red-coloured man,' a woman mutters.

'We heard it moaning,' Tumenti continues. 'I did everything to get near it but, after a few paces, the overpowering smell of death made me recoil. It's true, it stinks of death!'

Several repeat in chorus: 'Death!'

'Then it's someone who is dead returning to earth,' old Niumta announces in a resolute voice.

'The dead never come back to earth in an almost human form! What are you talking about? Their spirits must be reborn in a woman's belly to give them a human likeness! They would not appear like this, without warning, as monstrous adults!'

'They have never come back like that, but perhaps they have been warning us about such a reappearance with all those new things, those strange things we have seen or heard about,' Niumta replies.

Silence falls. Despite her age, the old woman retains her authority. And we hesitate to contradict her. Even Tumenti fails to reject the suggestion.

'Yes,' he says. 'That's possible! I am nevertheless astonished that I've never had any premonition of this change! Astonished that none of the circle of the Men of High Degree received one either!'

As if talking to himself, Ngargala whispers:

'Perhaps it makes up a part of the cycle of Life! Perhaps

it is a new form of Life that's come with Time!'

'It could be my son who died many Great Assemblies ago.'

After she has spoken these words, Niumta stands up and, without asking anyone's advice, sets off with an assured step to meet the one she takes to be her son who has returned from the world beyond. Behind her back, her daughter-in-law, who has little liking for her, makes a mocking gesture. Tumenti, Wongiman, Mandji and I follow her, full of curiosity to take another look at the incredible apparition on the path of the Woman Goanna. The others walk behind us. Tumenti makes a sign that we should put down our weapons.

The monster hasn't moved. At the sound of our approach, its body twitches, its head turns towards us. It watches us coming towards it and reveals no sign of aggression, no fear. Its eyelids are puffy and it has difficulty keeping its eyes open. We cannot see the pupils. The creature's smell overwhelms us.

'It is normal that he should smell like the dead! Seeing that he's just come back from the dead! But look! He looks like my son. Yes! It's him, it's Guningbal!'

I am thinking that only a mother could recognise her child despite such an altered appearance.

'The poor thing, how ugly he's become!' Niumta chimes in, gathering up enough courage to touch his face. 'Look at his forehead! It looks as if it's disappeared, it doesn't extend above his eyes. Hardly surprising that he has trouble keeping his eyes open!'

'And his nose!' exclaims the wife of the living-dead, who does not want to be outdone by her mother-in-law. 'The nose he used to have was so nicely rounded at the nostrils. It now looks like a hawk's beak. How horrible! And his mouth! He hasn't any lips! It gives him such an evil look. No! This is not my husband.

Besides, if it was him he'd recognise me!'

The stranger does not stir. He lets Niumta take one of his hands and count his fingers.

To see better what is going on, Kamal shoves me aside and draws nearer, with her little girl Diktali in her arms. But at the sight of the apparition, the child lets out such a cry of terror that her mother steps back straight away, pointing her fingers at a flight of pink cockatoos. The baby lifts her little face towards the cloud of feathers and her screams change into soft warbling. Two little boys, who have been sheltering all along between the thighs of grown-ups, clinging to them, slip to the front of the gathering. One furtive look at the monster and they, too, run off howling.

The True Men have just sat down, a little way off, to discuss the matter. They do not want to be influenced by Niumta's emotional reactions. It is a serious problem. In effect, if this is not a dead person who has returned to earth, it could only be a dangerous visitor from the spirit-world of another people. For none of us imagines the possibility of finding ourselves face to face with a white-skinned stranger: no one can imagine that anyone would be insane enough to violate the first of the laws laid down by the Ancestors, insane enough to unleash their wrath in the face of such sacrilege! Mad enough to abandon their protection and plunge into the terrible dangers posed by the malevolent spirits of an unknown land!

No, no one could imagine such an absurdity even for an instant!

Seated in a circle not far away from it, we watch the 'monster', who does not seem to be troubled by all this upheaval. He – if it is a man – looks harmless enough. We discuss, we reflect, we dwell on the ideas and suggestions each of us makes. Then, when we decide at length to confirm Niumta's intuition, the Woman Sun begins her descent towards the dead. The red-faced man, whom we are no longer calling a monster, is well and truly a dead person who has returned to earth; and he could only be Niumta's son.

The son, who has turned so ugly, sits down. In the way that human beings sit. He looks utterly exhausted; he lets out a long sigh as he gazes at us. We look at his hands, curiously thick and gnarled, a little less ruddy than his face, but made repulsive by the brownish spots on the back.

With repeated gestures, he makes us understand that he wants something to drink. Niumta goes off quickly to cull a succulent plant, which she holds out to him. The creature, who seems to us more and more a human being, utters some peculiar sounds, expressing himself, without doubt, in the language of the dead. With a foolish look, he is holding the plant at the ends of his fingers; disappointment is clearly visible on his face. His eyes travel around our circle and, with a feeble gesture, he drops the plant. Astonished, Niumta picks it up, muttering:

'I am sure he is my son! But like the newborn, he has lost his memory. It will be necessary to teach him everything again.'

So she puts a stalk in her own mouth, extracting the sap by chewing it, and spits out the sugary juice in one long spurt. Then she holds out another stalk to the red-faced man. He takes it, looks at it, smells it and shrugs his shoulders in resignation. At last, hesitantly, he lifts it to his mouth, chews it at the end of his lips, then gobbles it avidly. His eyelids are a little more open.

'Look! His eyes have taken on the colour of the sky, the colour of the beyond!'

We all rush forward to look at this unimaginable apparition! Blue eyes!

At the sound of Niumta's voice, the living-dead raises his peculiar looking face to her, and I notice that his skin is moulting. Perhaps it is about to regain its fine dark colouring! Silence falls. Tumenti asks Niumta to see if her son-turned-ugly has retained his sex. Niumta hesitates. Then, with care, she puts her hand to where the creature's sex should be. The red-coloured creature recoils, then, no doubt too exhausted to resist, lets her do it. She succeeds in penetrating his thick new skin and draws out a small sex entirely white and, oh surprise, not circumcised! Consternation is evident on every face. But Niumta will not admit defeat.

'In the beyond, the penises of the dead grow long,' she declares authoritatively.

Mother and son look at each other. We think that they are in silent communication, for the one we think of, without knowing too well why, as Guningbal smiles sadly at her.

'He is too weak to come with us,' the old woman decides. 'I will camp with him not far from here until he gets a little of his strength back. We will catch up with you later.'

In his prison, Nari lets out a long sigh and, only for himself, whispers:

'Yes. That's how our first encounter with one of our invaders took place! The unconditional death of Time had just been announced!'

5

From time to time in the bush, not far from the prison, the morning wind stirs up the red dust, bending the large thorny bushes, shaking the tops of the ironwood. Mischievously, the Woman Sun climbs over the long mountain range. She enjoys making the boisterous little world far beneath her sparkle with her light.

As a colony of pigeons flies past, her light diminishes, then grows joyful once more as the cloud recedes. At the base of a rocky outcrop, resplendent at this hour of the day with a coppery glow, a troop of emus is slowly making its way. Far behind them, a stray male jiggles its plump body in rhythm with its steps. Seven chicks, with striped plumage, follow behind, thrusting their long necks in front of them now and then, just as their father does.

Its body rearing on its front legs, flourishing its long bifurcated tongue, a brown-skinned monitor lizard crawls out of a thorny bush. After stopping briefly, it leaps, like lightning, on a wagtail much too preoccupied with pecking. But the bird notices it, calls out in distress. Immediately, hundreds of its kind soar from the scrub, rapidly forming a compact flight, cackling, whistling, chirping. They make ready to dive on the lizard, then soar again, calling even more loudly, to land not far from the enemy's head. In the face of this attack from the air, the lizard gives up and disappears in a cleft in the ground.

The shape of a dingo, all skin and bones, appears on the crest of a sand hill. Its russet hide, hardly lighter in colour than the sand, is etched against the stark blue of the sky. It moves rapidly, its ears pointed, tail horizontal, now and then lowering its muzzle to the ground. Suddenly it leaps at great speed towards a small bush, emerging with a small stray emu between its powerful jaws.

Sheltering beneath a flowering wattle, the two night guards try to forget their miserable life by firing at a mob of a hundred or so kangaroos making their way to a distant region, where they know that a shower of rain is about to fall.

Nari, the prisoner, does not notice the return of day, the noises around him, the oaths reaching him from the outside. He remains immersed in the past.

Like the sun, the moon and the stars, like day and night, he is ceaselessly travelling with his people, leaving one path for another, and yet another, identifying himself with each of them, accomplishing one sacred journey only to embark on another. Each of them master of the ritual in turn, he and his people are aware of their own importance, they think that they are irreplaceable, charged with a heavy responsibility that gives meaning to their lives.

The abundance of edible plant life, of game, their familiarity with sources of water, both visible and invisible, in short the hidden but very real generosity of the desert give them time for long moments of leisure. A leisure which, according to their mood, offers opportunities for lengthy meditation, for long periods of communication with the environment, for sitting around with nothing to do, content to be simply aware of the Life within each of them, of the eternity of the moment; time for philosophical discussions without end; at least when not making useful objects, inventing new poems, new dances, new songs for a coming ceremony. Efforts energised by the care to be as expert as, if not more so, than the Sparrowhawks, the other moiety of their people.

Sure enough, the old man remembers, there were quarrels, young men and old fighting over women; sometimes strangers carrying one of them off and, most often, the strange behaviour of Guningbal, the living-dead, which brought on difficulties of a kind not encountered until then. These small incidents of everyday life, important but always secondary, emphasised the vitality of the group.

One day, Niumta sits down next to me to complain about her son, the man who has returned from the land of the dead.

'I am very unhappy. My beloved son has forgotten all his kin, those of his blood as much as those linked to him by the Dreaming, marriage and alliance. And it goes without saying, the various ways of addressing each of them, too. You yourself know well enough how lacking in politeness he has become!

'He even refuses to carry out his obligation to help others, refuses to share, refuses to hand his possessions around! I am ashamed. He is upsetting our people's way of life, and also his trading partners', who will abandon him one day or another. Tumenti has tried everything. Alas, his mana, no matter how renowned, has no power over my son.'

'What else can we do but wait a little longer? I've often tried to reason with him. He seems, nevertheless, to pay more attention when we remonstrate with him nowadays than he had when he arrived. I get the sense that he is making a great effort to understand.'

That was how I tried to raise her spirits. In truth I was just as worried. Nari can hear himself saying for the hundredth time:

'Believe me, Guningbal, nothing good can come of your determination not to hand things around. Why don't you listen to us? Look how worried you are about losing the flint you don't want to lend to anyone, which you think you hid out of sight several weeks back, though the children told us about your misdemeanour long ago. What is more, you are growing distrustful. Distrustful of everyone, so afraid are you that someone will take it from you. You must realise that it would be much simpler to let everyone use it. And don't you see, what's more, the trouble this attitude is causing you, that you are responsible for allowing a detestable sense of envy to arise among our people? For you were lucky enough to trade your kangaroo skin for an exceptionally fine piece of flint; it is particularly good for cutting and we would all like to make use of it.'

'But it's mine, all the same. I can't understand any of this ridiculous attitude of wanting to share everything. To each his own!'

Then I left him, aware of his inability to change his mind, even when recognising how well-founded our remarks were. At that time he was spontaneously turning his back on all our customs. Something seemed to be blocking his ability to reason things through. He puzzled me more and more. How could I have understood him?

One day, I come on him by surprise as he is eating the tail of a kangaroo he has just killed, alone and in secret.

'Don't you know that you should offer the best portion of your catch to the others? That the tail of a kangaroo is precisely the choicest bit?'

'It's not on! Why should anyone be so stupid?' he replies, with a smile, with those childish words he always uses.

'I have already told you that this rule imposes a restraint on the urge to hunt game for pleasure, that our laws only permit us to kill for food. We must act in a way that makes sure that game remains abundant. Killing a kangaroo in secret, as you've just done, without sharing the meat with your people, represents an intolerable waste. Can't you understand that at least? Try to remember that one fact!'

'How could I remember it?'

From the look on his face, which has suddenly grown sad and thoughtful, I know that he is telling the truth.

'All the same, you wouldn't want to leave the remains behind for scavengers! At least help me take them back to the camp.'

'All right! No doubt you are right. But game seems to me so abundant!'

'Thanks to our respect for the laws. Another of our laws forbids a man to look at or even address a single word to his wife's mother. I've told you that a hundred times already. So, don't do it when we get back to the camp, or when your wife's mother comes visiting. Otherwise you'll find yourself in even greater trouble. And we will too.'

'But all the same,' he says bursting into laughter, 'she's a fine woman, much better looking than her daughter! She isn't old, she's the same age as me,' he led me to understand, more by gesture than words.

'Our wives' mothers are never elderly because their daughters marry when they are very young. It's precisely for that reason that such a prohibition exists. Do you really remember nothing of that?'

'No. Nari. In the land from which I come, everything is different!'

'In the land of the beyond, those who have vanished from earth submit themselves to the same laws as in the land of living. Your ideas, your behaviour are too strange for us to credit what you are telling us.'

Guningbal shrugs and says nothing.

Once more I realise that I am wasting my time, that it does no good trying to instruct him. He acts as if he were the only one on earth, without rules or laws to obey. His attitude is that of a dreadful individualist! But he likes me very much and, curiously, I return his friendship.

Later, he launches into an elaborate explanation. I come to understand vaguely that in the other world he was forced to stay inside a dwelling made of stone, which he could not leave; he got nothing to eat, or so little that he often had to fight for it. He managed to escape and, thanks to the help of several groups of black men, made his way west over a long stretch of time, burying himself in holes in the ground to avoid being disturbed by people of his own kind. Until we found him.

As I was expressing my doubts, telling him that, this time, he was depicting an image of the world of the vanished far too gloomy to be believed, he stared at me for good a while, but did not go on. From the look on his face, from the tone of his voice, from the waves his whole being was sending out, I know that he is not lying. He is telling me what he believes to be true. He has entirely forgotten his life in the land of the dead, as much as his life among the living. He is making things up. But why?

He still smells of death. It is true that he has no concern for cleanliness. He refuses to rub his body with sand, to remove his body hair, to coat his hair with mud in order to plait it. Since he has shed his old skins, he stinks a little bit less. Once red, the surface of his body has changed, and it is covered now with altogether repulsive brown patches.

Just like his mother, his wife is unable to reconcile herself to the fact that her husband, who had been so carefully brought up, should have turned into such a bumpkin.

'He is not the same. I've given him a good rubbing with my churinga, with his too, but nothing happened. He no longer knows what tenderness is, he has completely forgotten the wonders of the game of love! I cannot believe that Guningbal would have forgotten! He has come back to earth in the body his mother gave him, but he forgot to charge it with the spiritual body which had been engendered in him.'

I am of her mind. He acts like a sleeping man who has been brutally roused, before his spirit, wandering somewhere to visit a distant relative, has reintegrated itself with his body. A phenomenon which, in such cases, only lasts an instant!

We do not know what to do. Clearly, our laws have not foreseen such a predicament. We dare not be as severe with him as we would be with another living creature for fear of insulting the beings of the invisible world.

Night has fallen. The most influential men of our group, shocked by the story of the kangaroo killed in secret, discuss, for a long time, all the infringements of the laws committed by the son of Niumta, who has returned from the dead. After much hesitation, they decide to have recourse to a rite of purification. If, as they fear, no change ensues, then they must run the risk of offending the invisible powers by bringing the case of Guningbal in front of the tribunal which meets to deal with such difficult matters: crimes, incest or acts of profanation against important laws. A smoke signal is immediately sent up to warn the members of the group.

From the following day on, the men of my camp discuss the preparation of the site where the meeting will be held. Tumenti is in charge of the ceremony. He gives the order for a circular cavity to be dug, symbolising a sacred waterhole. Then it has to be surrounded with a crest of sand, two hands in height. It is at that site that our Man of High Degree will enter into communication with the Rainbow Serpent, the most powerful cosmic being, the one whose magical agent is starlight. He will ask him to absolve Guningbal and to return him to the right path.

On the morning of the appointed day, the men and women of the Grey Falcons converge on the chosen place. And, until evening, everyone sings, dances, exchanges finery, all rejoicing that they have come together to safeguard a common cause. Guningbal is behaving as disgracefully as ever, and poor Niumta remains squatting, solitary next to her small fire, not daring to look at anyone.

A little before nightfall, the Wise Men and the Men of High Degree enter the circle marked out by the crest of sand; they sit down, with their backs to the raised part, facing the centre.

Tumenti gives the signal. The rhythmic sound of sticks struck against one another fills the dry air. In a low voice, on three piercing notes, the men intone the appropriate ceremonial chant before the didgeridoo sends out the enchanting sound of the Sacred Energy. The waves emitted by the chant surround the onlookers, seep into them, leading them little by little into reverential silence. Far behind them, the women leap up and down in the one place, then they interlace their steps in a dance-pattern intended to make it easier for Tumenti to communicate with the Rainbow Serpent.

I have been charged with the task of leading Guningbal to the centre of the symbolic waterhole.

A song rises, signalling the start of the meeting. My task begins.

I look my strange friend firmly in the eye; with an encouraging smile, I take him by the shoulder and gently push him towards the centre of the depression, without his showing the least resistance. I am always astonished to see how silent communication is possible between us.

'All right, all right, old man! I'm coming, but it's only for your sake!' he shouts at me.

Tumenti and several of the Wise Men make their way towards him, carrying wiris, wooden vessels filled with water. They sprinkle his face and body. They invoke the cosmic being concealed in the sacred waterhole. They beseech him to cleanse Guningbal of all his faults, so that he may find again his proper place among us. Guningbal, looking at me with laughing eyes, taps his forehead with a finger, not at all impressed by the gravity of the moment. I know that he will never change! But his predicament enthrals me. You do not run across a savage in an adult frame every day!

Some weeks later, after the anticipated failure of the purification ceremony, old Niumta finds, at long last, the right solution: she asks the Wise Men to agree to recreate the invisible body of her son, who has grown so ugly – that is to say, to start fashioning him into a True Man again. Hoping, without doubt, that recovering his Memory will also restore his good looks!

The Wise Men agree, as does, to the surprise of all, Guningbal himself.

Nari, the old man, is experiencing once more another period of isolation that follows these events. Here he is now in a place forbidden to the uninitiated.

His body is resplendent in its physical maturity. It has conferred on him the greatest ability through the development, one by one, of all of his sensory faculties, his bearing and his capacity to withstand exertion as much as pain.

It is at this time that he begins to know how to channel the Cosmic Energy before attaining a state of total relaxation. To achieve that, he has learnt how to shut his mind to every sensation, every idea reaching him from the physical world. Transformed in such a way, he manages, therefore, to enter into fleeting contact with the influx of the sacred energy, diffused from the sky to the earth and imprinted with the primordial Knowledge.

He continues perfecting his interpretation of texts disguised in the symbols of stone carvings. One day, as he is struggling with an image symbolising a certain object, a representation he cannot connect with the sequence of other representations, Tumenti explains it to him with a simple glance, by letting his gaze rest on a spot just long enough for Nari to understand that he will find the solution there. After reflecting for a long time, he solves the problem at last: the maxim which he had recognised behind a simple sign symbolises, in its turn, a simple word. And this word must be translated like a poetic symbol; poetry which, according to the degree of Instruction, would remain a mere poem or else would transform itself into the representation of a knowledge concealing within itself yet another truth. He had received the revelation of the symbolic symbol.

Later, he discovers new maxims hidden in the designs on the stone tablets, in the familiar songs and tales or in sacred stories. Little by little, the riches of the latter reveal themselves. Their multiple contradictions, to which he has access now, make him question what seemed to him, up to this time, the truth; they have made his philosophical speculation advance magnificently. Each revelation has to do with the formation of the world, which until then he thought he knew so well; they lead him, after that, to new subjects for meditation, enlarging his vision of the world. Slowly, he progresses along the path of discovering what he now thinks of as his ideal self.

The man skips rapidly over some of his recollections. He lingers over others, pauses, giving himself time to hear the sounds, smell the scents, relive the feelings attached to certain images. Abruptly, like a dart, one of them forcefully blots out the others.

He sees his initiators, some years later, sumptuously decked out, moving around his body, which is stretched out on a human litter of bent backs. He hears them intoning sacred texts, admires the frenetic dancing, as jerky as it is rhythmic, smiles with feeling as he hears the low register of the didgeridoo, the dry sound of stick hitting stick.

One of the participants approaches. With a swift movement, he lifts my prick and, with a rapid gesture, makes an incision along the whole length of the underside. Despite the agony, I do not flinch. I have become the absolute master of my body. Blood is trickling.

'Now you have a hole in every way similar to that of women. You are bleeding like a woman bleeds when she is menstruating or giving birth,' one of the participants whispers to me. 'From now on your are endowed with both male and female organs.'

I see a smoke signal rising into the sky. I know that it is announcing to my mothers, who have stayed behind in the camp, that it is time for them to confirm my transformation, and that Waela, my favourite, should confirm it with all the strength of her love. At the sacred site, the rite continues with fresh dancing, with prolonged chanting.

I remain lying on my back, my mind entirely blank, not knowing whether I am still on earth or whether I have been projected into the blessed Alcheringa Time. Have I returned to the Time of the first Creation, when men and women were not differentiated from one another, when our kind were all hermaphrodites? One thing is certain. The trial which I have just endured will allow me to let my blood, which has become the vehicle of the sacred energy, mingle with the Wise Men's blood, it will allow the sanctification of young men, of objects or places, impregnating them with fragments of my own divine nature flowing within it.

When the Woman Sun begins her descent towards the land of the dead, I am led out of the shadows. I am capable of transcending my rational self in order to understand certain mysteries. The rhomboid, an object of the greatest sanctity, the 'voice' of which makes women, children and the uninitiated flee, no longer holds any secret for me; I have laid eyes on the great churinga shared by the Sparrowhawks and the Grey Falcons, the concrete and visible sign of the eternal Dreamtime. In truth, much more than that, for this is the Dreaming which, in its material form, allows men to penetrate it.

Other sacred objects have been revealed to me, they are also receptacles and transmitters of the might and strength of the Ancestors, those innocent representations which the uninitiated ascribe to the sacred vital energy.

I have my own personal churinga, an oblong stone, on which the engravings represent the sacred story of my Dreaming, the giant Ancestor, neither human nor animal, the Man Dingo of Alcheringa Time. Within this perfectly smooth stone, there lies the essence of what I was at the beginning of Time, my spiritual double beyond Time, which I cannot lose without immediately losing my life. I share the secrets of the Wise Men. Like they,

I have become one of the repositories of sacred rites, religious myths and symbols. I have at last recovered the great part of my memory of the Eternal Dreamtime. I know who I am. I am a sacred being. This so much wished-for revelation fills me with wonder. It casts me, equally, into humility.

How can I not remember the sense of fulfilment I experienced that evening! A fulfilment I relished in the calm of the last of the periods of isolation that I had recovered. But how can I not equally recall the smoke signal announcing the return of another of the dead to the living? News that made me leave abruptly the spiritual world to find the physical world once again, that world which was turning more and more treacherous and deceitful for me.

6

Weariness overwhelming him, the old Aborigine must have found it difficult to recall the years that followed. He sighs, turns this way and that, conscious now that the night has turned cold. A horse snorting not far from the prison arouses a forgotten emotion with brutal force.

I am sitting with Guningbal, the living-dead, on top of a rocky outcrop, in the place where the Emu Dreaming stopped on its journey. I am careworn because the sky is ceaselessly announcing the return of other living-dead. Finding a place again for so many men in our system of aid and mutual obligation is not going to be an easy task. Messages have arrived from the east, the west, then the north and today from the south. What is going on? Why are so many of the dead coming back to earth in the form of white men? With the skin of corpses!

I gaze at the blue sky, terrified by the thought of seeing another of these messages appearing there. Why such apprehensiveness?

Guningbal has not caused us any trouble for a long time now. Over many years, he received Knowledge. Since then, he has become once more what he had always been before his death, one who obeys the laws, like all of us. A good Guardian of Creation. Certainly, his mother and his wife are disappointed because he has not recovered his former good looks. What does it matter! For the group, that is truly without importance; if other dead people return, we now know what attitude we should strike straight away. And we will easily enough find a solution to the problem of how to give back to them their place in the Dreaming group. So then, why this anxiety dogging me day and night?

Guningbal breaks the silence. We have become very friendly. He knows how much anguish it causes me that so many of the dead are coming back to earth. Once again, he wants to convince me that these creatures have nothing to do with the world of the beyond. Once again, he explains how he and the other men with white skins arrived in our land. With a piece of clay, he traces a map of seas and imaginary lands on the rock face to show me where his country is to be found. I know that he is sincere. Nevertheless, despite my dreams, which speak to me of a great catastrophe soon to be unleashed by an evil force I cannot identify, I refuse to believe what he is telling me.

Suddenly, in spite of myself, the truth overwhelms me, more forcefully than a blow from a club! The notion that people would dare to leave their country to invade ours has become irresistible. It can only be that! I finally accept as the truth something I have been pushing to the back of my mind: the so-called return of Guningbal's memory is simply a result of our Instruction, an Instruction which has made him one of us. Should I impart these thoughts to my people after what I have realised this evening? Once again I hesitate: then I try to forget that flash of insight, I persuade myself that I have misinterpreted the dreams of these last nights, misunderstood what Guningbal has explained to me. It is so unbelievable! With such grave consequences for us. Besides, who would believe me? Who could possibly be in a position to envisage that people could have abandoned their duty as sacred Guardians, abandoned the omnipresent protection of the Creators of their land, that they would have set out to invade the territories of strangers, territories charged with unknown powers, territories where everything could only be hostile to them. Who could believe that someone would be capable of violating the strictest of interdictions, that of leaving the place where the Great Heroes of the Dreamtime commanded them to live forever?

Such a criminal act would prove, beyond any doubt, that these men had never received Knowledge, that they are ignorant of all the Sacred Commandments, of all moral laws, judicial and social. It would prove that their human nature has remained trapped in the condition of a savage. They would represent therefore a lesser kind of humanity, as certain of our trading partners from remote places were whispering. Which none of our people wanted to believe. Their ugliness, their smell, the imperfect pigmentation of their skin would confirm that.

'If all that you are telling me is true, that would prove that your kind has never had a civilising Hero.'

'We did have one, who came down from the beyond to deliver Ten Commandments to mankind. His moral rules touch on yours a little, since they require men to love and help one another. But he went away without establishing the multiple rules of kinship which your people know, those inalienable ties which surround mankind with inviolable laws, obliging them to respect the Commandments in those ways.'

'One sole Great Ancestor? Who, moreover, seems to have known human nature which remains prisoner to material things, because, in fact, he had only expressed how he wanted human beings to behave!'

'In reality, I don't know a great deal about these beliefs. With us religion does not have the importance it has for your people. I, like many others, turn to God only when I am enduring great misery. But I have never understood sacred things, have never felt a communion with the Cosmic Energy in the way I have found with your people.'

We allow the silence to shroud us once more.

Our wanderings in the dry season slowly lead us back to the world of plants. My gaze comes to rest on the immensity of the landscape, where green is more in evidence; it announces that the end of the desert is near. I know that when they are screened by the surrounding plant life, my extrasensory faculties of perception will not function at their highest potential. I regret that. But the instant when that thought is born in my mind, I become aware of the first stirrings of a second sight. My body begins to shake, and I have trouble swallowing. My lips intone some words without my having caused them to move. A blinding vision overwhelms my mind. I see several members of the Grey Falcons in a state of panic. I cannot make out what alarms them so.

The vision vanishes. I breathe hard, concentrate to such an extent that I feel that my body is ready to burst. My temples are twitching, my body heat rises even higher. And another image comes to me. A man wounded by some kind of fire-spitting monster. The vision fades. Am I really awake? Have I not simply dreamed everything? Slowly, I recover from a great expenditure of energy.

My gaze scans the horizon once more, sweeps over the endless plain. At the moment when my field of vision reaches its extreme limit, I notice two slender shapes emerging from the place where the ochre glow of the sun cuts off the blue of the sky, along the entire length of a straight line that vanishes both in the east and the west. I recognise Wongu quickly enough. He is returning from a visit to his wife's people, members of one of the groups of the Sparrowhawks. A little behind him, Wotjoba, his wife, and, behind her, their two dogs. With Guningbal, I go over to meet them.

Soon, panic makes me tremble just as much as my friend is shaking. His hurried pace, his jerky movements, his stiff posture, all these confirm what the waves sent out by his body have already told me. He calls out something that I do not understand, and I am astonished that he is raising his voice in such a way.

We are now face-to-face. I notice large drops of sweat on his face, and that he is controlling the trembling of his limbs only with difficulty. Wotjoba joins us; her eyes popping from their sockets from fear, she begins crying and moaning in the way women do after great catastrophes.

'Be quiet!' Wongu orders her. 'Let's get away from here, or they will find us.'

And, all of a sudden, I know that my vision was not a dream. Despite that, I hear myself asking him:

'Whom are you talking about? What is going on?'

But Wongu pulls me towards the outcrop. In a few instants we are at its base. With difficulty, we slither into one of the openings in the cliff face and, on all fours, make our way across a maze of fallen rocks, the only access to the cave of the Crow, which is illuminated by an opening at the top. There, my two friends sit down, raise their weary eyes to me. Their dogs are panting, seemingly just as upset as their masters, for they creep away to hide in a hole.

'Go on, speak now. No one will come here to look for us.'

Wongu leans forward, swallows hard and, at last, begins.

'I can hardly control myself. It is so unbelievable! Now then: first of all I noticed a cloud of dust, inexplicable because there was no wind and, instead of rising straight up as in a willy-willy, it sped towards us. We were with Wotjoba's brother. Without knowing why, we ran off, driven by our instinct, to hide behind a mound and lie flat to the ground.

'When the cloud of dust got nearer, fuzzy image of monsters emerged from it. Imagine, strange furry animals with four legs, legs as high as your shoulder, supporting a long horizontal body, with, at one end, a massive neck and head a little like a grey kangaroo's, and, at the other, a huge tail hanging down, with long hairs, and above the slightly arched back there was the trunk of a man, whose white face was the only thing to protrude from its weird, dark, loose skin. The draught of their career made that skin flap, for the animals were travelling extremely fast, perhaps faster than kangaroos; they moved their legs in a strange fashion, with unheard of force! They made the ground shake, and we shook too, but from fear! A strange smell reached us, enveloped us. How to explain that smell? No! It is not possible.

'Sensations, questions followed one another in my head, getting tangled with each other until I was no longer able to master them. A foul stench, I thought. Two-headed creatures, neither men nor beasts! Creatures of the Dreamtime?

'Then, when that thought struck me, I lowered my spear, which I was getting ready to hurl. Wotjoba's brother did the same. We could do nothing against the creatures of the Dreamtime.

'At that moment, for an inexplicable reason, one of the monsters seemed to take fright. It stopped abruptly a little distance from the place where we were hiding, reared on its hind legs flailing the empty air with its front legs. I had time to notice its huge nares before we saw what we took to be the natural extension of the animal tumble to the ground. We were struck dumb with astonishment!

'Straight away, the "thing" that had fallen off got up and—Nari!—it was a living-dead, one of the dead, who had come back from the beyond on the back of this unknown beast. Another of the living-dead! I don't know why, but I was reassured! These were not legendary beings, beings which I should not have feared therefore! I am still as much flabbergasted by all my bad reactions as by the fear I had felt!'

'What did the others do? How many were there?'

'There were three. When the first fell, the others stopped straight away. I saw that they managed to stay on the animal by sitting astride its back. All got down quickly and went to stand around the man who had had the accident, to make sure no doubt that he had not been hurt. But that one stood up, and spoke, pointing with his hands, as if to explain what had happened to him.

'Apparently reassured, each man gave his animal something to drink from a large receptacle carried on one of the beast's flanks. Then, talking all the time, they lit a fire. We gazed at them for a long while. They did not seem to send out any bad waves. After we got over our fright, our curiosity increased. Since they carried no spear, nor club, nor boomerang, and because Guningbal has never harmed us, we came out of our hiding place to go over to them.'

'At last you are going to understand that I have been telling you the truth,' Guningbal, who seems as concerned as Wongu, whispers to me.

'The first to notice us called out, obviously afraid. A terrible noise rent the air, it bounced off the rock face.

We stayed where we were, without budging, looking all around us to find out what was going on. Then I thought that the noise had come out of the nares of one of the animals. At the second outburst, I saw that it was coming from the curious elongated sticks one of the living-dead was holding perpendicular to his face and pointing towards us! I saw a ball of fire shooting out of the stick. Fire-spitting sticks! Yes! Fire! And that fire has unbelievable force. It hit Wotjoba's brother who was killed straight away, blood pouring from every part of his body! But before we could get our courage back, the men and the beasts had already disappeared. I think—'

Wojtoba, recovering her spirits, interrupts him:

'The foreign people of the far east are right. These evil beings are not the dead who have come back to earth. They are monsters disguised as men, monsters!'

'At last!' Guningbal mutters.

I look from one to the other, overwhelmed, horrified at the thought that they have just proved Niumta's so-called son right, horrified that my premonitions have come to fruition.

When we emerge from our hiding place, the monsters are gazing at us from the top of the cliff. Their elongated sticks are spitting fire again. An intense burning sensation pierces my leg, at the same instant separating my body of flesh from my astral body. The latter, hovering a little above the ground between the two warm edges of the rock face, contemplates my wounded body for an instant, to which it is still attached by a flimsy thread. Suddenly, as if sucked up by the waves emerging from my flesh, it falls back, to mingle with it again. I have kept my life.

Alerted by my two friends, several of the men come to

look for me, to take me, with great care, back to my own people. Straight away, Tumenti, accompanied by an old woman, diagnoses a broken tibia. He takes hold of my foot, the woman my knee, and, gently, they put the bone back in place. Then, while continuously chanting some words, the rhythm and sound of which should augment the efficacy of his actions, Tumenti pushes the flesh back into place with light taps of his fingertips. Next, he starts making long passes with his hands above the wound to impregnate it with the healing power diffused by his palms. The old woman massages me with concentrated oils, a remedy she always carries with her in a little bag slung around her neck.

'As you know, it is up to you to take charge of your own recovery. With your mental powers, you must activate the memory in the broken bone until it remembers its healthy state and is ready to recover that state as quickly as possible,' Tumenti tells me.

After several days of rest, I am carried to a sacred rock, a nanja, renowned for helping recalcification. Quickly enough, I am restored to health, retaining in my memory only the presence of these lesser creatures on one of our eastern paths, close to the desert.

Then more news arrives along the chain formed by our trading partners, confirming what we know already, but something my people have never had the courage to concede: Guningbal had told us the truth; none of the dead has returned to earth. White creatures have invaded our country to steal our land.

The rumour which has been spreading from the coast informs us that the white creatures have never received Instruction, that no law seems to govern their behaviour, that they cannot disguise their reactions, as Guningbal had done in the past. They don't even have any religion, unless it's that of work! And they did not come unaccompanied. Strange animals came with them; animals which drained most of the waterholes of the far east. The memory of something I was told about during my childhood, the cow which we took for a spirit, returns to my mind. Only abnormally abundant rain could have impelled them to penetrate so far into the west!

In the evening, we discuss this disquieting news for a long while; we ask ourselves where these pale creatures could have come from. Once again we put the question: what could they want with our country, about which they know nothing, not the topography, not the sacred sites, nor the dangers of the malevolent forces of those places, which could overwhelm them without anyone being able to combat them, since none of them knows anything about them, and none of their Great Ancestors would be there to help them! No! We cannot understand it.

In spite of everything, following the prompting of our whims, we make our way towards the east, negotiating the maze of paths leading to the Sacred High Places, where the plant world begins to take over from the mineral. The path is still singing the great songs associated with it. Over long days we become the path once more, forgetting the vicissitudes of our material life.

So now we have arrived at the edge of the plant world. Days pass. Unlike in other years, the further we travel the more sparse game becomes. This anomaly distresses us. The prospect of a fine roast at the evening halt is no longer a certainty prompting the recovery of energy, joy and gaiety. For two days now, we have been living on what the women have been able to gather and on the few small marsupials and lizards they have caught.

The evening halt! The air is sweet, perfumed with the strong scent of mint, eucalyptus and wattle in full bloom. The sky embraces the last red flickering of

Okerka's cape. An interminable flight of pigeons cuts off the light for many an instant. A colony of wattle parakeets, perched on their favourite tree, bid the day farewell. A flight of thousands of red-tailed cockatoos passes overhead, describing a perfect arc to descend in hovering flight, coming to rest a few paces from us. Hardly have they touched the ground before, with an inverse movement, they soar up to the sky as if with one mind. In their harsh voices they call out 'Good night' to their Dreaming-brothers, to the human beings descended from the same Great Ancestor.

Then silence falls. It is the time of day when the colours of the evening shroud us in their unreal veil, when the waves sent out by the sky and the earth unite in a perfect harmony, impregnating all that lives with itself.

Nevertheless, fires spring to life in a heavy silence broken now and then by grumbling. The children feel the adults' ill ease and seem to be shattered by it. The youngest, snuggling against their parents' breasts, are sucking on a teat for reassurance, burying their heads in the long breasts.

'As long as we don't lack for water, all will be well!' says Mangala the almost-dead in an astonishingly strong voice. 'I saw so many things in my youth, when, for ten Great Assemblies, the rain stayed away from our land!'

But the younger ones make fun of Mangala's hardships. They guffaw, gobbling large roasted grubs, which make up a little too much of the food we eat. Then Guningbal's voice commands everyone's attention, for he rarely speaks out:

'Why are you so sad? You won't die of hunger! In my country, some people never have anything to put in their mouths. Not even a scrap! To survive, they must steal from other people, people who often make themselves sick by eating too much. I don't understand you. Such are my thoughts.'

No one believes his story.

'Stealing a woman, certainly! A woman is unique and love justifies the act. But stealing food! As if Mother Earth did not produce enough for all! And the less courageous, the less able, the simple-minded, are they not fed by their many relations? How could it be otherwise in your country? That is the natural behaviour of every group of True Men! If what you say is true, your country must really be inhabited by creatures who are less than human. Such is my thought,' says Mau, who has hardly any liking for Guningbal.

'You will not make us believe that men can make themselves sick by eating too much while watching others starve to death,' one of my mothers shouts at him. 'Enough of your stupid stories! Your imagination has led you astray! Why would Mother Earth feed some better than others? Don't we all belong to her in the same way? How do you explain your unbelievable ideas? I'm listening.'

'On the other side of the sea, where I come from, people do not belong to the earth.'

'How can we believe your other notions when you tell us such whoppers? People who do not belong to the earth!'

'I know how difficult it is for you to imagine such an error! But that is how white people think. They are persuaded that the earth belongs to them. Even more unbelievably, that the earth is the exclusive property of some, and they alone have to right to hunt, to harvest food from the plains and forests. When they find a starving person killing game for a little food, they hang him, or, at least, lock him in special constructions called prisons. A place where air hardly penetrates, and the sun, the sacred vital energy never does. For some time now, these wretches have been sent to prisons built in your country. You will see, they will steal your land as soon as they can. Possessing land! They always dream of that! Yes! They will steal your land, you can be certain of that.'

Those who are still listening to him shrug, or smile indulgently, with condescension. Despite the return of his memory, despite his behaviour, which has become perfect, Guningbal remains a rather strange creature, a man whose imagination is mired in evil; for everything he tells us about his life among his own people is too horrible for us to believe. And the objects and tools he describes, trying to please us by telling us about them, are too inexplicable for us to take them very seriously at all! Certainly, no power, and above all not the power of those lesser creatures, would be able to fashion them.

As for me, once again, I am tempted to believe him. Every piece of information about his former life makes me reflect on the primitive mentality of men trapped in the constraint of bestiality are likely to have. Without our Great Ancestors, without our civilising Heroes, we would be at the same stage of development! Without them, we would never have reached a state of consciousness, of higher intelligence. Could men so primitive still exist? Unmindful of all their sacred duties, of all the possibilities of rising above their human nature? Difficult enough, indeed, to believe such an obscenity in an age like ours.

7

Early in the morning, a missionary arrives at the prison. The guards, who are barely awake, look at him in astonishment.

'I've come to see a black prisoner. He's called Nari.'

'A blackfellow? Nari?'

'He's tall, with a white beard.'

'Right-oh, they're all tall. Come with me. Perhaps it's the one who hasn't eaten anything for a week.'

The clergyman steps inside the cell, looks at the prisoner. Straight away, his face reflects, in turn, surprise and disbelief, followed by concern and alarm. His eyes dart from the prisoner to the guard, fix on the latter as if to seek confirmation of what he has just seen. He manages at last to exclaim:

'He's here! How can this be? God in Heaven! He's here!'

'Seeing that you asked for him, you must have known that he is here!'

'Nari! What are you doing here?'

At the sound of a voice he recognises, the old man returns to the world of perceptions.

'Why are you in prison? Come on, get up.'

The prisoner sits up, crouches on his heels and casts a glance, as astonished as it is questioning, at his visitor.

'Who told you about me?' he manages to say, in his

own language, after a few seconds.

'Mashubi. He told me that he had tapped into an image he received from the lands of neighbouring people. This image showed you shut inside one of the whites' wiltjas. Of course I don't believe any of that rubbish. God has not given us the skill to see into the distance. Then, I had to ride over here to get wine for the mass. And this morning, without knowing why, I found myself outside this prison. I felt bound to find out whether what he'd said was true. So he's a sorcerer, in league with the devil! What will I do about him?'

'You know as well as I that Mashubi is one of the Men of High Degree, that there is no evil in him. It is merely that he has powers superior to yours. What do you want here?'

'To help you get out. Your people stopped singing alleluias after they found out that you are in danger.'

'You can't do anything. I stole a calf.'

'You, a thief? Come on! You, a cattle thief?'

'You don't understand. You can't do anything for me. Go away.'

'You've really stolen a calf?'

'Yes.'

'I can't believe it. I've gone to the trouble of teaching you that God—'

'Leave it.'

The old man lies down again and turns his back on his visitor.

'I am going to pray for you. And see what I can do. I'll come back tomorrow. To think that I was going to make a good Christian of you!'

The prisoner does not listen to him. Without giving the missionary another thought, he plunges back into the past.

I remember. I am married. I have a good lubra who, thanks to her mothers' advice, gives me sexual satisfaction. However, my love for Natati remains very strong, now and then even managing to distract me from my spiritual life. Oh, not for long because, in truth, only the latter really counts for me. My true discontent arises precisely from that.

Because my life of eternal wandering no longer satisfies me. I feel the need to refine the True Man, the Wise Man I have become. I have come to understand that I must proceed even further in esoteric Knowledge, to extract from my body of flesh and blood, as from my intangible body, the force and power it has still not yielded to me. Only the fashioning of a Wise Man of the highest degree would allow that to happen. The effort is immense and the outcome uncertain. I hesitate.

My intuition tells me, however, that I am capable of overcoming such a difficulty. And, according to my elderly father, even before my training, my body was already shining with the luminous aura particular to men of the highest degree.

I want so passionately to be someone who is able to walk with impunity over fire, to climb an invisible rope towards Waeruward, the world in the sky; someone whose spirit moves on the wings of the wind, who has the gift of being everywhere; who can read the thoughts of his fellows just as he can read traces left behind in the sand, not unwittingly as the others do, but because he wants to; I want to be one who sees events unfolding in the distance whenever he wishes; who knows the future and can warn his group about dangers to come; who takes possession of others' minds for a good cause. I want to be the one to take care of my people, help them with the problems of their everyday life, for which our sacred stories are not always a great comfort; and the one who struggles against evil powers. I want to be all that. Not for prestige, authority, but because that is the only way to pursue the imprecise quest I am following. My entire body and my mind launch themselves on a spiritual quest, a communion with the Sacred Energy.

Such are my thoughts over several moons.

After a final period of reflection, I take at last the decision to share my desire with Tumenti.

Shaken by the violent emotions these last thoughts provoked, Nari is shivering on the floor of his cell; he stops the images of his life unfolding.

For the first time, he becomes aware of the formative role Tumenti has played since his childhood in the emergence of his vocation as a Man of High Degree.

It is in large part thanks to him that he has possessed, since that time, a fine insight into the manner in which the minds of others function. Since his early years, his old father helped him to record in his memory a flood of information about people's general behaviour, but above all about what is reprehensible, explaining to him that loss of health most often results from an imbalance between these two phenomena, a knowledge essential for treating a stubborn illness after the usual methods of healing employed by old women.

The healing powers of the Men of High Degree most often come into play thanks to their ability to set beneficial forces free over the patient in cases where the disease was caused by their contrary, that is to say the powers of certain malevolent Men in command of magical powers. It was accordingly that capacity which he had to develop.

The magnetic power of his hands had already cured many wounds, transmitting a little of his energy to the person lacking it, or, otherwise, removing the harmful surplus. He has also become aware of the power of the waves sent out by his voice. And his hypnotic powers make a tentative appearance.

Tumenti has taught him about most of the symptoms of curable diseases and the symptoms of those beyond hope. In the latter case, it will be necessary for him to become adept enough at explaining to the patient and his group the inevitable outcome or the reasons why he failed. He had helped him just as much to glean and classify in his mind the attitudes of local groups, whether of clans and tribes, a knowledge indispensable for flushing out a criminal whenever the need arose. There still remains much for him to do. But his studies rely only on his courage, his aptitude for observation, his memory and his concern for the welfare of others. The most difficult thing will be to make the powers, the mana, of the Men of High Degree spring to life once more. Powers which are in an embryonic state in all human beings, that only an ascetic life, a steadfast will and completely ignoring the self can succeed in setting it free. For that, he will have to endure psychological and physical trials of a most terrifying kind. He hopes that his courage and determination will prove strong enough.

Tumenti and Mashubi will be his masters. On condition that he fashions a dream, a very precise dream, which alone will give him access to their instruction. For that, they tell him, he must go away for an extended period of fasting and solitude in order to meditate on death until it pursues him in his dreams.

The old black man conjures up with force his memories of the time of his training as a Man of High Degree, as his people say, that final, lengthy journey of initiation as a shaman, as others will come to call it. To achieve that, he controls his breathing for a long time, rids his mind of the parasites which took possession of it with the sounds and the voices of the prison, emotions which his memories have made surge again. Finally, he manages to channel the Cosmic Energy and, after a few moments, achieves a state of total relaxation.

So he returns to the past. He becomes, once again, the proud, dignified man of a bygone time.

My two masters lead me to an unfamiliar site, an immense flat expanse, covered all over with the ochre blood of the Unjtiamba Women, an exultant colour which the sparkling azure of the sky seems never able to meet, so far away is the horizon. Here and there, tufts of karingana, one of our medicinal plants, perfume the warm air with the scent of mint.

We come to a stop in front of a rocky outcrop. The two men explain to me that a Man of High Degree with unequalled powers was buried there. A little time before his death, he spent many days, many nights lying on that ledge. There, by means of an unknown power, he had engraved all his knowledge into the mineral. For eternity. In order that other men might benefit from it.

'Look, Nari,' they say, 'when we are at a little distance, pointing out two identical tall rocks separated by a narrow fissure, their perfectly smooth walls glistening with flashes of the quartz embedded in the pink granite. 'In the Dreamtime, two of the Unjtiamba Women sank into the earth in this place, so giving birth to these two rocks. And they made sure that these two mineral forms would surge out of the ground, absorbing the Knowledge locked within their nuruntunjas and their churingas. Today they, too, continue to diffuse that Knowledge. But only to certain of the True Men, those who are endowed with the correct mana.'

As I look at them in some astonishment, they continue:

'Yes! That is how it is. All the Knowledge of the Primordial Times has been retained by the mineral of our sacred sites. Mineral, that other form of Life to which we owe so much. Such is our Instruction. The rock in this place will help you fashion your anticipated dream. On condition that you are thoughtful and that you meditate upon the greatest possible number of myths and legends concerning death. That you mingle all these representations until a new truth emerges from them.'

With these words, they leave me, promising to return when they have had six nights' sleep.

I am lying on the warm sand, surrounded by the soft shadows of the night, close to my little fire, my sole companion for six long days. Not far from me, a marsupial mouse emerges from its burrow concealed beneath the rocks and scampers off in search of a morsel of food. In the distance, a dingo sends up its love call. I hear a night bird agitating the air with its powerful wings. I love this semi-darkness, which was the darkness of the first ages, before the birth of the Woman Sun.

I raise my eyes to the sky. Tonight the Man Moon is revealing his entire self, adorned with his most beautiful starlight. He seems to be smiling at me. Without cease, my gaze returns to him. And that is when he sends me a message. He, Bahloo, who formerly transformed human beings into mortals to punish them for not wanting to help him search for what he called his dogs, snakes in truth, has now consented to help me dream of death, his vengeful invention.

For long moments, the memory of stories about this terrible chastisement, stories I heard in my childhood, in my adolescence, memories of the successive deaths I endured during my long formation as a True Man, all unfold inside my head, superimposing themselves, mingling late into the night. After life ceases, there is neither reward nor punishment. Dreaming about it should hardly cause me torment. Without knowing why, an entirely different experience, oh how unsettling, precedes what I have been longing for, while fearing it, too, all along.

I can sense my yowie, my astral body, leaving my body, as it often does, to go wandering at will throughout my sleep. But this time, Tumenti's is waiting for it, hovering above my camping place. And our two spirits set out, invisible, on the path of the Man Emu where one of our relatives is visiting a group of the Sparrowhawk Dreaming. Tumenti takes possession of her spirit and orders it to go to declare her love for Nepa, my maternal grandfather, the man she loves in silence. We then return, to reintegrate ourselves within our own envelopes of flesh.

I awake. The land at the horizon begins to sparkle. I remain stretched out, without stirring, trying in vain to recall my dreams. I have trouble concentrating, for all of my senses are answering the call of the life around me.

I breathe in the dry air with relish. It is suffused for an instant with the smell of sand mingled with the scent of eucalypts and a solitary wattle. My flesh tingles with well-being at the first caressing rays of the Woman Sun, who is now entirely visible. I wonder at the thousand sparkles of the vermilion cloak she drapes over the desert, an immensity of sand and rocks of all sizes where shadows, carmine, mauve or violet, change in intensity at every instant.

Is this a presage? Some forty paces away, two large monitor lizards are rearing up, struggling vigorously. In that posture, their height is impressive. But even taller were the Men Lizards of Alcheringa Time.

An eagle with a cuneiform tail appears in the sky. Its wing span, the size of a human body, casts a huge shadow on the ground. As if warned of its presence, the two lizards separate, still rearing on their hind legs; they start running off in opposite directions; in a few seconds, as if by enchantment, they vanish into the immensity of the desert.

Time passes. The heat becomes difficult to endure. I have seen the Man Moon die and, for several days, I see him recovering. Complete fasting, the burning sun, solitude, the interrupted meditation have made me terribly feeble.

Despite everything, I continue meditating on death. All through the day, in the infiniteness of the desert, the burning rocks send out their heat with a whisper; in a low voice they sing to me about eternity of the true Life; slowly they diffuse through my spirit the Knowledge with which they have been impregnated. They lead me to understand that the essential part of my being is immutable, eternal, and that that alone is of any importance. Slowly, they manage to make my apprehensiveness about the dream of death disappear. My communion with them is such that I lose perception of my body of flesh. Several times, I fall into a swoon. Several times, my consciousness raises itself towards the higher spheres.

It is then that death enters into my dream. It takes hold of my spirit, removes it from of my body against my will, leads it in a rush to the bottom of a black chasm. And in this chasm, made of a material more compact than flint, I am tossed about at a dizzying speed. I struggle mightily against the despair of not being able to escape this infernal rotation. But, little by little, the unknown material absorbs me; in a long spasm of suffering, I feel nothingness engulfing me.

The dream goes on and on for days. My screams awake me. Ever since I have been capable of accomplishing the feat, I memorise straight away all the terrifying experiences I have endured. Will they give me the right to receive the Instructions of the Men of High Degree? I am too feeble to attach any importance to that any longer.

On the appointed day, Tumenti and Mashubi appear next to me. They inform me that the meeting between my ethereal self and my old father had been my first victory. And my dream about death had been an excellent dream.

'Forget about it forever,' they command me.

I have succeeded! They agree to fashion me into a Wise Man. I am happy. I manage to stand up. I have the right to a frugal meal, the first for many a long day. Then, without delay and despite my weakened condition, we set out for the camp again. After these days spent in solitude, I am truly glad to take up again the life of the group, the long wanderings, sharing everything, our joys, our sorrows, food; lengthy discussions in the evening under the starry sky; the marvellous fellowship that arises among men in the course of a difficult hunt, when someone else's skill and astuteness prove as gratifying as your own.

Since I experienced the dream of death, I sense that many relatives are wonderfully close to me, as if they made up a part of me. I perceive us as one and the same entity; an entity which, one day, will dilute itself anew in the primordial Energy from which it issued, from which we have all issued. This revelation changes my relationship with my own people, rendering it extremely easy.

And sure enough, after my ascetic life, the joys of love invade my body and mind. Nevertheless, I am glad when the time to retire into solitude arrives once more.

Slowly, with infinite patience, with a calm mind, with meditating, with remembering, Tumenti and Mashubi suffuse him with their esoteric knowledge; they insist on physical and mental exercises intended to render his material and spiritual body more receptive. Nari learns even greater indifference to the small cares of everyday life, true parasites of the spirit. After his earlier training, he has learnt, like all the Wise Men, to neutralise that part of his consciousness which blocks access to the information possessed by the unconscious. Today, he must learn to master it completely so as to remain in unbroken contact with the knowledge he carries within himself. Better, he must grow capable of harnessing the unconscious desires of his people.

It is at this period that his extrasensory powers are definitively confirmed; that his telepathic gifts increase; that premonition and the ability to see distant things come to him more and more frequently. It is at this period that he enters with growing ease into the parallel world.

At last the day arrives when Tumenti and Mashubi,

accompanied by two of the other Men of High Degree, surprise him once more in his place of retreat. The time of the first examination is about to arrive. Strangely, he feels no apprehension.

Speaking all together, telling apparently trivial stories which they manage to make dense, confused in outline, pronouncing one maxim after another, mixing up myths, slipping small mistakes into them, they wait for him to pick out straight away, by replying almost simultaneously to each of them, symbols, philosophical propositions and also to identify physical and mental techniques. And his replies come, rapidly, spontaneously, without the need of any reflection on his part, because his whole being has memorised these concepts for all time; they impregnate his blood, they are forever flowing through his whole body of flesh. And his brain is able to recall them with dizzying speed.

The old man experiences again the state of marvel which the discovery of his immense ability procured for him. He recalls his extreme weakness, the mental alertness increased tenfold by all the extrasensory faculties that manifested themselves when, over the course of days, he was plunged again into the delights and torments of solitude.

Then the memory of the vision of Tumenti and Mashubi walking along the path of the Monitor Lizard Dreaming makes him leave behind the present he had recovered for an instant.

Stretched out on the sand, my eyes shut, I capture what is in my masters' minds. I see what they see, feel what they feel. After two long days, they reach at last the place where I am; they lift me up and help me walk for what seems to me an eternity. They plunge me in a waterhole and confine me to the care of the inhabitant of that place, the Rainbow Serpent, the all-powerful cosmic being. I am shivering in the liquid element, I have trouble holding my breath. I lose the sense of sight.

But that is when I enter into communication with the being of the Dreamtime. I sense my spirit fusing with its at the moment when a piercing pain slashes through my head, bringing with it a vision of lightning flashes like those during a most violent storm. I feel that the whole of my body is about to explode in a thousand sparks. I cannot tell one limb from another.

Soft, musical voices cut through the blur of my panic and, gradually, I grow calm. Small creatures, neither men nor birds, rise before me. Their song, softer than a caress, assures me that they will always be my friends, always be at my side to help me. Always!

Abruptly, I am sucked down even deeper. I hold my breath the best I can. I am choking. My last effort of will to defend myself leaves me. I feel that I am snatched up by the being of the Beginning. I slide into its entrails, a deep, black bottomless pit. Strangely, my mind stays alert. Suddenly, the Rainbow Serpent surges from the pit, running off to spew me out in a place far removed from there.

Here I am now, all alone, in a foetal position, in the immensity of the red plain, at the base of a white gumtree. Little by little, the rhythm of my physiological life reasserts itself. My sight returns and my four limbs obey my brain. The glow of the perfectly distinct seven colours of the rainbow overwhelms and dazzles me.

Then I have a new vision, that of my two masters searching for me. They make their way slowly; the ritual designs painted on their bodies strike my eyes. A few moments later, I hear Tumenti's voice above me:

'Look at your body, Nari. It is no longer that of a man. It has become the body of the baby you once were.'

Saying this, he raises me with one of his hands placed under my right armpit and, with the other, he seizes the rainbow, the colours of which are so many soft but solid ropes. Passing from one to another, slowly, without effort, as if propelled by the gamut of shadings, he climbs them as far as Waeruward, the world of the sky. There, he hurls me violently down to the celestial ground. The shock momentarily stops me from living. My astral body watches as Tumenti inserts a maban, a small piece of glistening substance, into my infant's head, two others into my ankles. Then, with his index finger, he opens my abdomen. With slow and precise gestures, he begins to pull out my intestines and all my other organs.

Then, with infinite precaution, he places one by one other mabans, small, round beads of crystal all of the same size, sparkling like stars, inside the gaping hole. I hear him intoning a sacred song over my open abdomen. The warm timbre of his voice, its slow rhythm comfort me again.

Then, filled with terror, I see him descending to earth again by letting his hands slide down one of the colours of the rainbow. There, he picks up a small snake with the same name, hidden in a waterhole. To my great relief, I seem him climbing up towards me, approaching my still inanimate body and placing the animal between the life-giving, empowering crystal objects.

I see him pulling on my flesh to close the wound, passing his hands slowly over it. After a moment, I feel the warmth of the waves discharged by his palms.

Tumenti sings, in time with his movements, they themselves in rhythm with the words of the sacred formula. His litany seems to increase the warmth spreading over my belly; it becomes unbearable. But, slowly, my flesh recovers and my wound vanishes without leaving a trace behind.

Throughout this long operation, my physical body regains life slowly, twitches with pain, then leaps joyfully at contact with the mabans; and from pain once again. I can sense it seeping through all eternity.

At last everything contracts and normal life returns again.

Now, my yowie continues hovering for a time above my envelope of flesh, still that of a child.

Then Tumenti puts this envelope of flesh under his arm and descends to earth again on the same magic rope. My master puts me down in the middle of a circular space surrounded by dry branches, with which he makes a fire. I can vaguely discern Mashubi next to him. Both, in their hoarse voices, intone formulas which must get me to return to my adult body. The power of their words, the power of the waves they discharge and the power of their rhythm merge together in the overheated air circulating above our heads; they revive my vitality. I become aware of the warmth around me. Little by little, my invisible body is made one with my body of flesh. I rise from the dead.

Mashubi makes me drink a long draught of my two masters' mingled blood, blood sprinkled with shards of crystal, other powerful mabans. My strength returns.

Mashubi comes up to me. He grasps my head and, with a rapid movement, ritually breaks my neck, marking it with a black stone heavy with the power concealed within it. Then, with a stick glowing at the tip, he pierces my tongue. The pain is terrible, and I need all the help of my newfound winged friends not to faint. I feel my body of flesh vanishing again as the ethereal part of my being disengages itself from it, irresistibly attracted by a living circle of light, golden, soft and chanting, at the centre of which a dazzling, swirling silver shape seems to want to breathe. With all my strength, I yearn to be swallowed up by it forever. At the same moment, an atrocious pain wrenches my flesh and, in that swirling mass, from which I cannot remove my eyes, in a flash of lightning, in a rush of love, I glimpse the supreme perfection of what we call the Mother! I am transfigured, transformed for ever.

I concentrate all my will so that my mind may recover the far too fleeting image which has just made a new being of me. Alas! Despite all my effort, against my inclinations, I am brought back to the world below. I already know that no everyday word, that no sacred word would be able to describe, would be able to explain the experience I have just undergone. Lying on the ground, I fall asleep.

When I wake, I have become a Man of High Degree, a man commanding the highest Knowledge, of great power, one who mediates between the worlds of the living and the dead. I have now been admitted into the company of those of our people who command esoteric and advanced mental knowledge. I feel satisfied, serene. Suddenly, I capture a message, and then I know that I will not be able to climb any higher into the memory of the Eternal Dreamtime. I have attained my ideal self.

8

The Woman Sun climbs slowly over a mountain range as old as Time, which has been transformed by wind, rain, the searing heat of day and the icy cold of night into a rocky skeleton. It is soon set ablaze by her coppery golden rays. Like the Man Moon, Okerka looks down with contempt on the huts of the little settlement in the back of beyond. She curses the leprous stain on the earth she illuminates and warms; she does not care greatly for the newcomers, human beings drained of colour who ignore her completely or flee from her to shelter beneath roofs they have made out of some unknown material! She yearns for people whose dark skin is in harmony with the landscape, those brown men who greet her each morning, addressing her throughout the day. It has been thus since the dawn of Time. But, she thinks, wholly disrespectful though they are, the newcomers also obey the rhythm of my journey over the earth to the land of the dead.

When she reappears, the daily life of the whites goes into full swing again. The scraping of chairs, metal pitchers clanging against one another, the voices of those who are barely awake ring out in the prison. These noises do nothing to disturb the calm reigning in one of the cells. On the bench, an untouched bowl of soup is waiting for the flies to come to life. The black prisoner, lying motionless, still curled up on the ground, continues watching the scenes of his life as they unfurl.

After attaining the status of a Man of High Degree, here he is resuming his normal life, the life of the group.

Yes! I realise very quickly that my people think of me as a stranger. That makes me sad at first. Then I understand the reason for their reaction: most often I am withdrawn from the world down here, having plunged body and soul into the intangible world, indifferent to petty daily cares. My young wife seems to be reconciled to that. I have a good lubra.

Tumenti is growing old. He is losing his skill, becoming less sure of himself. His influence is on the wane. More and more often, I am the one to give advice, to heal, bring rain, apprehend someone guilty of a crime, thanks to my ability to see into the distance, and even to determine whether to mount a punitive expedition. My reputation grows.

Here I am on the path of the Man Emu. It is carrying us with lively steps towards the Great Assembly which has been arranged for the occasion of the circumcision of young men from the two moieties of our people. It is our turn, the turn of the Grey Falcons, to be responsible for the rite. For this occasion, we have invented new dances, new songs. My wife has captured some new verses that came to her in a dream from the world of the Invisibles. She offers it to the Wise Men of our various groups. If all acknowledge that it came from the parallel world, it will be adopted, it will bring new blood to our rite.

At each place where we stop for the night, we practise our dances, for it is necessary to perfect the rhythms and steps. We must give the best of ourselves so that the ceremony equals and even surpasses the one for which the Sparrowhawks were responsible last year.

As we are travelling, we think about our many obligations towards our blood relations, towards those of our kindred, our many close relatives, our Dreaming-brothers, and our trading partners among other groups of the Grey Falcons or Sparrowhawks; finally towards those partners from other people whom we will be meeting. On this occasion, it is for a particular reason that these thoughts provoke our spirit of competition. Because in order to receive from other people properly, it is necessary to know how to give properly. That is why I can sense a certain tension among my people. Confronted by imperatives of this kind, they are going to be obliged, once more, to bring the best out of themselves, to demonstrate, as much as possible, that they command the qualities of their ideal selves, of the Sacred Being they once were.

After an instant, the rhythm of our steps and of the path of song make me forget about the coming festivities. Here I am again coursing through Alcheringa Time, far from the petty problems of the world below.

Suddenly, the image of our appointed partners from a people of the far east comes forcefully into my mind. As is the custom, they are waiting for us at the crossing of our paths, ready to exchange certain of their possessions with us. I capture the telepathic message sent out by one of them: something is upsetting them, making them afraid. I fall in step with some of the Wise Men.

And, in effect, when we reach them, and after the usual greetings have barely finished, they start talking all at the same time. They found that some of their watering places had been polluted or depleted by animals belonging to the white-skinned humans, the migloos as they call them; the strange wiltjas which these creatures build are becoming more and more numerous on their north-eastern paths. Each of the migloos brings the inevitable herds of bulls, cows and calves, abominable sink holes that guzzle the last drop of water, devour the smallest scrap of vegetation. In that region, they say, wallabies are becoming rare, killed by 'fire-sticks' or displaced by these new animals that eat up their food. As for the emus, they have practically disappeared; in a few moons, millions of flightless birds have been reduced to little groups of twenty or so individuals; a great deal of luck is needed if you are to come across them, because they have changed their usual habitats. Also, their meat and eggs are becoming sparse over there. Finding food each day is affected by it.

'We thought we might find the abundance of earlier times again by coming west,' Ardana, one of my partners tells me. 'But there is nothing. You are also going to find, no doubt, that your next watering place has been polluted or dried up.'

Our group listens, horrified. Sitting in the shade of a karingana with the scent of mint wafting from it, we spend a long time learning about the invaders. We are not too sure what to make of all that. Finally, disheartened, we set about exchanging goods.

I see my people forming a group around an object which makes them call out 'Ah!' I go over to them and discover, at the centre of circle they have formed, a man holding a strange cutting tool, an axe, as we learnt to call it, the blade of which is, quite simply, incredibly sharp.

'From what kind of stone could it possibly have been made?' someone asks.

'This is not stone. It's some material from the world of the whites. This tool came from the far east; reaching me by means of many successive barters. It is mightily effective. At first, we did not dare make use of it, for fear that it might posses some malevolent power. Then, after several tests without disastrous consequences, we have adopted it.'

Our eyes linger on the whites' axe, bemused and envious.

I go back to Ardana and ask him if it would be possible, at our next meeting, to procure such a tool for myself. My group would be ready to pay a very good price.

My old friend laughs, and says that what I ask is truly very difficult, but that he will do all he can. And we get down to the transactions of the day. I exchange with him the skin of a red kangaroo, rare for a long time now on these paths, for a sharkskin, wonderful for polishing weapons and other useful objects. I watch Wongu haggling bitterly to get hold of a strange piece of cloth woven from the bright red fibres of some unknown plant. A piece of cotton, we will learn later on. His partner is a crafty old devil and, as usual, he tries to get as much as possible out of the exchange. At last he accepts the long flint with a sharp point Wongu offers him.

When individual transactions are finished, my group decides to acquire the rights to a dance and a song which some of us have known and wanted to use for a long time. In exchange, we offer the other group balls of red and yellow ochre, an earth not to be found in their country, and therefore indispensable for their ceremonies. When we reach an agreement, the shadows cast by the vegetation stretch to their greatest length over the ground. We leave at last, hurrying to reach the evening stopping place.

The following day, we find, indeed, that our watering place is dry and that, all around, the ground has been soiled by the migloos' beasts. We have to dig to quench our thirst. Something that would not be too serious if the absence of water did not also signify the absence of game. Disappointed, anxious, we follow the path again, impatient to arrive at our next billabong, a small pond concealed in an island of rock, a place which, because of the complete absence of vegetation, would have no attraction for the whites' animals.

All of a sudden, children are running towards us, calling out, speaking all together, a flabbergasted look on their young faces.

'Come, come quickly!'

They lead us to a clump of low-growing wattle as they all babble at the same time, without our being able to understand anything.

'There!'

They poke their fingers into the branches, all the while holding our dogs back.

A dingo is in its death throes in a pool of blood; one of its paws is half caught in some sort of a giant maw, with large and sharp teeth, made from a material resembling that of the axe. It must have been there for many days because its body is reduced to a skeleton. We stand frozen in front of this incomprehensible sight. One after the other, the members of the group crouch to look at it; they stand up straight away crying out in astonished voices, then in horror and terror. The suffering of my Dreaming-brother throbs through my whole body as soon as my gaze comes to rest on him. I am looking at him as if I myself had fallen victim to such an atrocity.

'We must finish him off,' someone calls out. 'We must put and end to his suffering.'

I go away. It is not I who can put an end to the agony of my brother – I have never killed a wild dog, never tasted its flesh. Law, to be sure, forbids killing or eating a Dreaming-brother; doing that would be to fell a part of yourself.

A spear takes flight and plants itself in the animal's heart. A few twitches, and the calm of death descends over the body. There follows a respectful silence for the spirit of one of our dead which might have taken refuge, for a time, in the dog's body. We are all moaning, moving our heads from right to left, as if refusing to believe what we have seen.

After hesitating a little, I remove the corpse from its hiding place by pulling on its hind legs. I drag with it the 'thing' responsible for this horrible agony. I tap the sides with my spear in an attempt to free the animal. Without success. The women send up cries of woe, and the men all have a lugubrious look on their faces. We are all tormented by the thought of how our Great Dingo Ancestor will react to such a profanation, by the thought that this malevolent act is without doubt that of a people who own a path parallel to ours, with whom, however, we have never had any trouble. We discuss, for a long time, what could have led its members to commit such a terrible deed.

Guningbal speaks out:

'Your neighbours are not responsible. This,' he says pointing to the object, 'this had been sent by the whites. If it is not with their fire-sticks, then it's this way that the migloos are trying to make your animals disappear, our animals now that I am one of you.'

We look at him with questioning faces.

'What are you talking about? The whites' power is not as dangerous as this!'

'Do you want us to believe that there are killing stones in their land?' one of the women asks, as she is about to sit down a little further away so that she can put her child to her breast.

'You can see clearly enough that this is not a stone! More probably it's a half-broken shell.'

'No! This object is made of metal, the same material as the tool we saw yesterday, especially made for killing animals.'

Now seated in a circle, we are all lost in our thoughts, once more not knowing what to make of Guningbal's words.

'So what kind of beings, then, are these migloos? It must be that they are cowardly and vicious enough to kill animals in this way, not to recognise the suffering they are inflicting on them, not to suffer when they are suffering! Where could creatures capable of carrying out such horrible deeds have come from? I wouldn't for all the world want to meet one of them!' says the pretty Mureimurei as her crying baby is trying to crawl up onto her haunch.

'Me, I don't believe this story. It's an object from the beyond, from the beyond of the people of the east whose paths cross ours; an object saturated with their evil forces, which are more powerful than the whites',' affirms the almost-dead.

'Sure, sure,' say some.

'How can we tell?' others reply.

A dull sound makes our eyes return to the dingo. Guningbal has just prised open the strange maw without any difficulty, obliging us to think more carefully about what he had suggested. A long silence follows. We disengage the animal, and carry it a little father away to hide its body under some stones.

I lean over the object, trying to figure out how it works.

'One of us could have met the same fate as the dingo. If we are really dealing with a malevolent object belonging to a neighbouring people, the danger is immense!' says a man, who never believes a word that the living-dead, the son of Niumta, says.

'That's certain. It couldn't have been the migloos. I've heard people say that apart from their fire-sticks they possess no other mental capacity!' one of our young men replies.

'Which doesn't stop them from being very dangerous,' says Guningbal with conviction in his voice.

'Our friend is right,' Babaka says at length. He is another partner of Wongu, whose paths penetrate deep into the south-east, and who joined us at yesterday evening's camp to help prepare for the next ceremony.

'At the Great Assembly,' he continues, 'your people will put you in touch with many things you know nothing about. You will come to understand the real danger threatening us.'

No else one speaks. I return to the dingo's corpse, to conjure away the wrath of what might be the spirit of one of our dead. I go away to sit on my own. In a muted voice, with the rhythm of two sticks struck against each other, I recite the appropriate incantations. Ones I consider appropriate, for I have never had to deal with such a situation.

Pensive as much as careworn, we continue making our way along the path. In the evening we reach, at last, the creek where our billabong lies concealed. Smiling with a sense of well-being, our gaze strays to the place where we are sure to find a tranquil surface of limpid water. But our eyes come to rest on the huge rumps of three animals cutting off that longed-for sight. Three tails are wagging their ridiculous pompoms; one of them is raised, and the beast drops an enormous pat of stinking, steaming excrement. Heads down, indifferent to our presence, the animals continue gorging the liquid of life. Of our life!

Recovering her spirits more quickly than the others, one of the women picks up a stone and, with a precise action, aims it at one of the beasts' flanks. It jumps, takes fright, turns around and flees into the rocky maze, taking the other two with it. We can hear the fitful noises they make as they are running over the stony ground. Of our clear and transparent water, there remains no more than a muddy, nauseating pond, with trampled and flattened edges, which no longer retains, in all likelihood, the least trickle of water from the spring.

We have just met our greatest enemy, two cows and a calf.

9

Here we are, after all our trials, Sparrowhawks and Grey Falcons gathered at last at the ceremonial site.

Although the rite should be conducted with exceptional fervour, only the images of yesterday's meeting swirl in our minds.

We are squatting on our heels on absolutely circular lines traced in the sand of a creek-bed, which have been marked out with the dust of red ochre, as we listen to each of the participants speaking his mind. Every piece of news gleaned by all of our trading partners – of the east, of the west, of the north-east, of the north and of the south – proves more difficult to believe than the other.

We are obliged to do more than turn the evidence over in our minds. Not only is it true that the living-dead do not exist, as our friends from the east tell everyone, but the migloos, some lesser kind of human beings, have invaded our land. And they are approaching the network of our twisting paths at the edge of the plant world; they are steadily advancing west!

'For the moment,' says one of the Men of High Degree, 'we are seeing only the few animals that have managed to escape from the pens in which they are confined near the whites' wiltjas. Tomorrow, it is likely that we will be seeing as many of these as the tribes of the far east complain of seeing. So, just as it is over there, farewell to our watering places, our kangaroos, our emus.'

'We'll kill the cattle!' someone jests. Everyone laughs, no one takes the suggestion seriously.

'That would be easy, they're always confined behind posts, in unbelievable numbers, near the whites' wiltjas.'

'Have I understood correctly what you have just said? Do the migloos keep innumerable animals in confinement near their shelters? But why?'

'That's the mystery, for they don't kill them, except the odd beast or two from time to time.'

'You are meaning to tell us that they enclose all these beasts for nothing? That there aren't enough of them to eat all that meat?'

'Well, yes! That's just it! Unbelievable but true! Sometimes there are no more than three or four of them, and they guard hordes of captive animals! They own many more than they need! Yes, you have heard correctly, many more! I've though about this a great deal, I can't really understand why they do this.'

'To dry up our watering places,' Mashubi answers in a bitter voice. 'To dry up our watering places to stop the kangaroos breeding! In a word, if I understand what you are saying, they want to destroy our land to see us perish there!'

'I know nothing about that. That is, in any case, what will happen, whether or not they want it that way. And, behaving as they do, they don't experience any of the pleasures of the hunt, they destroy all the plant life around them. So I can't understand what they are doing. I've heard it said that they behave as if they are ignorant of the blessings of our Mother Earth; that, on the contrary, they flee from her and shut themselves behind lifeless stones piled on top of one another; or behind sturdy timber stockades, even cutting themselves off from the sky with roofs without openings. People insist that they have no respect for it. The only thing they know how to do is to concern themselves with material things, without finding enough free time for things of the mind. No one has ever seen them meditating! One of my trading partners, from the Diyari people, managed to get inside one of their wiltjas. He assured us that he felt sick in there because beneficial waves could only penetrate it with great difficulty. One of his trading partners, who lives not far from the sea, told him that over there these lesser beings chop down entire forests!'

'Entire forests! What are you trying to tell us?'

'That's what I've heard from several of my partners from the people living near the coast. It is a serious problem for them. Every day, they see game disappearing at the same time as the timbered country and the watering places disappear, all in step with the arrival of these new animals. It is getting essential for us to drive out those whom we must call our invaders. Essential to make them return to their own land.'

We listen in disbelief.

'Here and there, some groups tried hard enough to fight the enemy with the psychic powers of the Men of High Degree. Without success. Then they decided to join forces to enhance their chances; they asked us whether we wanted to join them. It concerns you too, because each day the invaders are growing more numerous and they are making their way west, bringing with them more, and still more, cows and calves. What do you think? We can't just sit around while they invade our own lands, and make us starve too, in turn. We cannot sit around with folded arms, waiting for the great balance of the Dreamtime to be broken. What will happen to us then? What terrible punishment will fall on us? We must do something.'

Men and women agree with him, they ask a thousand other questions. So that we can think things over, I withdraw, together with the Wise Men of my group. Our experience of these things is confined to Guningbal, who now possesses Knowledge – he is a fine man – and, certainly, to those insane horsemen, the murderers of Wotjoba's brother. Our spies are still looking for the person responsible, who must recompense the family because they are suffering great hardship as a consequence; but despite the help of our partners from other peoples, we have never been able to obtain even a scrap of information that would point out where to find the white murderer, so that we might make him respect our law. However, this business is only an isolated instance, and, after lengthy discussions and much reflection, we have decided that we do not have the unqualified right to condemn all white men, for these are white men, for acts which were probably committed by certain irresponsible people among them.

The last crimson rays are vanishing from the horizon when we reach an agreement to take part, at least, in an extraordinary assembly made up of the Wise Men and the Men of High Degree of several friendly peoples to the east and the north.

The women who, for their part, have for long been considering the problem, are also in agreement about accepting the invitation to the meeting set down for the next full moon at the site of the Woman Honey Ant, far to the west, a site still unsullied by the presence of white men, its watering place allowing such an important assembly to be held. Despite the late hour, our messengers, armed with their message sticks, set out straight away to take our reply to the organisers of the assembly - small dark shadows, each vanishing in a different direction.

When we fall asleep, we dream of malevolent spirits, of cruel migloos, of enraged Ancestors. And we will need long days to accept fully the truth of all we have learnt in the course of one evening.

The appointed time arrives. The drought persists with brutal force; it is particularly severe this season. It bakes, it burns the plants best armed against its malice. Patches of water, ponds, pools have disappeared, and, in most cases, the water beneath the ground is no more than reddish sludge, not fit for use. What is more, we do not linger on our way along the path, as is our usual custom. We are in a hurry to reach the meeting place for a refreshing bath, delighted that the meeting is to take place next to such a supply of water. Situated at the extremity of a small promontory, it is contained in a huge cavity of orange-coloured granite rock, fed by the slow trickle of a gentle spring. A thick carpet of spongy moss filters this stream of clear water. Emerging out this greenery, which is as fresh to the eyes as to the touch, the sparkling white of a eucalypt proclaims the victory of trees over the mineral world; for all around, on the barren slopes of a mountain range, there are only boulders, stones, pebbles or rocks, worn down by erosion, barely marked here and there by the greenish grey or carbon black of a few bushes just managing to cling to life. To the south, a gap in a narrow gorge leads the eye towards the limitless flat expanse of the stony desert, a plain all sparkling with the fire of white quartz, black rocks polished to perfection by the sand-laden wind, fragments of transparent chalcedony, yellow, red, brown or black jasper. A land fit for meditation if not for everyday life.

The arrival of the participants, belonging to three different peoples, builds up over several days. And, very soon, the various encampments transform the landscape. Set well apart from one another, each place reunites members of the same Dreaming.

At last the meeting of the Men of High Degree may take place. It is held in a small creek-bed, at a little distance from the encampments, transformed into a meeting place of the occasion. The meeting may commence.

The less well-informed groups listen. Then the participants speak in turn, never interrupting whoever happens to be speaking. After lengthy discussions, long moments of silence, of reflection, all reach an agreement that, if we are united, the intangible strengths of our spirits will prove our best defence. We others, whose surprise does not stop increasing, hesitate to join in. But after seeking information from several groups of strangers, we are obliged indeed to believe what the speakers had said! And we understand at last that we have no other choice.

It is decided that, in secret, each Man of High Degree, on the same day and at the same moment, will point the Bone at the nearest invaders; it will take possession of their minds to impress mental images on them, making them believe that their vital organs are being gnawed by worms. This notion will not leave them for several days. By means of this self-suggestion, they themselves will bring about the inevitable death of these organs.

Our lethal powers will have to be disseminated after a public ceremony, in the course of which all the True Women and Men who are present will also let loose their weak, innate powers against all the white men. That time, the images would have to be of such a nature as to bring the latter to their death in three or four days' time.

The difficult thing will be putting in place the revelatory signs of the Bone in order to point them in the direction of potential victims. We consider ourselves adroit enough to accomplish that.

In the days that follow, we spend much time thinking up the most effective means of succeeding with our attack. In order to accomplish it, we must represent, with symbols, all the living beings who have been drawn into our drama: the cattle in the first instance, the subhumans, as we have come to think of them, and, it goes without saying, ourselves, the despoiled people. Three groups of dancers mimic the behaviour of one or the other of these groups. The dancing and the singing, preceded by the execution of ritual paintings on the ground and on our bodies, enhance the dissemination of our collective forces.

Having settled the essentials, we invent songs that draw their strength from their rhythms, and address the new reality we are facing with words which do not evoke the same image for all: the bulls, calves, sheep, horses, killing-sticks, 'white men's eyes' – objects which, it seems, compensate for their poor eyesight. Some days later, the preparations get under way with the properly intoned chants.

Men representing the migloos smear their faces with white clay: then their legs, their arms, their trunks with red, yellow and black, in order to imitate the different kinds of skins that cover the invaders. On top of their heads, they shove a basketwork copy of a vaguely oval object which, it seems, the latter rarely remove. The others finish making a manikin out of an assemblage of branches and creepers, also representing the white man. Those representing cattle adorn their backsides with a long plait made of thin, flexible vines, the ends of which imitate the pompoms of those strange animals. The men of the third group have an easier game to play, for they represent what they are, black men, furious at witnessing the violation of the greatest of their Commandments, against leaving one's own land to steal the lands of others.

Something their laws had not foreseen, so unthinkable had it seemed! There is no doubt that they will have no difficulty feigning rage.

Now we must prepare the ceremonial ground, situated in a semicircular space, surrounded by high cliffs glowing in the sunlight. We pluck grasses and branches from the sandy soil. So we have a large round surface, perfectly smooth, ready to receive the sand, tinted with white, red or black, on which we are going to trace the symbols of the Tutelary Spirits.

I pick up handfuls of black sand, which I am going to sprinkle from my fingers while I walk in such a way as to trace out the long slithering path of the Rainbow Serpent. In the same way, the other Men of High Degree trace various symbols with distinctive colours. I still remember the fervour which overwhelmed me in the course of this tracing, I can still feel the magnetic fluid, absorbed by the coloured mineral trickling from my hands, which it transforms into a field of powerful forces, those best capable of attracting the Sacred Energy, our ally.

When everything is ready, the perfect circle formed by this arrangement sends out waves to encourage the success of our attack. At nightfall, the members of the three peoples are sitting all around it. Total silence falls.

After a short but intense moment of concentration, the participants lose their individuality; they become the personages of our ceremony, those who will create an event in order to project it into the future.

The beef men are the first to appear; crouching, hands flat to the ground, they move forward with the gait of cattle, slowly turning their heads, gazing stupidly into the distance while adroitly waving their basketwork tails back and forth. I am content because they are truly excellent, and that is important for the success of the rite.

The hunters arrive, with their bearing, their physical strength, their heightened mental powers, enhanced by the form and colour of the symbols painted on their bodies. They pace unhurriedly, bending their knees slightly, holding their spears horizontally in one hand. Their feet hardly touch the ground, just like hunters who are able to put themselves in position without even a twig creaking; their heads lean forward; one hand placed as a visor above their eyes; they gaze to the right, to the left. You can sense how much they are concentrating, living out the exceptional seriousness of the moment.

A few paces away, now assembled into herds, the beef-men go on with their mimicry. The hunters approach them with caution, encircling them. Then, having reached the appropriate distance, simultaneously raising their horizontal spears above their right shoulders, each targets an 'animal', reckons the force of propulsion, so that the weapon will only scratch the beast's body. Three of the beef-men fall. The others scamper off to save themselves, leaping over the spectators seated in a circle around the show.

Then two hunter-dancers approach the slain 'game' and mimic a scene of flaying, while others light a fire for cooking.

Here come the dancers representing the subhumans who surge from the other side of the scene, each armed with a long killing-stick. They come and go, as if running, the gestures they make are far too quick, jerky, they are wiping their faces with the backs of their hands, addressing one another in ridiculously loud voices. Some pretend to be horsemen tending their horses, others raise an elbow as if to drink, then stagger heavily. It takes them many a long moment, for the white man lacks powers of observation and cannot see too clearly, to discover at last what is going on, only a short distance from them. Straight away, without concentrating on what they are doing, they all raise their rifles, fire, miss their targets. Before they have time to realise that they have failed, and on account of their deficient hearing, they are speared by three hunters, who have stealthily crept up behind them.

The audience laughs, calls out 'Ah!' in satisfaction; the noise grows louder when two men set fire to the manikin representing the invader: a symbol of his coming defeat. At twilight, the flames illuminate happy faces, lips murmuring in a low voice the words of the newly invented song, the final accomplishment of our mental attack, which will be repeated over five long nights.

That evening, we regain our confidence. And, for several months, to strengthen the malevolent forces unleashed against the migloos by this ceremony, the True Men and Women activate, every day and for long stretches of time, their various mental powers. And every night the men qualified to kill at a distance point their Bones in the direction of the subhumans. The killing Bone, our infallible weapon throughout all of time! A weapon that kills everyone it is pointed at. With hardly any exception.

Yes! I remember the difficulties the men endowed with the skill of killing at a distance were to meet in accomplishing their mission against the whites, who proved difficult to approach. It was necessary to have recourse to a rite: having their feet covered, by those privileged to do it, with wilpatias, highly secret shoes made of emu feathers, which leave no trace on the ground, and are reserved for their use alone. Then employing their finest hunters' strategies, to approach the white man's wiltja and leave behind the object which would reveal to him that the attack of the Bone is about to take place. A revelation which would begin to affect his moral senses, rendering him even more vulnerable to the second part of their task.

I remember the long moments these men then spent, each squatting on his heels, next to a few pieces of burning wood, far from everyone else, bathed in the silence of the desert. Heads lowered, rubbing against their chests their sacred stones, their personal churingas, the replicas of their ideal selves, endowing them with the powers of Alcheringa Time, they will enter into a trance.

By means of a narrow plume of smoke rising from their little fire, which spreads their will on the wings of the crystalline air, they had to capture the spirit of each of their victims. It was then necessary for them to convince each of them that evil is gnawing away at his vital organs, just as they must have been fearing ever since they discovered the object symbolising their imminent death. Slowly, the killer had to insinuate himself into his prey's mind, to make the hideous face of this evil sprout; that horrible image, haunting, impossible to evade. In a few days, the physical and moral suffering would have turned more and more violent, less and less tolerable, and, at last, it would have led to death.

Soon, all the migloos we knew about had been pointed at.

Then, for several moons, with everyone in an anguish of anticipation, we watch out for the least sign of success, gazing every moment at the sky to look for the appearance of a signal announcing victories from the other regions. And I, like the others, spend each day inspecting the horizon! All in vain.

The moon comes and goes. Then years. The sub-humans are still there. And their nightmare animals seem endlessly obliged to multiply.

10

We were amazed at how quickly events unfolded after that! Amazing, too, the unaccustomed length of the drought that took hold a little later on!

Yes! I remember moments of great discouragement when our group could find nothing more to eat, when having something to drink represented a question of life and death. We had to make long detours, without cease, to find underground water, digging deeper and deeper to reach it, or else walking for most of the day to reach places where we knew we could find a kurrajong, the water-tree, which yielded us hardly enough liquid to avoid dehydration.

Despite everything, our wandering continued, our situation growing worse each time we turned back towards the east. More and more frequently, days after leaving behind the settlements of the subhumans, we would come upon stray cows and calves. And that signified the pollution of our watering places. I remember the birth, at that time, of a feeling of hatred of a hitherto unknown intensity. And how surprised I was by that.

However, none of my warning dreams spoke to me of lost hope! I still had faith in the future.

We are walking in a single file, careworn, sullen, ill or in great rage. The harmony of the group is no more than a distant memory. Most of the day is now taken up with finding food. And in spite of that, we often go hungry. We no longer have enough time for meditating, to be aware of the Life within us, to communicate with the living things around us. We no longer have the leisure to make lengthy preparations for our ceremonies, to entertain regular relations with the other groups, as we did in earlier times. We seem to exist only in order to find something to eat! We feel diminished, like animals lacking intelligence!

Sometimes, to avoid the whites, we need to follow paths that belong to people we do not know, whose malevolent powers we fear; as they fear ours. Also, the songs our paths are singing have lost their reliability.

The path is no longer a transcendental place, only a thoroughfare we must follow. A mere trail leading from one point to another. Yes! Great change begins at this time. It is difficult for us to keep travelling while continuing to make our hearts sing.

I quicken my pace, hurrying to arrive at a little pool concealed beneath a heap of stones which no white man should have stumbled on. Wongu and I are now some paces from the place. Abruptly, while signalling to the others that they should stay behind, we hurl ourselves to the ground, trying to hide behind tufts of spinifex. In front of us, two men are lying on the ground, not far from the billabong, spears and throwing sticks scattered around them in a strange way. They do not stir, the way they are lying on the ground fills us with suspicion. In the sky, a bird of prey appears. It is hovering above them. It remains there, immobile, a certain sign that the men are dead. The bird begins to turn slowly and starts to descend, making for the corpses, but when we leap to our feet it soars quickly, filling the overheated air with its harsh cry. We draw nearer and stand, stupefied, mute, in front of corpses horribly deformed by decomposing flesh. The others have joined us. Like us, they cannot take their eyes off the two hideous corpses.

A cry snatches us out of our inertia. I am the first to reach young Aripoko, who is lying near the crystalline water of the billabong, which she had certainly been lapping avidly.

I see how twisted she is with pain, crying, weeping, raising her imploring eyes towards me. At the sight of her revolting features, the women set about uttering prolonged groans of sorrow and fear. Her father leans down carefully, putting an arm under her head, the other under her knees, and carries her far away from the watering place, suspecting straight away that it was responsible for her sickness. After a few steps, he puts her down in the scant shade of a solitary itara. In a hubbub of comments, cries, weeping, our group has followed him, panic-stricken at the thought of the malevolence of people living not far from this place, with whom we share the pond. Who, apart from them, could be responsible for such a monstrous act?

And I, the Man of High Degree, the great thinker, like them, and without hesitation, despite all my skill at keeping a cool head, think that they are right. I am even convinced that, in addition to the deadly crushed grasses which they had scattered there, they had charged the water with waves capable of causing great evil.

I go over to the young girl to make her take, as quickly as I can, an antidote I always carry with me. I call up all my willpower to empty my mind, the only means of gaining access to my paranormal state as a Man of High Degree. I place my hands on the back of her head, her temples, her face. I feel the warmth in my palms increasing, increasing even more, reaching its highest degree at the instant of greatest concentration, the final discharge of the magnetic fluid, which I transfer to the small body. I try to visualise the evil which the waves must have dragged to the surface. I make passes over her with my hands, from head to foot, and I can sense that my Vital Energy is leaving my body for hers. At the same time, I make use of the power of my voice, which has proved effective so many times. I recite some words, the sense of which escapes me but words I know to be imprinted with the infinite power of the Great Ancestors who created them. A power retained, for a time, by the multitude of the Men of High Degree who have been pronouncing them since the dawn of Time. Words whose sonority, rhythm, represent an ineffable potency. I place my lips on her stomach and suck as deeply as possible on her skin in order to draw out the alien substance responsible for her illness. All in vain, for she dies that evening.

It took us a long time, a very long time, to understand that the malevolent powers of our neighbours had nothing to do with poisoning of the watering place. We needed a very long time to discover that the subhumans alone were responsible for that.

In the face of all obstacles, our life as wanderers continued. It led us back towards the mineral world, where the migloo had not yet dared to venture. Penetrating it, we suddenly felt more joyful, as if freed from an unhealthy presence.

I can see again the meeting of the Wise Men which took place a few days later, after all the members of our people, Sparrowhawks and Grey Falcons, had returned to the desert for the ceremony of the Great Assembly. After celebrating the rites necessary for preserving our world in the image of the parallel world, we have come together so that each might report on the condition of the paths.

The sum of the situation revealed itself as grave: our

mental attack had no result. New territories have been laid waste, new paths were seeing game growing scarce, more and more watering places were becoming unusable because they were polluted or guarded by the migloos' guns. In consequence our usual itineraries could not be followed.

The conclusion is obvious. With death in our souls, we realised that our attack had been pointless: the whites revealed themselves to be wholly impermeable to the power of pointing the Bone.

Why?

No one could answer the innumerable questions we put to ourselves.

We, the Wise Men and Men of High Degree, who were once so proud, dropped our heads, lost in our sad thoughts, humiliated, depressed. We were worried about seeing our influence diminishing, for nothing good could come to our people now. But it is certainly true that, after so many failures, we had already lost our credibility!

Kapari, one of my trading partners from the far east, who is visiting the Grey Falcons, takes up the discussion.

'I have heard that the whites exploit the powers of the coastal tribes to protect themselves.'

'The powers of the coastal tribes? We've never heard of powers so superior to ours! Have they improved their skills with the help of the subhumans?'

'That could be so, for they live near the migloos. They helped them track down people guilty of theft or acts of sabotage perpetrated by our people; they sent them signals about the movements of our groups; without them, we would have far less trouble combating the invaders. Because they, they see nothing, understand nothing, and get lost if they stray, no matter how short a distance from their encampment. The newcomers from the east say that these black collaborators would be able to cast a halo of protective waves all around the invaders! A halo of waves isolating them from our mental attacks! It is clear enough that the subhumans would not be able to resist us without the help of the True Men of the coastal people. Whatever the case, we have reached a dead end. Also, with your permission, I am going to put an idea to you which might, perhaps, be able to lessen our difficulties. Listen: eight or ten moons ago I saved the life of a migloo.'

We look at him, not understanding what he wants us to make of this. But, imperturbable, he goes on with his story:

'This white had strayed into the mineral world. I found him all alone, in the full heat of the day, lying under a kurrajong, practically unconscious. I quickly gave him something to drink from the liquid trapped in the tree, saving him just in time from dehydration. Then, when he had recovered something of his senses and a little of his strength, I helped him return to the plant world, where I knew he had been living for several moons with his horrible animals.'

'And so? In what way could this be of interest to us?' asks Djingili, who always speaks before he thinks.

Most of us have already understood: for politeness's sake, we let Kapari finish his argument:

'Well, soon afterwards I went back to my people and thought no more about it. But today, I realised that the law of reciprocity places that migloo under the obligation of helping the one that saved him, that's to say me, whenever I might ask him. And, if you agree, I will ask him.'

Djingili, who has understood at last, tries to let him know it:

'You are going to ask him to share watering places with us!'

No one goes to the trouble of answering him. After

lengthy discussions we reach an agreement. In exchange for services rendered, we will suggest to the white man that he use only the billabongs to the south of the creek bordering the path of the Man Lizard and leave for our use those to the north of that creek. The bargain seems to be of little advantage for us, but we do not have any choice. And it is more worthwhile to have less clear water than we had before, rather than abundant water polluted by cows and calves! We agree to try the experiment.

We set out one morning without clubs, without spears, without boomerangs, as a sign of our desire for peace, still confident enough about outcome of our enterprise, bold though it be; still capable of high spirits as we make our way.

Yes, there it is. We arrive downwind, without being seen, without the white's dogs' barking. We crouch behind a low shrub. Dumbfounded, I am looking for the first time at a migloo's wiltja. All the noises, the smells escaping from it overwhelm my senses. Disfigured nature, unrecognisable as far as my gaze extends, casts me into deep consternation, into a terrible anguish. I can't believe what I am seeing. All the trees had been felled. What a catastrophe! How will it be possible to forestall such a disaster!

'A wiltja like this for sleeping in!' one of us whispers.

'He shuts himself inside during the day too. Odd, isn't it?'

'What did he use to build this shelter?'

'Tree trunks cut lengthwise. He uses a strange tool for that, an implement which looks as if it had been made from the same material as the axes some of us have been able to get hold of. A substance that cuts better than the best of our stone tools! How many trees have been sacrificed for that useless shelter! And, to my mind, injurious to health! Look, the animals have been shut in too, behind wooden barriers, without a roof this time.'

'What an idea! If they were running free, these animals would be easy to spear whenever necessary.'

'But why don't they eat kangaroos?'

'I don't know anything about that. A few days ago, in one morning, this migloo killed fifteen of them! Fifteen! He left them where they were, without making sure that they were really dead, without making sure that they were no longer suffering. One of my people found them and distributed them among his family. If he hadn't done so the scavengers would have had a feast! A little farther away, there were two dead females with their young still in their pouches; he collected them. My relative has still not come to terms with such carnage. He is convinced that only the mentally retarded could act in such a way!'

'And all these strange birds, they are also shut in. What does he do with them?'

'I don't know. For some days now our youngsters have been on the lookout to observe him. They saw him pick up a dozen eggs. To do what with them? So many eggs just for himself!'

'He doesn't have a wife?'

'No! And that's not normal either!'

We remain lost in our thoughts, our eyes fixed on the unbelievable extent of country that had been denuded.

'Right! Go on Kapari, go over to see him.'

Kapari, suddenly a little less confident, crawls on the ground for a good while, so as not to reveal our hiding place; he then stand up and goes off, head held high, with an air of assurance, despite feeling apprehensive and having no weapon. We see him entering the place where the subhuman lives.

'Will he know how to make himself understood?' Wongu whispers.

'Oh! I think so,' replies one of the brothers of our

messenger. 'For some time, in exchange for a knife, he helped out another migloo, who had settled even farther to the east. Their vocabulary seems rudimentary. It only deals with material things.'

Time passes. The waiting seems long to us, longer than it is in reality, for the unfamiliar smells and noises make us nervous and impatient. A cow utters a lugubrious cry. A dog barks in a peculiar manner, a strange dog! Now one of their birds sets about making loud cries, all 'o' and 'i'. A plume of smoke rises from the roof of the wiltja. In my mind, I register every one of the numberless things lying around, as if they had been abandoned on the ground, from which every trace of life had been removed. Ground which looks as if it had been skinned, like an animal. I notice two curious circles of timber, parallel to each other and perpendicular to the ground, approximately five hands' span from one another; they are absolutely perfectly formed; in the space they mark out, poles sticking out of the inner surface join at the middle, probably to keep them together. Between these two circles, there is some kind of large container made of symmetrical planks placed on other timber supports. What possible purpose could this contraption serve? And why such a large container? It must be some kind of a container, because there are bundles of dry grass in it.

But here are Kapari and the migloo coming out of that peculiar shelter. Kapari gestures, indicating the creek. We see his lips pronouncing the word in our language for water, then, without doubt, translating it into the dialect of the invaders. He repeats it several times, pointing his index finger at the white man's chest; then he stretches his hand out towards the watering place to the south; next he taps his own chest with the palm of his hand and straight away points to the north, repeating the word for water. So he looks questioningly at the other and waits for his reply.

After a short silence, the latter makes signs again, the same as his. He has understood! But here he is now bursting into peals of laughter, throwing his head back and slapping his thighs; then, without a word, he turns his back on us and goes inside. Doubtless, we think, to consider our proposal. He could not decide on such an important matter so quickly! Like us, Kapari is sure that he will come back to give us his answer. Also, with a gesture, he signals to us to come nearer.

'I don't know what his laugh signifies. He is given to such peculiar reactions! I believe he didn't recognise me. I should have remembered that subhumans lack all powers of observation, and that to their eyes we all look alike!'

The man comes out again, but, oh surprise!, with his fire-stick, his gun, as Kapari calls it. He fires into the air and seems to be aiming at us. What can we do? We flee, accompanied by his mocking laughter.

The shame! I feel soiled by shame. Yes! That day my life was pitched into an unknown world. A world which is going to deprive me, quickly enough, of the function that gives meaning to my life, to deprive me of my dignity, of my pride! And even more quickly of my self-confidence as a Man of High Degree.

Indifferent to our trials, the seasons determine our wanderings. Camps follow one another, rituals unfold, and the time for the Great Assembly of the two moieties of our people returns. Together, Sparrowhawks and Grey Falcons are going to organise the ceremony glorifying our common Ancestor, to seal their unity with a great mystic impulse, in joy and in plenty. Plenty?

Alas! After beating even the smallest parcel of land, setting a fire around bushes to make any game that might be sheltering there come out, our catch is meagre.

In the evening, gathered around a hearth illuminated by the harsh light of the Man Moon, the Wise Men of the Sparrowhawks and Grey Falcons stay silent, dropping their heads, lost in their sad thoughts.

The young Gooradoo stands up and, for the first time since he achieved his new status as a True Man, he begins to speak. We are very curious to hear what he has to say.

'I'd like to explain my reasoning to you. The celebration of the great unity of our people should unfold in faith, joy and plenty. As it has done since the dawn of Time. We all know the three things that must be observed in order to ensure its success. Such is my thinking.'

A silence. No one moves a muscle, waiting for what is to follow.

'Now, we have established that the path of the game which had been created here at the edge of the plant world by our Great Goanna Ancestor no longer shelters anything but a few marsupial mice and other small game fit only for women to hunt. We all know that the invaders are responsible for that. Such is my thinking.'

A fresh silence, this time prolonged.

'So, the whites lay waste to our territories, kill our game unnecessarily, refuse to discuss the problem with us, refuse the compromise we offer them. Their sole objective seems to be simply to suppress us. In these new circumstances, more than ever, we must be united. That is why it is important, much more so than formerly, that the celebration of our common Ancestor, the Woman-Honey Ant to whom we owe our unity, must succeed. Such is my thinking.'

Then, as if hurrying to finish, he continues, speaking rapidly. His listeners, taken aback, are impatient to hear what he, this young man, is about to say.

'That's why I think that we, the Wise Men and the Men of High Degree, whom our people trust, must do everything to ensure the success of this ceremony. And no matter how. Such is my thinking.'

A murmur of approbation runs around the listeners. Gooradoo goes on:

'So, this is what I propose. Three days' journey from here, I know of a herd of cows and calves enclosed in a pen a spear's throw from the wiltja of two new migloos who have come into the region. There are about twenty animals there. Let's go over there, kill a cow, cut it up on the spot, and bring the best pieces back here. The whites are killing our kangaroos. Well then! Let's do as they do! Kill their cows, their calves. That's what I, Gooradoo, want to suggest to you.'

A long silence follows. I am thinking that he has spoken well, that the force of his personality surpasses that of certain of today's men of influence, that he will quickly succeed in rising to a position of importance, replacing individuals less forceful than he is. Then, how many thoughts were crowding around in my head! In theory, he is right. For what he suggests is good strategy. But what will be the consequences of such an act? Are we not about to embark on a path that will prove dangerous for our future? Dangerous, or beneficial for the ceremony on which our future depends?

Another man begins speaking.

'I agree with Gooradoo's reasoning. And acting in such a manner, we would be within our rights. However, we must consider the consequences of such an act. We know nothing about these animals; we do not know from which Great Ancestor they have descended. Taking their life, without knowing anything about it, suppressing the Sacred Energy flowing in them, could be dangerous. Such is my thinking.'

For a long while, we try to imagine the possible consequences of such an act, what might be the reaction of the two whites to the loss of one of their beasts. We reach the conclusion that, whatever the risks might be, we have hardly any other choice.

When we have worked out our plan, chosen the itinerary for reaching the place where the migloos are, determined how to get into the enclosure, how to get the beast out, the place to kill it, Bahloo begins to sink in the starry sky; the cold bites agreeably into our skin, which still bears the imprint of previous day's sunlight. In the grandeur of the night's beauty, beneath the benevolent gaze of those of our people who have ascended to live on the stars, we fall asleep at last.

Why do I have such yearning for the instant that prompted me to join in the resistance against the invader, that changed me in their eyes into a cattle thief? Why? Doubtless because I still had, at that time, confidence in myself, the certainty of being able to help my people put that incredible nightmare behind them. Of which nothing remains today.

Even though we had linked, quickly enough, the idea of killing cattle with an idea of murdering rather than of hunting, we were often sorry that we did not run across these animals on the paths that were less and less well endowed with game. And I recall moments of great discouragement, when my group could find nothing more to eat, when finding something to drink posed a difficulty at every instant.

Once more, water became a crucial problem. Very often, only succulent plants gorged with sweet sap saved us from dying of dehydration. Searching for water and food became our sole occupation, our sole care. How can I not remember that period, which sent us on the road to turning us into beasts once more.

After many trials, here we are again in the desert where we find, once more, the life we have always led, without great difficulty in feeding ourselves, rich in leisure time, time to create art, for philosophical discussions, moments of meditation. And also, of course, fighting over women! We became once more the irreproachable Guardians of Creation. Never have I appreciated so much what the whites would later on call our customs and beliefs.

Our return to the east marked the mounting of our resistance.

Yet again, life became a struggle at every moment. Despite the terrible dearth of food, the ceremony of the propagation of the species had been performed. A few days earlier, once more, the lack of meat for the feast obliges us to penetrate into the greener regions, where we are sure to find cattle. And nothing happens in the way that it did the first time.

I see it again. At sunset, I set out with six other hunters, holding a shield at arm's length, protection against the fire-sticks of the migloo we are in danger of meeting. Guningbal has often told us and told us again that we are greatly mistaken, that our shields would be useless against the latter's gun; we did not want to believe him. Then, he insisted on coming with us.

We make our way swiftly, covering a good distance, at first one behind the other. Then our guide signals us to slacken our pace and lean down. All our hunter's instincts are on the alert. We advance, crouching in that way, from bush to bush, until the enclosure comes into sight. The light of the moon illuminates the landscape sufficiently for us to make out the dark shapes of the cattle. Two throws of the spear from the enclosure, we sit down under a thicket of scented wattle and decide which of us will place a vine around the animal's neck to drag it over to us. Guningbal seems the most capable of carrying out that task.

'No. I don't need a shield. I am telling you again that it's useless. If he catches sight of me, I'll talk to him in his own language to distract him. But in that case we will have to save ourselves very quickly.'

He stands, only to crouch and whisper that a migloo armed with a fire-stick has just arrived, that he is walking around on the other side of the pen.

'The Man Moon is giving us hardly any light tonight. You know well enough that the subhumans, who can't see too clearly during the day, are completely blind in the dark!' one of us whispers.

'That's true. In any case, at this distance, his gun can't reach us,' replies another.

'His gun can reach us,' Guningbal insists vehemently. 'What's more, when I get inside the pen I could alarm the herd; that could not fail to make him come over to find out what is going on. It would be better to wait. He's not going to stay there all night.'

'He's going away,' Wongu, who has just glanced over the top of the foliage, announces. 'He's going inside. Quickly, off you go!'

Guningbal stands up, half erect, and makes for the animals, his body crouching low. We see his shape advancing over the open ground. Ten paces are left before he can slip between the posts of the enclosure. But a terrible noise rends the air, and does not stop reverberating. Guningbal throws himself to the ground, where he stays without moving a muscle.

'He has come back,' one of us whispers stupidly. 'Fortunately at that distance he can't reach him!'

I signal to the others not to move and I stand up to go over to see what is going on, secure behind my shield. When I get close to Guningbal, the same terrible noise rings out again. A burning sensation tears through my chest. I fall on top of my friend. A final lucid moment to understand that the living-dead, Niumta's son, has just departed from life once again. Then, brutally, my yowie leaves my body of flesh and blood; my invisible self embarks on its difficult return journey to the world of the Invisibles.

11

The wet season arrives in the little township in the back of beyond. Huge raindrops drum on corrugated iron roofs. The fine smell of damp earth, mingled with the scents of wattle and eucalyptus oil, wafts indoors.

'When all's said and done, it's good to hear the rain!' one of the gaolers repeats for the third time in an hour.

'Yeah, but what a racket! Do you remember the gentle rain, the small drops we used to get back home?'

'You ask me if I remember! But all this din's better than having no water at all! Tell me, have you heard that they are going to finish the telegraph line soon? We are going to be in contact at last with civilisation! I don't know why, but that makes me glad!'

'Me too, even though I'll get nothing out of it. In fact, do you know how they installed it? With all that water between us and over there! I have trouble believing it.'

'They could only have laid submarine cables. They speak about a—'

'Stop, listen! I can hear a funny rattle. Better make sure it isn't the Abo who is refusing to eat. Perhaps he's about to croak.'

The sound of the door opening snatches the black man out of his reverie. Then, reassured, the gaoler shuts it again. Almost immediately the old man forgets about the present.

The time of one long generation has flown by. Why

did it become necessary for the spirit of the Great Dingo Ancestor to want to come back to life one more time? Why was it necessary for him, Nari, to return to the earth? He does not want to remember any of it. No more than remembering his new childhood, which he spent fleeing from the whites, rather than celebrating his Ancestors.

Despite all the difficulties they were experiencing with the invaders, whose numbers continued to grow, he underwent the lengthy instruction which allowed him to recover the memory of Alcheringa Time. In a new body of flesh and blood, he has become again one of the sacred beings of that era, once again he is one of the Guardians of Creation. For the past, the present and the future are coexistent.

He has, in the same manner, regained his status as a Man of High Degree and often presides at the assemblies held by members of that group.

His people's resistance against the invader has increased. That does not prevent the world he is safeguarding from becoming continually degraded. Each day a little more of the forests, of the air-borne game and of the paths disappears.

Nevertheless, the greatest worry for the Men of High Degree flows out of the new attitude adopted by some of the True Men, those who were formerly little heeded, because they were the least capable, and above all by young men who are still in the process of formation. These latter are more and more often in conflict with their masters. For, since they discovered with their own eyes or from hearsay the technological world of the whites, they no longer aspire, as their elders had done at their age, to receive Knowledge. Knowledge which, for the latter, represented the sole hope of ameliorating their way of life. They, they think that a gun for hunting, a horse for moving around rapidly, certain clothing to differentiate them better from the Elders, whose conservatism seems to them like an incapacity to adapt to the new world, confer on them far more significant prestige. That is their sole ambition. They have little faith now in traditional values. This is why they have trouble coming to terms with the isolation, the calm, the mediation imposed on them during their training as True Men.

More serious still, these youths, who have not yet emerged from ignorance, are beginning to neglect their obligation of aid and mutual aid, sometimes going as far as ignoring those pertaining to their Dreaming-brothers, the strongest of their kinship ties.

This irresponsible attitude is made possible nowadays by the opportunities to find food near the invaders' world, by doing a little work for them, by unscrupulously prostituting their young women, because that corresponds to the traditional practice of lending women: fear of being rejected by their own people, without whom they would not have been able to survive in earlier times, no longer functions as a sufficiently persuasive weapon.

Nari became aware of the birth of a notion hitherto unknown, because it used to be mastered, nipped in the bud: individualism. He knows that such individualism will inevitably lead to egotistical behaviour. As dangerous for men as for Mother Earth! For the network of aid and reciprocal aid, which, by links unbreakable except by death, binds together all the members of his people, binds them to the other people of the surrounding regions, who are themselves bound to other more distant people, as far as the sea to the north, to the south, to the east and the west, that gigantic spider's web spun by the civilising Heroes, the threads of which govern temporal life as much as the spiritual. This gigantic puzzle, as complex as it is astute, is nothing less than the vital nerve of a civilisation. The least little jolt can begin to shatter it.

Certainly, the prisoner remembers, we, the Men of High Degree, were long aware that renouncing this organisation, renouncing the interdictions associated with it would lead to the total disintegration of our world, to communal suicide. Nevertheless, despite the gravity of the situation, we did not lose hope in the future.

From that time on, the invaders chased us out of the regions richest in game, water, edible plants! And when, prompted by our religious duties, we ventured into those parts, they slaughtered us like animals. Whites kill anything that moves, indiscriminately, without making any allowance for the breeding season. Still more unbelievably, they kill without need! For the pleasure of killing! They seem to hold Life in contempt. Worst! To be the enemy of every living thing!

We gave up, a long time ago, trying to find the murderer of one of our people. The murderer who, according to our laws, must be punished, the only one to compensate the grieving family. We came to understand at last that all the migloos were implicated, that none of them would ever help us unmask the criminal since, in their eyes, we are only 'Abos', creatures they consider to be animals, to be pests, worse than kangaroos!

When we found the courage to accept this monstrous truth, every white man became an enemy. However, we hesitate wiping them out systematically for, although they are subhumans, there is Life within them. And we are not at all certain that that Life is not, in some manner, linked to the Sacred Energy impregnating our world. And spilling a great deal of blood, would that not run the risk of bringing down the wrath of the Heroes of the Eternal Dreamtime? And the unleashing of malevolent forces which the whites could let loose on us in reprisal?

So we continue to study their ways, the better to know them before learning how to struggle against them better. Our powers of observation, developed to their highest degree since the dawn of Time, because it is essential for our life as hunting wanderers, find a strange enough employment today. In effect, we require the same curiosity, the same alert senses, the same power of smell, the same aptitude to read footprints left behind on the ground to keep ourselves current with the movements of the migloos, the same knack of making ourselves invisible, the same tricks to attract the 'new game' wherever we want to, and, it goes without saying, the same control over our nerves. But this time we are facing a dangerous species, the first we have had to confront.

In effect, we already know practically all about the migloos; and we know that they are almost entirely unaware of us. Nevertheless, hiding at the outskirts of their settlements, we continue spying on them for whole days at a time, unbeknownst to them. This attitude has allowed us, among other things, to find out how they work with their livestock, what they do to stay on the back of a horse, how they operate their weapons. For each of these actions, we have memorised, with great precision, every one of their gestures. This has made it possible for us to know how to aim and fire without too much practice, how to become reasonably expert horsemen fairly quickly and occasionally valued herdsmen.

It is thanks entirely to our skill as hunters that, strengthened by despair, we are still able to conduct our ceremonies at the sites in the east, High Places too sacred to be abandoned without struggle.

The time is long past when my forebears relied on their mental powers to make the enemy leave. For a long time now we have been fighting them with our own weapons. But today, we must recognise clearly enough that this mode of defence is hardly effective. We continue, it is true, killing a few whites, but not without a greater number of our people having to leave their own lives behind; these attacks do nothing to make the thieves flee from our lands.

It is at this time that, in the course of a meeting of influential men, I suggest a new kind of resistance: to try to unsettle the minds of the two new whites we have discovered in a part of the east which had been spared until now. That is, creating a climate of insecurity all around, and even inside what we now call the cattle station. I suggest that we foster extreme tension among the migloos by linking up our acts of sabotage, theft of cattle, raids on their plantations; frequently performing provocative pantomimes and jeering at them; but also by attacking the convoys of provisions sent by the people who have raped the coastal lands.

'Are you advising us to establish a climate of insecurity, of terror if need be, in order to make the migloos incapable of exchanging their produce with their own people. In a word, to try to starve them out just as they are starving us?' one of the Elders asks.

'I think that this tactic remains our only chance if we do not wish to lose the sacred site of the Lace Monitor Ancestor. I believe in effect that only such warfare can save that site. Such is my thinking.'

After lengthy consideration, lengthy discussions, the meeting accepts my proposal.

So, for some time, we were confident enough of our future success, for we knew about all those things that the nerves of the whites were almost unable to withstand, that they could not be compared with our people, who have been made, by necessity, harder than flint in the course of our long training as True Men and in the course of our life as hunting wanderers. After reaching that decision, the hope that we would see our invaders fleeing for ever surged again.

The memory of my first raid! It was a matter of digging up the large tubers that had been introduced by the invaders, which the newly arrived migloo had trouble enough cultivating. In our land! That should have given us the right to a part of the harvest. But for a long time now, we have known that it was useless trying to assert our rights, whatever they may be.

Most of the white men live without women. They steal ours whenever they can. We are going to profit from this behaviour: in anticipation of our coming action, we decided that, two moons in advance, Kamal is going to seduce one of the whites.

For several days, she has been loitering around their dwelling, sweeping the ground as she has seen them do, spending time squatting on her heels just outside their door. At last, one evening, the younger one shoves her inside the wiltja. She manages to make it impossible for him to manage without her. In the days that follow, she agrees to do the housework, to look after the hens; she offers to water the vegetable patch every day.

A moonless night. The raiding party has assembled. Their number is equal to the fingers of four hands. Sitting on the ground, each smears the soles of his feet with several coatings of blood, obtained by pricking the calf, or perhaps a vein in the arm, or the underside of the sex. When the covering is sufficiently thick, we stick them with feathers, which the women have provided for us. Without a word, we wait for the preparation to dry before we stand up, making sure that we leave no other trace on the ground than those of our sacred shoes. Then we leave.

We make our way in a single file towards the site that had been despoiled, each armed with a woman's digging stick and large nets. Arriving in sight of the plantation, in spite of the dark night, we crouch in the tall grass growing there; motionless, we are on tenterhooks, waiting for the agreed signal for the action to begin: the call of the gugurgaga, the morning bird, repeated twice, which must send Kamal on her way, once the dogs have been shut away and the two whites have gone to sleep. At the least emergency, we will be warned by the call of the same bird, repeated three times, for the newcomers are incapable of being surprised at hearing the song of a daylight bird in the middle of the night.

The night is warm, the air charged with the smells and sounds of the white world. In the distance, the dark shape of a cow seems to be coming towards us. Will it let out its lugubrious cry, will it raise the alarm? Rooted to the spot, as much masters of our nerves as we are during a difficult hunting expedition, we wait, without letting out the least breath, without making a sound, all our senses alert. Softly but distinctly, the signal rings out. Once, twice. Then no more.

So we make our way towards the pen, crouching, sticks and nets at arms' length. We climb over the barrier and find ourselves in a space covered with perfectly aligned potato plants, which had been abundantly watered this very evening by our accomplice. Straight away, as it had been agreed, we quickly cut off, with a knife, the tops of the plants and place them carefully on the ground. Then, still with haste, some of us gather the tubers, others arrange them into piles to put them in the nets, which they then hurl outside the enclosure. We need little time to finish the harvest. Then, in the holes left behind, we replant each of the tops with care, making them stay upright in a mound of soft earth, trying to give them their original appearance. Then, always with the same haste, always silently, without trampling on a single blade of grass, without disturbing a single pebble, without leaving the least trace behind, we vanish into the night, after announcing our departure with the repeated call of the morning bird.

The plants take several days to wither, and we are far away, and our accomplice too, when the owners realise their misfortune, our little triumph over them! Convinced that they will not hurl themselves after us in pursuit! For no white has ever done that; none of them has a good enough knowledge of the region. And all knew that they would be incapable of finding black people who have the skill to make themselves invisible. What is more, in this particular case, they looked with extreme suspicion on every tree of the timbered savannah behind which an 'Abo' and his spear could have been hiding.

That evening, I experienced the same emotions, the same joy as in the course of a difficult but bountiful hunt. Above all, I experienced the immense satisfaction of having gained a victory over the enemy. Yes! That evening I was still proud of being black!

The two whites would not have had time to collect their wits, to get over feeling ridiculous because we were already following the track leading to their dwelling for another act of sabotage, more severe than the first.

This time it was a matter freeing the forty cows and calves in the corral, to lead some of them into another region where we would set them free, so that they would reproduce and replace the game which had practically vanished from there. The other half would be killed not far from these subhumans, in a hollow known only to us. That done, the plan we had hatched would have been accomplished, so that the migloos would become aware of our misdeed even before realising that their cattle were gone. Beforehand, to avoid being pursued, in the unlikely but always possible case that they would come on us by surprise, we will have speared the three horses.

We discuss our tactics for a long time; then determine the role each of us is to play. We attend to the smallest detail.

But another great difficulty arises. Since we no longer have an accomplice there, the two dogs prove a real handicap. To spear them would be too risky. Only one solution: poison.

The previous evening we stuff the carcasses of two wild geese with lethal herbs smeared with blood, in sufficient amounts to obtain a result during the night, while the whites are asleep. I am given the task of hurling them into the strange, low construction to which the dogs are tied with a long metal chain.

At the hottest time of the day, when the two migloos escape the heat by sheltering indoors, I approach their house, on the side opposite from the dogs, downwind. Soon, I am moving forward, my back to the wall, doing my best to stay in the scant shade surrounding them. Reaching the corner, I see the animals, lying side by side, flattened by the heat. The wind stays with me, and they do not notice my presence. I hurl the two carcasses, with precise aim, in front of their noses and I half-turn without making them bark; they are too busy chewing on the unexpected food.

I go back to my team, who are hiding not far from there, among a clump of dwarf cycas growing in the middle of sharp-bladed grass, difficult for a horse to traverse.

The afternoon draws on. The usual sounds of the farm reach us, the chickens' clucking, a horse neighing, tools and buckets noisily thrown to the ground or picked up, and, from time to time, the loud, always so loud, voices of the whites, for their hearing is as poor as their eyesight! They are going about their business as usual, without betraying any particular sign of nervousness. For the last time they cast a few grains to their fowls, distribute hay to their cattle, carry buckets of water to them. Our water! Then they shut their chickens in the shelter where they perch. Finally, as they do every evening at the same time, they go inside for a drink, before their last meal of the day.

Still squatting, we wait in silence, absolutely still, exchanging a few observations in the language of signs. The evening adorns itself with the magnificence of the setting sun. The grass of the savannah sways gently under the last of the breezes, dons a vermilion veil to await the coming of night. Here and there, the dark shapes of trees emerge from it, crowned with their topmost branches that merge into the incandescent glow of the Woman Sun. Then bright orange gives place to softer magenta, which is soon dissolved in the blue of the night. The serenity of the moment makes us forget everything! Once more, we ask ourselves why the migloos seem to flee from the most privileged moment of the evening, just as they do early in the morning.

The first star appears in the sky, followed by its friends. Soon the Milky Way unrolls its carpet of fine diamond dust. And I ask myself whether the upheavals that have visited our world might not also have affected the starry world, since it too is shrouded by the veil of the Sacred Energy. I ask myself what the inhabitants of the world up there think of a new and decidedly recent form of resistance: making the invaders flee by unleashing a drought as intolerable for them as for their animals. To achieve that, the Men of High Degree have stopped the rain falling. A decision which, for the moment, seems to trouble us more than it troubles our enemies.

Time passes, the men stay silent throughout, lost in their thoughts, as still as rocks. My instinct tells me that the right moment has come. I give a signal and, as arranged,

Wongu goes off to spear the horses. Calmly, we listen closely to the sounds of the night, as we wait for the song of the morning bird to spur us into action. Above the plain, a dingo calls out to the Man Moon. Not far from us, a bird of prey utters a wise 'book-book' immediately followed by the frenzied squeak of a marsupial mouse caught by the bird's headlong dive, carrying it, for an instant, above our heads.

And here is the signal. Without haste, always alert, we walk in single file. We reach the corral without hindrance. One by one, we leap inside, with long intervals in between, so as not to frighten the animals. Only a little shuffling and a few muffled sounds of lowing greet us. Patiently, we wait for complete calm to return. Then, each of the six men passes a vine around the neck of an animal, leads it slowly towards the fence Mau is holding open. Pulling gently on their makeshift halters, they leave placidly, one after the other. So, as we had foreseen, the rest of the herd follows, surrounded by other men, who guide them with sticks, as they have seen the whites do it.

We get away from the station as quickly as possible, leading the forty head of cattle without too much trouble. Then we divide the herd in two: three men continue making their way south-west throughout the night, in order to set the calves and cows free to replenish the region with 'game'.

The other half of our raiding party makes for a narrow gap in a rock face concealed, despite it height, by the perfectly vertical trunks of three palm trees. On the ground, a thicket of thorny bushes obscures the entrance to a sandy creek-bed, once upon a time the site of an immense expanse of salt water.

We know of a narrow path through the vegetation, just wide enough for an animal to pass.

Without too much difficulty, the beasts make their

way one by one through the opening, squeezing past the two rock faces and emerging in a circular space. We lead them to a makeshift corral, constructed the previous evening. They go in easily. Calmly, we secure the enclosure, happy to have accomplished so easily the first part of our undertaking.

Steadily, even though it is getting late, we drive our spears into the head of each of the beasts, in the same spot where we have seen the migloos making holes with their rifle bullets. And we are rewarded, we too, with instantaneous death. Once more, we acknowledged the superiority of the invaders' materials. The tips of our spears, made of metal or the sharpened shard of an old piece of china, cut through the thick hide much more easily, burrow much more rapidly into the flesh at the vital spot than our traditional weapons. Those armed with the latter have to repeat their actions several times, complaining, in hushed voices, that they missed out on the opportunity of getting hold of those tips for their spears.

At last all the beasts have been felled. The sand is covered in blood, it flows in narrow streams along each rut in the uneven the ground.

Such slaughter makes us feel ill at ease, for these animals were no more aggressive than ours, and we know nothing about their Ancestors! Will they not come to avenge themselves for such a carnage?

It is necessary now to cut open each abdomen to look for the heart. We do not have as perfect a knowledge of the anatomy of our victims as we have of the animals of our land: so it takes us longer than we had envisaged.

Each of the hearts we remove is placed in a bag. The work seems interminable. At last, a short while before the morning star appears in the sky, burdened with our booty and twenty poles, half as tall again as we are, we return to the whites' station.

As soon as we get there, we quickly place these poles all around the corral, and, even more hastily, we fix a heart on top of each upward-pointing tip. Then, just as silently as we had come, my companions go away, merging with the immensity of the savannah at the instant when the morning bird's laughter announces daybreak.

I am on my own, lying flat on the ground, a few paces from the enclosure, which has the blood of twenty hearts dripping onto it. I am sure that the colour and contours of my body make it merge with the barren ground; as long, it is true, as I stay completely still. The art of mimicry. The art an expert hunter must command. So, like a piece of stone, my gaze fixed on the enclosure, I wait patiently for the migloos to awake.

At last I hear the hammering of boots as the first of them comes out, those boots whose smell is a precious ally whenever we are following the whites' tracks. He calls his dogs in an ever more impatient voice. I can see him walking around his dwelling, to see what is going on. His cry of horror, followed by oaths, informs me that he has just discovered the corpses. He comes running back, rushing to the door, calling out his companion's name in an anguished voice. The latter, a short, red-headed man, his face pocked with freckles, who smells even more strongly of death than the others, hears him, shouts, comes out, and both run, almost jostling each other, to the carcasses of the two animals. Then, still running and shouting, they make for the corral.

The sight of the hearts impaled on our poles, which are still dripping blood, brings them to a dead halt. They stay rooted to the spot, speechless, for several moments. Then they raise their arms to the sky, swear, hurl invectives at the bush, where they know that we are hiding. As one, shouting all the time, they rush towards the enclosure in a last, ridiculous hope of finding that their fear is baseless. So, at that moment, seeing them unarmed, I leap to my feet, execute three dance steps not far from them and, in their language, shout three insults I have learnt for the occasion. Before they can get over their surprise, I throw myself to the ground once more, crawling for a good while, zigzagging like a lizard towards the west. When I am a good distance from them, I send them in the opposite direction by hurling a stone into a bush, at a spot where I known that the light of the rising sun will hurt their eyes, making them lose some precious time. Quickly, with a fire-stick that has been kept glowing since the previous evening, I set a clump of spinifex alight and, at the moment when the two whites turn their back to me to make for the place where they heard a rustling in the leaves, I stand up to throw the firestick on a dry patch, knowing that the fire will go out by itself, but will delay my two enemies for a good while.

So, very quickly, exploiting every unevenness in the ground, every clump of vegetation to make myself invisible, I straighten up and move off as quickly as I can.

None of us had any premonition of the disaster that would follow a short time after this raid.

That day, Mangala, the almost-dead, finally died. Her funeral had to be held in a small creek bed, difficult to reach but, we were certain, unknown to the subhumans. Several groups of Grey Falcons and Sparrowhawks had just arrived there. Many others were absent, perhaps because, fearing the presence of whites, we had been unable to send messages into the air, perhaps because the journey was deemed too dangerous, given the need to cross many devastated tracts of land. These absences caused great anguish for all of us.

I can still see my own people, dressed in mourning garb appropriate to their degree of their kinship. Some were covered in a layer of red or white ochre, as thick as a finger's breadth; otherwise it was black charcoal. Red clay mixed with fat had been smeared over the hair of the nearest male relatives of the deceased; some women, 'dressed' in a covering of white clay, had circled their bloodshot eyes with a white ring of the same substance. At that time we used to grieve for the loss of one of our people with such intensity!

The women remain sitting around the body. Some are sobbing, others utter a long, piercing lament. Weeping and moaning all the while, here are some driving the pointed stalks of yams into their skulls, others are violently striking their heads with a sharp piece of flint or with a digging stick, managing, in an instant, to pierce or slash their leathery scalps. So blood is trickling slowly down their faces, it mingles with the white clay, making them unrecognisable.

Seated around the women, the men are groaning, weeping. Suddenly, as they are gashing their thighs and raising the pitch of their lament by two tones, some of them stand up; they shove their sister aside to hurl themselves on top of the dead woman. The women help them stand up and put their lips to their companions' wounds. A veritable frenzy of suffering seizes everyone, the men continue slashing their thighs, and the women set about striking themselves with clubs. By means of this suffering, this violence, they all wish to prove to the spirit of the one who had vanished, now soaring above them, how great is their sorrow, how much she and her body, which had been her shelter since she last came to earth, had been loved and respected. We hope just as much to encourage her to be reconciled to the idea of leaving us; with these thoughts we hope to help her find again the road to the world where her Dreaming dwells, the world of the Invisibles. We do everything in our power to avoid giving her any reason to avenge herself on us.

The dead woman has just been lifted onto a platform which had been placed beforehand in a tree, when I hear a sound I cannot yet recognise. Before I am able to identify it, I see a dozen white men on horseback, each holding a rifle at the end of his arm, arriving at the far end of the creek.

I cannot believe my eyes. Then, a feeling of horror turns me to stone. They draw nearer, surround us without slackening their pace, their mounts' hooves vanish in a blinding, suffocating cloud of red dust. Having come within twenty paces of where we have assembled, they circle around us, frantically galloping all the while, they take aim, fire several times, shouting, laughing, and hurling insults at us. I can see once more all that horror.

Men, women and children are killed at one blow. In the unbelievable confusion that follows, I manage to get away far enough to find a hiding place, in a tuft of spiky bushes, where I play dead. I see Wongu crawling behind a bush and remaining stock still. Mau joins me, his shoulder bloody. Powerless, we observe the progress of the slaughter.

As if intoxicated by the smell of gunpowder, by the howling, the moaning, by the Life that is slowly oozing out of dozens of bodies, by the death that is now floating in the creek, the whites continue shouting, gesticulating on their frantically circling mounts; they call out joyfully to each other, fire again at those who are already dead. Then, when the moaning dies down, they stop at last. As the bodies become motionless, the subhumans, weary of shouting, weary of cursing, fall silent.

In the tangibly heavy silence that follows, they alight and hurry to where the bodies are heaped. Each rider grabs one of the corpses by the feet, drags it over to his horse. They shove them, some more adroitly than others, across the halters of their mounts and quickly leap on behind them. All leave, yelping, shouting, laughing, their shapes barely discernible in the air saturated with red dust, heavy with blood. Before leaving the creek, with a last blast from their rifles, they make the air shake, as well as the mineral, the plants and the few survivors.

Shocked, incapable of moving, I stay prostrate for a long while. With Mau at my side, who is as speechless as I am. I can now see those that survived emerging from the heap of bodies; stunned one moment, soon panic-stricken, they rush to the foot of the cliff to bury themselves inside a cave. A few moments later, all of us find ourselves there. Of the fifty people who were here this morning, there remain no more than twelve men, fifteen women and five little children. We spend a good part of the night huddling against one another, trying to comfort the most seriously wounded, filled with panic at the thought of the fate awaiting us, by the dead whom the invaders have stolen from us, by those who remain piled on top of one another not far away. Fear prevents our affliction from revealing itself. Slowly, great distress replaces our panic. Very quickly, it gives way to horror at the prospect of all those spirits that will soon show their wrath if we do not manage to recover the missing corpses, if we do not succeed in offering them a funeral ceremony, as we must. Thirst and hunger are soon added to our moral torment.

A little while before dawn, after long whispered discussions, we take the serious decision to leave our hiding place and make our way to the nearest watering place. The moment we arrive there, a woman utters a shriek of fear, which she stifles straight away, believing that the migloos are still somewhere around. She points her arm at a tree. The cold light of the Man Moon plays on the face of Batalja, whose body had been tied upright against the trunk. We look at the surroundings. One by one we find the bodies of our dead, similarly tied to trees around our waterhole. A warning from the subhumans for those of our people who will be coming here to slake their thirst.

12

Some days later, when our minds started functioning normally again, it becomes urgently necessary to pose a question none of us has yet dared to put. Who betrayed us? Which of the young participants revealed the secrets of our funeral ceremony? How might we lead everyone back to respecting our traditions?

In order to understand, the prisoner returns to the time of his youth, when the conservative authoritarianism of the Elders also seemed intolerable to him too! How ill did he and his friends take it that those old men were married to all the young women! How much did he suffer because Natati would henceforth be the wife of one of his elderly fathers! Yes! He too had rebelled! But at that time, the Elders were not at all concerned, for they knew that such a frame of mind would pass. Or they knew what had to be done to make it pass.

And, in effect, the Elders discovered one day that certain of the young men were beginning to put the harmony of the group in danger. To avoid such a situation, after lengthy discussions, they decided to ask them if they wanted to submit themselves to the discipline of 'Punj' and learn its secrets. A privilege, they said, which would assure them a measure of respect and would above all bring into play the return of their memory of Alcheringa Time. The young men guessed easily enough that this was a way of removing them temporarily from the group. They hesitated for a long time. Then, anxious to recover something of the Dreamtime, of commanding all the secrets of the world of True Men, they agreed.

The scent of burning wood that morning! The caress of the soft crystalline air wafting familiar sounds to him! The hoarse voice of a woman, a dog yapping, a child's cries! All this seems so real to the prisoner! So real despite so many years, despite so many tribulations.

I leave the camp with my friends and my grandfather. He leads us to the njudanu, the place where we must meet the Assembly, which is being held at the time of secret business, dangerous or forbidden – a gathering made up of the most influential men of our people.

We find other young people there, from the Sparrowhawks and Grey Falcons. We sit apart, waiting. Our apprehensiveness increases with the heat of the day. We do not say anything, exchanging impressions from time to time in the language of signs. I can still see Wongu's long fingers signalling, calmly with graceful gestures, that once again the old men have found a way of silencing us. At last someone comes to fetch us. They place all of us at the centre of a tight circle of seated men. The striking sound of the didgeridoo can still be heard. We begin with a dance of purification, indispensable for cleansing our spirits of anger, of our little rivalries and our material cares.

When we have recovered our calm and serenity, an unfamiliar chant rises. A sacred, secret song, the song of the Punj which, from its very first notes, makes all the fibres of our bodies tremble with emotion. The smell of the small fires around us, the odour of the masters surrounding us, made up of a mixture sweat and pigment, the smell our bodies secrete because we are troubled, the fact that we are deeply moved, followed by a violent onrush of collective love, all this outpouring captures and holds prisoner the waves we are sending out. My head is swimming! Fatigue accentuates my altered state of being. And the song is repeated and repeated until dusk, piercing, annihilating our efforts to stay alert, making us lose, little by little, perception of the world down here.

'Diwarni*!' the singers call out, raising their eyes to the sky.

This word rings out with such force, with such fervour, that they send shivers of emotion all over my skin.

'Diwarni!' they repeat with the same intonation of respect, profound faith and beseeching.

And once more, the vibrations of this word reverberate in the depth of my being, increasing the shivering.

'The name of our Mother, the Supreme Being,' we are told in a whisper, commanding us to blend our voices with those of the celebrants.

Trembling with emotion, love and compassion, then overwhelmed by a hitherto unknown sense of elation, we find the courage to call out that august name, the name of her who gave us the gift of our divine nature. Then, I can feel all of my body, my whole spirit rearing towards her light, as if sucked up towards the heights that are hers. I am transfigured. I can sense my astral body fusing with those of the men around me. And in a flash during this communion, we glimpse perfection, we become Diwarni again. The intensity of what I am feeling is such that it thrusts me beyond the tangible world, high enough towards a superior consciousness, one I would never want to leave. Alas! We must come down to earth again!

Our masters lead us to a distant place, in the silence of the night. They take all our ornaments from us. They

* A name invented by the author.

order us to speak no more, address not another word to each other. They deprive us of our names, designating us, among themselves, as mere 'flesh'. I feel humiliated, mortified as I have never been! I have lost all my dignity!

I ask myself a thousand questions. What have I become? What is any of us, obliged as we are to huddle against each other, naked? Can we return to the primordial embryonic condition, just as we were before the Supreme Being created us? I manage to control my behaviour, but I am oppressed by great anguish. I regret having accepted the discipline of Punj! Punj, as I now know, the public name of our Mother, the sacred Life Energy.

We sleep only for a short while. The frosty dawn arrives. Another interminable journey gets under way. Time passes. The Woman Sun rises above the horizon. We keep going, facing her red light, which sears our exhausted eyes. Under her ball of fire, we catch sight of a circular depression in the ground, filled with a multitude of moving waves, unreal, disturbing. We are more and more dazzled. We make our eyes into slits. What form of life is this? The sound of the didgeridoo hammers into my head as it has never done before: the throbbing of the Life Energy! Yes! That is what I hear, the heartbeat of her at the Beginning.

In my mind, I invoke her secret name: I ask her to help me look her in the face. Slowly, my eyes grow accustomed to the sparkling clarity, to the colours. But it takes me many moments to recognise our masters! They are crouching, unrecognisable beneath their sumptuous regalia, their bodies covered with ochre, with the down of a white bird, and plants similarly attached to the skin, slender dry leaves. The trembling of what covers their bodies blots out their physical shape, transforming them into a fluid entity, such as the sacred waves of the Mother when she descends to earth to scatter her Divine Energy.

Suddenly, the men stand up and with astonishing unanimity, launch into a frenetic dance. Their limbs come and go with unprecedented violence; they thrust their bodies forward, straighten up just as abruptly, leaning sideways until their thighs are horizontal, stamping on the ground at the same time with too great a force for it to be human! Then, still in unison, they sit down and start shaking their shoulders as rapidly as bees agitate their wings. The dance goes on without end. I have never seen such a dance. I am deafened by the sounds, dazzled by the colours which, without cease, are coruscating in front of my eyes, overwhelmed by the smells, the spellbinding rhythm. Unable to think, we are led to the centre of the dancers where, naked, conscious once more of our humiliation, we must dance with them.

Later, our initiators take blood from veins in their arms, from beneath their sex. They fill receptacles with it. Blood spurts into my eyes, into my ears, into my navel, between my lips and onto my feet. I am overcome by trembling, because I am certain that at this instant I am receiving our Mother's blood.

With each heartbeat, fragments of the Soul of the World seep into my human form, as it happened at the beginning of Time; the rhythm grows faster, and with it my sense of a veritable immersion in that energy, of communion with the whole universe. Then, strange sounds assail me, neither human nor animal; they increase in volume. Men punctuate the rapid cadence of their singing with the noise of two sticks striking one another. Above them, shrouding them in security, the heartbeats of the one we call Mother continue. We are now led over to the heat and smoke of a fire fierce enough to dry the blood covering us. I am choking, I am overwhelmed by giddiness.

It is then that a prolonged buzzing sound roars in my

ears, seemingly engulfing my whole body. A terrible anguish overwhelms me, for this strange noise, which makes the air tremble, twists the flames, stirs up the sand, this is the voice of the Mother! The voice that makes women, children and the uninitiated flee far into the bush. I leap away from the fire to escape, as I must, whenever that sounds rings out. But energetic fists restrain me.

'Look!' orders my father, beside whom stands my maternal uncle.

The terrifying sound stops at last. Slowly, I grow calm again.

'Look at this!' he insists, showing me a large piece of wood sharpened at both ends, one of which, pierced with a hole, is fitted with a long strand of plaited hair.

I look up at him with astonished eyes.

'This churinga, this highly sacred object, is the receptacle of the might of the Ancestors who are associated with the sacred Life Energy. To understand this mystery, it is necessary for you to rise above your reasoning self. It is the passage that leads us into the Dreamtime. It represents the concrete and visible sign of the Dreaming, of the Eternal Dreamtime. With it, you will receive the revelation of this Dreaming. Life and the force emanating from it reach mankind thanks to its intervention. Our Mother's voice propagates itself through the vibrant humming of this rhomb whenever you make a rapid rotating movement above our heads by holding it with this thread.'

Dumbfounded, incredulous, I gaze at the object covered with red ochre, the blood of the Unthippa Women. After a short silence, my father continues:

'With this initial revelation, you are taking your first step into Alcheringa Time. You are emerging from the shadows. Other churingas will be given to you later on. All contain part of the Knowledge of Alcheringa

Time. From now on you will share the grave secret of the True Men. I have nothing more to add.'

No! That was not necessary. I knew that death was the sanction against the least reference to the secrets of the Instruction.

'This evening,' my maternal uncle continues, 'you will sleep with this rhomb under your head. Its powers of transmission are immense. All the more so because it is very old. With it, you will make your way forward very quickly towards your past in the Eternal Dreamtime, the Time with an ever present reality, which stands at the base of Time and manifests itself through it.'

My masters make me lie down. Squatting around me, they intone a sacred song, gently rubbing my back with a sacred object which, slowly, diffuses its divine essence through my body and spirit.

'You have become a Sacred Being,' they whisper as they stand up, while the didgeridoo continues to surround us with its otherworldly sound. 'Every day this rhomb will help one of you to remember.'

With these words, our initiators went away.

Yes, the prisoner thinks with a sigh, it is true, I too had rebelled. But after the ceremony of Punj, as a consequence of I know not what mystery, I protested no longer, I accepted with good heart my many obligations as Guardian of Creation and supported the authority of the Elders far better.

At the time of the drama of the burial, the world of the whites had already more attraction for the young than a ceremony from which they hoped to gain no benefit.

Certainly, agreeing to reveal our funeral ceremony in exchange for the gift of a few useless objects, that young man did not imagine for a moment that the deed would unleash such horrors! We could not understand how the migloos had dared to carry out such a massacre! At an equally critical moment for all living beings, that is to say for the whites as much as for the blacks! At the instant when the spirit of a dead person hovers above everyone! Were they creatures primitive to the point of not recognising the power of the dead?

Despite my apprehensiveness, the old black thinks, I was obliged to flush out the guilty one.

With a leap of courage, I put myself into a receptive state. Little by little the vision of the traitor rises in front of me. And plunges me into deep depression. For this is a young man in whom we had such great hopes, a young man who would have become a True Man of the highest degree without much difficulty, who should have been able later on to ensure that the line of the Men of High Degree, of which our people stood in such need, would persist.

When we arrived to look for him in the bachelors' camp, this youth had already fled. A great sorrow overwhelmed us. Sadness over the loss of one of our great hopes, sadness for the decadence into which he was in danger of falling.

13

The prisoner tries to make his memories stop right there. But, implacably, the scenes of his life continue to unfold, making him live through events for a second time, events that he would have liked so much to forget.

Here are the Wise Men and the Men of High Degree of my people gathered for an extraordinary Assembly.

After each of us had spoken in turn, we come to a depressing conclusion: since the invaders had risked extinguishing so many lives, we must, ourselves, take the same risk. We no longer have any choice, from now on, blood will have to flow.

I remember the lengthy discussion about employing what should have been a powerful weapon. A weapon so powerful that it would have swiftly rid us of the subhumans; a weapon that would not have caused too many deaths, black or white! But, that day, in the course of another extraordinary Assembly, it was unanimously rejected. Too vile to be employed, too easy to use against strangers who are unaware of the extent of its might! In this struggle, we want to preserve our combatants' dignity! To perpetuate for as long as possible fidelity to our traditional combats; combats which exalt our skills as great tacticians, our physical and moral endowments; which respect the dignity of the opposing camp.

But our invaders did not even know the word dignity, they did not know that a combat must cease with the first death, if not with the first injury, unless men want it to turn into common slaughter, into the enemy of Life. They knew nothing about the behaviour of True Men, of civilised people!

That is why, in this struggle to defend our lands, it should have been imperative for us to know how to flout our ethical standards. That would not have been easy for us, for we would have been obliged to struggle mightily against an age-old pattern of behaviour, which has become a reflex action: it would have been a matter of mastery over the self, acquired painfully during our long formation as True Men, to serve a contradictory impulse. Many were still chary of opting for such behaviour.

Fire, which could have become a powerful ally, was therefore rejected. It represented much too great a threat for our land, even for ourselves! No! We would not use fire, the formidable force that became, according to tradition, our ally after one of the Sacred Beings taught us the art of mastering it. But a force which could only be used in exceptional circumstances, by taking into account several factors, together with knowledge of the seasons, winds, the state of the vegetation in the place in question, the likelihood of rain. What is more, to encircle extensive tracts of land, like those around the cattle station, many people would be needed to set fires in different spots, and then an even greater number to control them in order to prevent the blaze spreading over the whole territory. Without such control, we knew what force fire could exert, the conflagration it could start. A conflagration caused at times by nature itself, which could leap to the crowns of the highest trees with a muffled, violent sound, spitting huge clumps of sparks into the infinite expanses of the sky, then falling dangerously to earth far away, to start other fires which, in their turn, would grow monstrous and ignite others. A seemingly endless chain reaction! After such disasters, death hovered over the land. The vegetation, the animal life and we the people had to flee from the charred tracts of land and wait patiently for the next rains, which would make the fire-stunned seeds sprout. We were afraid that if fires were set in different places, even if they were scattered, they would join up and consume for all time the land of which we were the Guardians.

There was also the legend of the disaster that visited us long ago. A story concealing a grave secret which only the Great Initiates such as I knew.

Long ago, the legend said, mankind, having grown too numerous, turned extremely evil. Because there were not enough sources of water for all of them on Mother Earth, nor enough food. What is more, they did not have the time to receive the teaching of the Elders because they were too preoccupied with not starving to death. Their wickedness made them invent the 'fire of evil'. A huge blaze broke out all over the land. And it burnt every living creature, rising high into the sky, where it set alight the feathers of all the birds that had sought refuge up there. In order to escape, winged creatures plunged into the sea. To flee forever from the scorched world, they turned themselves into fish. Into fish with the striking colours of the ball of fire that made them flee from the bosom of Mother Earth.

Definitely, the ancestral fear of that legendary time, which is nevertheless always alive for us, and the wish to preserve our dignity prevented us from employing what could have rid us for ever of our invaders. Only a few undisciplined people had recourse to it, with indifferent success. That did not prevent us from intensifying our raids. As did the whites.

In order to accomplish that, the whites made incursions into our winter paths with numerous young black men from the people of the east, Guardians of the land bordering the endless water. They succeeded in persuading them to penetrate further and further west, where previously they would certainly not have dared to venture.

Like us, these young men had perfect command of the art of tracking, the art of observation, of camouflage, of self-control; like us they used the language of signs, so important for communicating when close to the enemy, without allowing it to realise that someone was nearby. We feared them more than we feared the whites. With the arrival of these young men, who were called police boys, the advantage represented by our skill to make ourselves invisible, incapable of being discovered, and therefore invulnerable, vanished. We only had the advantage of our intimate knowledge of the land, the protection that the presence of our sacred sites afforded. For these sites, we were persuaded, diffused benevolenvce over us at every instant. For strangers, these same places, which they knew to exist but could not locate, were no longer allies but, on the contrary, sources of a malevolent power. A power they feared more than anything else in the world. They believed it capable of unleashing its force against violators of the most important Commandment, a Commandment they shared with us, to acknowledge the interdiction against straying beyond your own territory.

Under the influence of the whites, but also intoxicated by the power of their new weapons, their new life, the first clothing they ever had worn, their sketchy familiarity with the invaders' language, they thought that they had gained superiority over people like themselves. They considered themselves invulnerable. What is more, without having properly thought about it, they did not take into account that interdiction connected with our beliefs, which had suddenly seemed to them a simple story told by old people to do with former times. But, from time to time, ancient fears surged again, growing stronger than their reason. Then the alarm provoked by malevolent powers hovering over the lands of strangers, into which they had dared to venture, the fear of the occult powers of the inhabitants, the vengeful spirits of their dead, all these ancestral certainties dulled their admiration for the whites, sprouted abruptly in their memory, filling them with panic, making them flee, abandoning the subhumans, and at the crucial moment of an attack, what is more.

Alas! Despite this potential weakness, our superior knowledge of the land did not carry much weight before those bearing firearms.

Yes! It was at that moment that our life ceased definitively to be Life as we had always conceived it. The change manifested itself as fleeing from the enemy without hope of respite, ceaselessly destroying living things, making blood flow, much too much blood! With the ever-present fear in our hearts of shattering the equilibrium of the Sacred Energy, the Soul of the World which envelops all living things, blacks as much as whites! How many times did I wish to explain this terrible threat to the subhumans I came across. Alas! I knew, we all knew their inability to profit from what we know, their inability to learn anything we might be able to teach them.

For the sake of greater mobility, in order to conceal ourselves more easily, we had reduced our groups to a few individuals, zigzagging around to find more undulating country, terrain more propitious for rapid flight. Places often far removed from the path we were following at the time.

Then the whites, who could easily spot us because of our evening campfires, started tracking us by night. So it became necessary for us to sleep without fire, our protector against the evil spirits of the shades; without its heat and the sense of caressing security it sent out. It often became necessary for us to eat uncooked food, or to cook it over pathetic little flames, all the while beating down the smoke with plaited leaves to prevent it from rising to the sky. A dark time, in the course of which each day brought the news of the death of a good number of our people and, by comparison, few enough of the invaders.

For a long time, since well before the calamity of the funeral, we had contemplated an attack on the wagons carrying provisions from the coast. Each month, they made their way along one of the tracks leading to a cattle station inhabited by six whites, which had by then been guarded for some time by blacks from the far east. A new station established some moons earlier on our best hunting grounds, there where the path of the Yam Dreaming snaked. At the time, it was a matter of a mere act of sabotage, intended to demoralise the new despoilers, forcing them to flee. Now it was a matter of killing all the carters, then seizing their cattle and goods. This bloody act of resistance would prove to the spirits of those that had disappeared how much they remained in our thoughts; it would help them, perhaps, to reach the world of the Invisibles. So that they would torment us no longer. And the subhumans would at last understand how determined we were to send them back to where they came from.

We had carefully studied the route they would follow, a track marked out by the successive traces left behind by the wheels of their wagons. We chose the section most propitious for an attack, that is to say the part of the track most difficult to negotiate with those generally overloaded contraptions, so vulnerable to the least unforseen difficulty. Our choice had come to rest unanimously on a narrow, stony path, with cliffs on both sides, an abrupt declivity covered with a thick layer of spinifex.

By exploiting traditional trading circuits, we had put in place a network of voluntary messengers chosen from our trading partners and the partners of those partners, extending therefore, from people to people, all the way to the coast. Over there, one of our spies would warn the nearest man in the network about the departure of one of the wagons; the latter would immediately set out, with the message stick which served to identify him, to carry the news to another of our men among the people living in a region neighbouring his. So, from messenger to messenger, spreading by day as by night, the news reached us very quickly, thanks to the short-cuts we all knew. Considering the ever increasing number of collaborators among the coastal tribes, the operation carried the risk of betrayal. We took that risk.

As soon as the news reaches us, we go into action. As the Council of Wise Men had decided, a group sets out in search of large dead trees or trees that had been uprooted in storms. One night, with the aid of lengthy thongs, two teams dragged the roughly trimmed trunks, concealing them near the place where the wagon would pass. Men of a second group set out to find observation posts where they would position themselves to wait for the moment to act. They decide on which place to choose by calling out to each other. They come to an agreement about the signal: the cry of the curlew, the night bird, for the whites are still unable to recognise the songs of our birds. The observer farthest removed from the point of attack will send out this call as soon as he hears the sound of wagon wheels; the man next to him will send it on in turn, and so on up to the last observer, positioned opposite the point of attack. The last man will immediately signal his team, which will hurry off to drag the tree trunks across the track itself, making them overlap in such a way as to render removing them as difficult and time-consuming as possible.

The long-awaited day arrives. Concealed behind a tree, a rock, a hollow in the ground, a mere clump of grass, we are on the lookout for two days and nights. Two days and two nights without hearing a single voice, communicating from time to time with the person directly next to us only in the language of signs.

Several times, children sneak up to bring us a little food. Silent little black imps who seem to spring out of the ground, so well have they already mastered the art of making themselves invisible. They vanish just as suddenly, as silently as they had appeared.

At last, on the second day, as soon as the blazing torch of the setting sun approaches the horizon, enveloping the countryside in unreal colours, a simply delicious harmony, as soon as my spirit forgets all our troubles and attempts to flee towards the higher spheres, the call of the curlew brings me brutally back to earth, instantly unlocking the alertness of all my senses.

Soon, I can hear the rhythmic crunch of stones, of the kind that only the large beasts of the whites are capable of making; I hear the crack of a whip, then the voices of the carters, the breath of bullocks wafted on a sudden gust of wind; strange smells assail me, strong, unpleasant. In a cloud of dust, the wagon draws level to me. Without moving a muscle, holding my breath back, I wait for the coupling to pass; I then turn my back on the dust and quickly clamber up the rock face, taking a short cut to rejoin the group of my people farther up the slope, on each side of our obstacle of logs, just beyond the nearby bend in the track. During my frantic rush, I think how lucky it is that we are dealing with a convoy drawn by four bullocks in place of the usual two. Bullocks which must become ours in a few moments! When I am directly above the wagon and its noise, I stop to send my companions the warning signal. My two hands cupped around my lips, with all the power of my voice, I call in the manner of the curlew and immediately continue on my way.

Here I am now at the height of the ambush. I clamber down to hide in the narrow cleft in the rock face where I have concealed my spear. I make sure that our armed men are properly in position. A red cloud of dust rises to my right, still a little distance from the obstacle. All is going well: the migloos do not take the trouble to reconnoitre the dangerous thoroughfare, which could well have been blocked by a small landslide or by dead branches driven there by the wind. Surprise gives us an advantage! They hardly slacken their pace and reach the bend, travelling a little too fast.

No sooner has the wagon started rounding the dangerous bend, than one of the whites calls out and tugs on the reins with all his might, the other leaps to the ground to try to calm the terrified animals with his hands and voice. I remove my weapon from its hiding place, aim, and with a precise gesture, drive my spear into the driver's throat. He does not have time to put his hands to the wound before Wongu's boomerang crashes into his skull; he collapses without making a sound.

The other white man turns his head to the right, to the left, then towards his companion. Dead! He realises that he is dead! Fear stops from him calling out. He stays rooted to the spot, his eyes popping out of their sockets. Then, suddenly, he lets his hand, which he has been holding aloft all along, drop and turns his back on the coupling, leaping into the ravine, screaming in terror. A spear flies, hurled by Mau, who is standing in the middle of the track, behind our barricade. I see the weapon slashing the air, flying into a clump of foliage, then emerging to plant itself in the fugitive's thigh. The instant he collapses, another man's club smashes his skull. The two migloos are dead. The bullocks have been calmed down and, behind them, unknown goods await our pleasure.

The moment we sigh with relief, the danger signal reaches us. Straight away, we hide, weapons in hand. We do not have to wait for a long before two horsemen appear, trotting gently. Opposite me, Wongu hurls his club, I my boomerang. The two men collapse over their halters. The unforseen could have made us fail.

Without any show of contentment, without a word, we proceed with the second part of our plan.

One of our men removes the limp body of the driver from the seat to lay it out across the track, behind the wagon; another goes off in search of the other body, to place it parallel to his companion's. With Wongu, we leap into the front of the wagon, climb over the driver's seat to get to the goods under the cover. Our eyes light on two brand-new rifles, laid flat on top of the crates, next to a box containing a large number of cartridges. We hand them to the Wise Men who are charged with carrying them very quickly to the place chosen by the Council, where our people would be able to find them if the need arose. To speed up the inspection of the goods, some climb into the back of the wagon. They slash the tarpaulin with their axes; then they open the crates on the floor and look at the contents. They are filled with numerous unfamiliar tools, nails, cloth, clothing. As well, two iron axes are quickly handed down to the men on the ground, those keeping an eye on the track while they are waiting to take the goods, in order, in turn, to hide them quickly in the scrub. They linger over some clothing, picking them up by the armful, then, with heavy heart, leave the greater part behind. For nothing must hinder our escape. I discover bags of salt and sugar. I taste a little of the first, more fortifying than the other; I signal to Wongu to do the same. Then we quickly leap to the ground, hurrying to look after the animals.

Waga, one of my trading partner from the east who has come to help us, knows something about horses; he fits ropes around their necks. In a low voice, he calls out to two young men, who are hiding nearby, and holds out the end of a rope to each of them, telling them to lead the animals away. The young men grab hold of the ropes, ready to restrain the beasts if they try to escape. But for the moment, completely calm, the horses are grazing quietly on the grass we have put in front of them. The youths lead them off a little further and, laughing silently, pretend to climb on their backs. Wongu signals to them to stop; they cannot run the risk of not managing to ride them properly. So, despite their inclinations, they move off with slow steps, each at the side of one of the huge animals. Instinctively encouraging them in a low voice, surprised by their docility.

Then, with Wongu's help, I try to work out how to remove the shafts restraining the bullocks. In spite of the urgency of the moment, I notice the quality of these restraints, of the wonderful couplings, as supple as they are solid, made I am sure of cowhide. I note equally the skill with which they must have worked out how to make these headstrong animals pull their load. By imposing such labour on their brothers, did not the whites fear offending their common Ancestors?

As I am busying myself, I cast an admiring glance at the wheels, which I am seeing close up for the first time. Made of perfectly curved wood! Able to roll over such terrain! What knowledge and skill! The migloos' needs must be very different from ours, and their techniques probably correspond to those needs. Why would the Giants of Alcheringa Time, those who mingled themselves with the sacred Vital Energy, with the Soul of the World, why would they have taught us this fashion of working with the substance of trees impregnated by the same mysterious force since the beginning of Life! Why should we have the right to fell them? Cutting a few branches, as we do, does not rob them of life. Besides, why would we have the need to transport food since, in every place, nature is subservient to our needs. More exactly: used to be subservient.

Throughout time, we have struggled against accumulating material goods. An accumulation which could not fail to divert mankind from the search for the ideal self, according to our tradition. What would we do with such contraptions, since making our way on foot without haste, becoming one with our paths in the course of our endless wanderings, represents our Life? A life which keeps us in contact with the invisible sacred world, the only one capable of making us rise above our mortal state. Why do the subhumans need such skills, such reserves of food and beasts? Is their land so impoverished? Or do they have no spiritual beliefs? The same questions always return.

At last we manage to undo the halters and couplings. The latter makes me think of the blades of axes. What amazing objects, which they probably obtained thanks to their control over substances we know nothing about! While we are holding the shafts, the young men pull gently on the ropes to make the bullocks move forward. They pat their flanks, calming them with their voices as they have seen and heard the migloos doing. Without any difficulty, they separate them from the wagon. After casting a last glance at the contents of the crates, we take a few nails and, very quickly, we hurry off to hide in a cleft in the rock face, from which you can see over great distances, to the right and to the left of the invaders' track.

Sitting calmly, in silence, we inspect the surrounding for a good while. If the whites of the station had any thought of coming to meet the wagon, we could easily emerge from our hiding place to lure them in a direction opposite to that taken by our people. But, so protective a cocoon, only familiar sounds surround us: the murmur of the evening breeze, as soft as its caress, broken momentarily by the noisy chatter of a cloud of pink cockatoos perching for the night not far from us – they quarrel, vigorously flapping their wings – the cackle of thousands of green parrots on their way to a clump of wattle where they vanish, as if by magic, then, from far away, the despairing cry of a dingo searching for a female. At length the night wraps us in its heavy cloak, bringing other equally familiar smells and noises.

Then we emerge from our hiding place. As a final measure of safety, in order to mislead any possible migloo who could be watching us, we take a long detour before making for our camp. We watch the Man Moon's journey in the sky, and when he is shining directly overhead, we know that we are not being followed, that the whites are not worried about the delay of their convoy. We know that we have succeeded!

Yes! That was a truly great moment when we gathered, a long way from there, in the cave of the Man Wallaby, protected by the elongated faces of the Ancestors painted on its walls. We were proud of our victory over the invaders! Proud of being black!

Then, for several days, preferably by night, illuminated by Bahloo, who had grown large once more, we learnt how to mount, then stay on the backs of the horses, discovering how to do it from the memory we have retained and imprinted on our minds by observing the white horsemen. We also work out how to fire a rifle and, after the shock of the violent blow of the butt against our shoulders on our first attempt, we came to think that aiming with a migloo's weapon demanded less skill than you need to aim a spear. Very quickly, we became reasonably expert shots, expert horsemen, allowing the intoxication of speed and the power of firearms to give us an illusory sense of invincibility, a sense that could dangerously affect our reason. Happily, one of us always retained a head cool enough to drag back to reality the one that had been momentarily intoxicated with his new skills.

Then … then, I see the horses again during one of our evening halts. Placidly, they make their way to the watering place their instinct had detected. Now I can see them coming back to us with slow steps, and once again I am surprised by and admire their magnificently muscular bodies, their heads like giant kangaroos' shining with two soft eyes. I love these animals. I surprise myself by being able to feel so close to them, for nothing in our beliefs is connected with them, I do not know what Ancestors they have!

Such are my thoughts when I see one of them tumbling heavily to the ground, rolling every which way, neighing, foaming at the mouth, twitching violently before it is overcome by stillness of death.

And now the other is doing the same! Unable to believe my eyes, I remain motionless, incapable of taking my eyes off the two corpses. It triggers something in my mind, and I call out to my companions, who are busy setting up camp for the night, warning them not to drink, because the waterhole has been poisoned. Horror, sorrow comes crashing down over the group.

'The time has come to leave the east,' one man whispers.

For some time in truth, the smell of the minerals, the smell of the vegetation, the places where we came upon flocks of birds, the air itself, suddenly grown heavy, all that has whispered to us that it was more than time to leave. Nothing could hold us back any longer. We hid the two rifles in the cave, and without any regret set out for the mineral world, irresistibly driven by the imperative of our religious obligation, by the imperative, as much physical as moral, of the wanderings of the rainy season.

14

The path of the Woman Honey Ant. At first, we are travelling purposefully, without meditating, preoccupied solely with deploying all of our skill to make ourselves invisible. For many days now, we have been in the habit of making our way in the first glimmering of dawn, surrounded by the last cool veils of the night, going to earth for extended periods in places where the subhumans like to ride out in search of an 'Abo' to kill. Then we set out again, late in the afternoon, travelling until nightfall. This new kind of existence requires a great effort of will, and there is always someone to question it. Without success, for our safety relies on this to a large extent.

Then, as we move further and further away from the east, that is to say from the invaders, our way of life slowly regains its ancestral rhythms.

This morning, the singing of the path announces that we are approaching a mountain range, beyond which the whites have not dared to venture. Soon, indeed, the appearance on the horizon of rounded summits, enveloped by bluish purple, airy and constantly changing light, urges us to increase our pace. If all goes well, we will have settled by tomorrow evening for an extended stay at one of our favourite sites. Far from our enemies.

One of my fathers has great difficulty in keeping pace with this new rhythm; sometimes he requires the help of his two young wives to prevent him stumbling on the rutted ground. He has fine young lubras; they feed him well, as they feed his first wife, who has now herself grown old. Without the invaders, both could have had a fine ending to their lives.

Little by little, the vegetation grows sparse. Only a few scattered eucalypts grow on the brown ochre of the stony vastness. The white of their satiny trunks and branches is etched against the deep blue of the sky. Their elegant foliage trembles at the smallest gust of wind, as if to sing out its joy of life.

Soon, fear begins to leave us. But a warning dream makes uneasiness invade my spirit once more.

A dream, still so clear today! I am travelling with my group along a path which is difficult to make out. We have been walking for a long time, singing. We walk, we walk and we are forever walking, exhausted, parched. Arriving at the place where there should be a hollow, the sacred High Place created by the Ancestor whom we have come to worship, there is only an immense plain entirely covered with cows and calves. An immensity stretching well beyond the horizon. And these cows and calves are looking at me, laughing maliciously. Then, in the middle of this endless extent of hides, a great black bird takes flight, flaps its huge wings and starts calling out in the overloud and strident voice of the migloos: 'I am their guardian!'

So my group takes to the path again, and walks and sings the songs that belong to it. The group makes its way, more and more exhausted, without ever finding the reassurance of the sacred High Place. Little by little, it loses its strength, its moral fibre. And I, in my dream, feel weakness overwhelming all my limbs, doubt assailing my mind. My anguish becomes so strong that it rouses me from sleep.

The following morning, as we are breaking up camp at

the usual time of day again, I am still under the disturbing influence of that dream. I walk alone, physically and mentally isolated from my people; I try in vain to interpret the images and sensations of the previous night. As time passes, I grow more and more gloomy, preoccupied. Deep in thought, turning the problem over and over again in my mind, I cannot see what that message from the invisible world might mean.

Lost in my thoughts, I am greatly surprised to find myself already at the heart of the mountain chain. A little before crossing the narrow gorge leading to the so-much desired site, the members of the group, dispersed until then, reassemble. In single file, we make our way between the two smooth walls of sparkling red granite, all imprinted with the force of their Creator.

So I forget about my dream. Like my companions, I regain my confidence, my pride and my good humour, all of which had vanished during our sojourn in our despoiled lands. We are like plants that revive after rain. So exhilarated by the thought of seeing no migloo, no cow, no calf any more!

I am sightly ahead of the others, so eager am I to recover the peace of mind and beauty of this spot. My feet seem to fly above the scorching pebbles, and my body grows thinner effortlessly, to allow it to pass through the last narrow passage between the rocks. But, one foot still on the burning granite, I come to a stop, paralysed by amazement! What a terrible memory!

I make my eyes into slits to reassure me that what I see over there, in the distance, is not a trick of the light. No matter how hard I try to focus my eyes, the form remains the same, a huge black bird flapping its wings in front of a cross-shaped piece of wood! The bird of my dream! I remain motionless, mute. The others are hurrying to catch up with me. One after the other, they poke their heads through the opening in the rock face and see what I can see. Exploiting our amazement, some of the children escape from the women's surveillance, slither between our legs and tumble into the creek, laughing loudly. At this sound, the 'bird' turns, notices the children. Soon, it hauls its lump of wood up on its shoulder and walks towards them. In a terrified and terrifying voice, the women summon the piccaninnies, who immediately come back to us. Mothers and children go off to hide. As for me, I seem to be living out the continuation of my dream. Slowly, driven by an unknown force, I emerge from the tangle of rocks. Just as I am making my way towards the strange shape, the dream images still present in my mind slowly give place to those of the real world. Then I come upon a short, stocky creature, swathed in black, who is walking towards me with a long cross-shaped piece of wood over its shoulder. The expression on its face reveals great contentment. Yes! It seems happy to see us.

We walk towards each other. When it is a short distance away, it puts its burden down with a great show of respect, raises its arms to the sky, lifting the black substance, which accordingly takes on the shape of what I had assumed to be wings. He – for this seems to be man – then lets them drop, clasps his hands in front of his chest, looks up at the sky and in a low voice recites an incomprehensible kind of incantation. Still with the same show of respect, he picks up his wooden object, props it on his shoulder and makes a sign for me to accompany him. My people have joined us. Dumb with amazement, not knowing what world this apparition has come from, we watch him making for the steep path leading to our waterhole.

All my senses are on the alert to capture the vibrations sent out by this creature. But I detect nothing worrying. What should we do?

He turns around and gently and, with a broad smile,

urges us to follow him. After a short consultation, the Wise Men of the group decide that it would be best to find out what he wants from us and to get back to discussing what we should do about him later on. For, Wongu says, if he is a migloo, he has certainly not come so far all on his own, into a region so difficult to penetrate!

'Where are his cows and calves?' someone asks.

'Perhaps he hasn't any,' Mau replies.

'If he hasn't any he's not a migloo!' one of the women remarks.

At that moment, my eyes meet the little creature's. And, in that look, I detect only calm and gentleness. Instead of rejoicing, I am worried by this because, obviously, such a look could not be that of an invader! Mightn't a mimi spirit be amusing itself by taking on this new shape? If so, has it come as friend or enemy? Or could it be that he is a migloo unlike others of his kind?

We make our way, slowly, indecisive, still in shock, behind the little black shadow. But a new sensation is waiting for us. Beyond a tall bush heavy with its honey flowers, we discover some kind of solidly constructed shelter. Once more, amazement stops us short.

Here we are now in front of this peculiar wiltja, rooted to the spot, speechless, ignoring the little creature who is waving his arms around to make us understand that this construction belongs to him. Shaking off my surprise, I address Wongu telepathically. We decide to set about beating the surrounding countryside in search of other migloos and their animals that might be there. Discreetly, one after another, we leave the group.

Having explored the surroundings without finding any other alien presence, we come to the conclusion that the peculiar creature clad in black has come all on his own! Without cows and without calves! Difficult to believe that this is a migloo. How could he have managed to come as far as this! Would there be an invader capable of travelling farther than those of the east, who are more robust than he seems to be? Capable of finding water without the help of our people? The same question once again: is this a white man or a spirit?

After discussing this incredible presence, we go back to the others, who have stayed near the wiltja of the tiny subhuman or spirit clad entirely in black. The little creature continues smiling, explaining to us that this construction certainly belongs to him. To accomplish that, he places his index finger on one of the walls, then on his chest, several times. Then, with a questioning movement of his head, with raised eyebrows, steady gaze, he asks us if we have understood. And, since no one bothers to reply, he goes on with his mimicry. Suddenly, with the same show of respect as before, he grabs his cross-shaped piece of wood, holds it out to us, chanting, eyes raised to the sky. Then, always with the respect reserved among us for religious objects, he leans it against the nearest tree. With his eyes closed, he places his lips to the wood as if in veneration. And he turns to us once more, smiling again. We all remain immobile, still incredulous, we can't take our eyes off this person.

At length we recover our spirits. We sit in a circle around the fire which will keep what could be a mimi at some distance. Calmly, everyone expresses what he thinks of this presence. We fall into agreement: no malevolent wave is wafting out of this peculiar apparition, which seems truly enough to be made of flesh and blood; we can read nothing disquieting in his look. We come to the conclusion that, for the moment, it is best to ignore him, to wait until the others have arrived to determine whether he is a subhuman, and therefore an enemy, or a mimi spirit, mischievous but friendly. So we leave him, him and his cross, to climb a little higher, where the pool of water is situated. We signal to the women to join us. We are all reunited. Our happiness has flown away. A feeling of lassitude, of powerlessness, casts us into a pit of discouragement.

We make our way along the stony path, hard put to arrive at a place where fresh water is awaiting us. The bird in my dream is still pursuing me, superimposing itself more than ever on the little creature. Lost in my thoughts, I am walking without noticing anything. Suddenly, the abrupt stillness of the others brings me to the alert. Their eyes are travelling past a scrawny beefwood tree, to the right of the pool of water. My gaze follows theirs and, in turn, I see what they are looking at. A monstrous apparition!

As if turned to stone, we are staring at a misshapen animal, slumped on the ground, seemingly without legs, covered all over with fur the colour of yellow sand, a creature even bigger than a horse. A large cone-shaped lump rises from its back, followed by a long flexible neck, like a lizard's. Its large and elongated head is surmounted by two ears, ridiculously small for such an animal, possums' ears! Its jaw moves backwards and forwards, working a large and fleshy mouth, which opens now and then to reveal big, repulsive teeth. Astonishingly beautiful eyes, shaded by long, feminine lashes, shine in the midst of all this hideousness. When we come nearer, the animal lifts its head a little and inspects us with a superior air. But now it stands up, with difficulty, on its hindquarters, on long legs which have remained concealed until now, in all probability, beneath it. It lets out a kind of moan, as disagreeable as it is unfamiliar, then it hauls itself up laboriously on its front legs. Its height impresses us, but we stay stock still throughout, silent, not reacting.

The animal makes for the water, pulling on a long rope tied to the beefwood tree. When it reaches the pool, it lowers its head and begins drinking. Noiselessly, we sneak behind a bush to observe it closely. It is still drinking. And drinking still! With horror, we watch as the level of the water drops. Two piccaninnies run off to safety, howling with fright. But they bump into the little creature who is climbing up the rocky path to join us and, arms akimbo, seems to be stopping them from fleeing. The little boys are crying even more vehemently, running along each side of his black cape, without his being able to stop either of them. Then he smiles sweetly, and continues coming towards us with a limp, for, like our invaders, he has deprived himself of the benefit of allowing his bare feet to grip the ground, imprisoning them, instead, in huge boots. A mimi couldn't be so stupid!

When he reaches us, he makes us understand that the monster belongs to him. We are inclined to disbelieve him. Realising that we have understood him, he smiles even more broadly, then grabs hold of the rope restraining the animal. Not without some difficulty, he climbs on its back, sitting astride it, and, gesticulating, he makes us understand that he has come from the south on the back of this animal. And he gets down, smiling as much as ever, not having noticed that the women are making their way towards us with our six dogs.

The dogs suddenly notice the unfamiliar smell and, as if driven mad by such a stink, they hurl themselves at the monstrous animal, which takes off at a speed we would not have thought it capable of. The rope slips out of the migloo's hands; he does not budge, his face revealing surprise rather than annoyance. He begins calling out a name, while trying to pursue his peculiar mount.

The women laugh, give voice to 'Ahs' of contempt, the children are leaping with joy and we, the Wise Men, are hoping, from the bottom of our hearts, that this walking abomination will not come back soon.

That was my first brief encounter with a camel. A new calamity that befell our watering places!

Strange little creature. When he returns empty handed, he does not seem at all put out. He holds no grudge against anyone. Neither people nor the dogs.

In the days that follow, he walked with us, swathed in his long black cape, his cross on his shoulder, smiling without cease at one and all, bestowing rather surprisingly paternal gestures all around. From time to time, he gave us a part of the produce of his hunting. And my people were saying that this amiable person, without cows or calves, who knows how to share, could not be one of our invaders!

As for me, I was not so sure. But, if he was a subhuman, what was he doing here? What was he up to all the time he shut himself inside his hut? Without a wife! Odd, all these migloos without lubras! One morning, standing for a long while in front of his shelter, I could not stop myself peering through the branches. I surprised him naked, astonishingly white. Around his neck, he wore a thin strand carrying a small object with spiky ends. I saw him grasp this object with both hands, beat it several times against his flesh until blood began to seep, then raise his eyes to the sky, intoning some words, the rhythm of which reminded me of an incantation.

We discussed this for a long time, but we could not decide whether this act made up a part of some kind of initiatory rite. Was he a Man of High Degree from the world of the whites, rich in Knowledge? Did he possess mental powers akin to ours, the Men of High Degree? Alas! Politeness prevented us from showing our curiosity, no matter how great it might have been! And the barrier of language made things even more difficult.

Despite our forbidding them to do it, one day, while he was with us, the children discovered that he kept in his place vast quantities of the goods which he distributed so parsimoniously. He became suspect once more.

Later on, we came to learn that not only did he sleep at night shut in his shelter, while the sky, magnificently pure and starry, dispersed its benevolent rays on the world below, but that, in addition, he put a distance between himself and the health-giving body of Mother Earth by lying on a plank of wood placed on four tall stumps, the height of two hands!

Time passed. We learnt to accept his paternalism, which came to be confirmed more and more, since it was proof that he knew nothing about us.

And we liked that ignorance.

What is more, he made us laugh as he mimicked our activities in order to make himself understood. And he laughed with us.

The first time he laughed surprised us mightily, for we had not yet heard a migloo laugh. Nor even smile!

Soon, since he asked nothing of us, since not a cow, not a calf had come to join him, since the water-guzzling monster had vanished, we paid no more attention to his presence, despite being unsure who he might have been.

15

Without clearly understanding why, I felt myself attracted to the little black-clad creature. And he to me, for he often came to sit next to me, close to my little fire, even though it was at some distance from the others'. Without speaking, he watched me making a new weapon or an ordinary object. His presence did not in the least disturb the concentration indispensable to actions with which, at one and the same time, I had to give perfect form to the wood and to impregnate it with the benevolent waves of my hands, something essential for it to function properly.

We had come to regard him as a human being, a little superior to the subhumans: a spirit could not have remained among us for so long a time.

One day, he began asking me the names of common objects, then, later on, those of our everyday actions. I can see him imitating a man running, then turning to me with a questioning look. His mimicry counted for nothing in my understanding, for I was reading his thoughts; a little less quickly than the thoughts of my own people, but easily enough all the same. As soon as I answered, he rewarded me with a broad smile of satisfaction, mixed with astonishment, constantly repeating my words; then he raised his eyebrows to seek my approbation.

Very quickly, he began to master everyday vocabulary. I was sure that the other, concerning our spiritual life, our philosophy, would always remain inaccessible to him, even if I had decided to tell him about it. For our trading partners from all the devastated regions had told us time and again that the vocabulary of the whites dealt only with temporal life; nothing about it suggested a spiritual life! That indicated, without doubt, that their mental evolution had not reached our stage of development.

Slowly, as the days passed, the other families arrived at the site, settling down to the east or the west of the little pool, according to whether they belonged to the Sparrowhawks or the Grey Falcons. The little migloo, accepted or tolerated by all, came and went ceaselessly from one camp to the other; he stopped in front of every one of the small fires, laughed, tried to make others laugh, giving friendly taps on the shoulders to one or another, distributing tobacco to the older people, salt or sugar to the youngsters. Our number, still increasing, seemed very much to surprise, if not disquiet him. Physically, I thought he was getting tired, but his morale did not weaken, he seemed to me even a little elated!

After the clan gathered, he and his mimicry no longer amused anyone. He was completely ignored. For it was now necessary to prepare for the numerous ceremonies which must be held during the Great Assembly. All our thoughts, all our endeavours were called into action for these events.

Reunited once again, each moiety of our people was going to be responsible for one of these rites. Once more, under the protection of the Woman Honey Ant, our common ancestor, they were going to measure themselves against one another. From this competition between participants from the different groups, between mere partners a new dynamism would be born, the wish for everyone to be seen in the best light, to draw a little nearer, if not attain, his ideal self.

How great were my hopes! That year, I was sure, after

the dance of purification, the competition would be at its most intense. And the participants, by reproducing the deeds and acts of the Ancestor, would immerse themselves for a moment in the fluid of the Sacred Energy, again becoming for an instant the beings of the prehuman epoch, from which they were descended. Accordingly, after our unity was affirmed in such a way, we would regain trust in our ideals. The doubts entertained by some of us would disappear; we would be convinced that the real Life was to be found there, in the spiritual and secret life of our great Family, in the life that raises us above material vicissitudes, endows us with pride, with trust in a secure future, because, as always, that future would be the perfect replica of Alcheringa Time, the exemplary model, of which we were the Guardians.

Of a sudden, how great was my confidence in the future! How happy was I! How remote it was, my dream of a great black bird! Did my sojourn with the invaders and all the disasters of that period render me more conscious of the grandeur and beauty of our conception of Life?

I recall what I felt when I was helping to remove from their hiding place the engraved stones, some destined for instructing youths, others, extremely sacred, extremely dangerous for those not permitted to handle them, indispensable for accomplishing our rites. I can still feel the trembling of all my limbs when I placed my hands on the representation of the Woman Honey Ant, the giant churinga, a piece of mulga wood taller than a man, carved and painted in the distant past by the best mediums and artists of the cultic group of the Men of High Degree.

With what fervour did I refresh the colours of the symbols painted on the wood and, with the sharp end of a sacred stone, the contours of its carvings. So I reactivated its field of forces, which grew particularly powerful and dangerous again.

A few days later, I see again our entire family in front of a vast platform. I am there with the other officiators. It is once again my privilege to raise aloft the representation of our common Dreaming.

It is with real devotion, an ecstatic transport, that I raise this venerated object above our heads. For a few moments, while the women and children are weeping with emotion and are respectfully dropping their heads, and the men are gazing at it with love and humility, I feel transfigured, becoming once again the Sacred Being of Time immemorial!

The blinding perception of the divine unity that shapes us, that shapes me, the reincarnation of a Great Ancestor, the Great Ancestor of my people, without whom I am nothing, the perception of this trinity, making up in reality nothing but the one and the same Entity, transfigured me, plunged me into an immense and painful joy. For several moons, for one last time, we were the proud and magnificent Guardians of Creation!

Then, in an unexpected way, the ill omen my dreams had announced was revealed to me.

One of the ceremonies had just come to an end. Men and women were leaving the sacred ground to return to the camp, near the waterhole, a long walk from there. Soon, the officiators found themselves alone with their cult objects, which had to be put in a secure place. It was then that 'he' reappeared.

We had just discarded behind a bush the bark paintings made specially for the ceremony, for we gave no thought to their value: the mere act of painting them with fervour, the mere action of our hands guided by the invisible world had provoked the beneficial emotions of the rite. Once that was over, we no longer attached any importance to these representations.

We were tired, our bodies, which themselves had contributed to allowing us to enter into a parallel Time for a few moments, were still covered with their sacred designs. Our spirits were slowly coming down from the peaks in the sky we had glimpsed during the rite.

With infinite precaution, we began wrapping the sacred stones and the other churingas, which Men of High Degree were permitted to touch, when I caught sight of him.

At that instant, the images of my dream struck my mind like a lightning bolt. I found it difficult to chase away the black bird standing in front of me and seeing in its place the thickset little white man, swathed as always in his dark cape. He was standing in front of us, brandishing, with a look of displeasure on his face, one of our painted pieces of bark, and started to question us in his clumsy vocabulary about the meaning of these designs.

Very quickly, I throw a large piece of eucalyptus bark over the last of the sacred stones lying at my feet. To prevent him getting interested in it, I take the painted bark from his hands and pretend to explain its meaning to him. Saying whatever comes to mind, I point my hand towards the nearby tree, then to the design of his own symbol. He stares at me with an incensed look and vehemently taps the representation of the Ancestor.

'No!' he says with his head and finger.

So he tips his cross from his shoulder to his chest and says to me that this cross does not like people to draw representations of sexual organs! He then raises his eyes and arms to the sky, mutters a few sounds and, without consulting us, sets about cutting the bark into small pieces with his pocket knife. After carefully trampling on them, he assumes his habitual smile again, pleased, it would seem, that we had not prevented him from destroying what he obviously regards a dangerous monstrosity. Only the thought of our sacred objects still lying on the ground stops us from smiling!

The migloo makes a sign that we should follow him to the bush where all our painted bark lies higgledy-piggledy in a heap. Because he is watching us, we walk behind him with swift pace but, when he no longer bothers to check whether we are all following him properly, two of our people peel off noiselessly and, as invisible as spirits, go back to our cult objects to put them in a safe place.

Here he is now in front of the ilykuwara bushes. He stands up, makes a three-quarter turn the better to see us all, thrusts his right arm towards the clump of vegetation, and, with a disdainful and accusing air, he points his finger at our piled-up heap of works. With the aid of a few words, many mimic gestures, he makes us understand that he would like to burn all of them. To confirm him better in his delusion, we force ourselves to implore a little. Then, to get rid of him, Mau lights a fire. The migloo watches as the powdered wood grows incandescent as two sticks are rubbed together and the dry grass and twigs on top catch fire. Then, he himself adds a few dry sticks, and smiles with relief as he is standing in front of the flames that are now leaping higher and higher.

With obvious glee, he begins to burn our representations one by one. Without a thought for the sparks spurting onto the dry grass. Like the other migloos, he knows nothing about the art of managing a fire. We stamp our feet on them to prevent the flames from spreading. Soon, nothing but a little ash remains. Then the little white man stands up, smiles again, and congratulates us for what we did by giving us a few taps on the shoulder.

He looks at everyone for a long time. And now his face expresses disgust. He points to our bodies, still embellished with ritual designs; once again he shakes his head. He goes over to Wongu, puts his right hand on his chest and makes the gesture of rubbing off the sacred symbols. Wongu recoils violently, casting him a scornful look which cuts short any further attempt.

The images of my dream rise again: the little migloo is transformed once more into the black bird, the protector of cows and calves! The bird raises its eyes and arms to the sky; I hear him reciting a kind of short incantation, which we have already heard, then, turning to us, the bird, turned migloo once more extends his right arm in front of him, then points to himself, thrusts his arm to the left, then to the right, where he keeps it for a few moments, gazing at us intently.

'God will help you,' he says in our language.

And he turns abruptly on his heels and leaves us.

We remain where we are, without saying anything, convinced that the cross which was traced above our heads irradiates our bodies with the waves created by the mental powers of the little migloo. But what waves? The moment when he was making that sign, I was observing him carefully; I am sure that he wished us well. But could I still put trust in my intuitions concerning this kind of unknown man? Why does he stay here, close to us? Why does he now interfere in our religious life, just as he had interfered in our daily lives? He helps us without the obligation to do so, which is in itself incredible enough! Even worrying! For this cannot but be to the detriment of the people of his own country! Why has he left his companions? Could it have been that his companions had driven him out? Why does he never asks us to give him anything in exchange for the way he helps some of us? His behaviour is certainly far from normal!

Such were my thoughts as, still rooted to the spot, we saw him making for the entrance to our holy storing place. Straight away, with all my might, I sent out the mental order for him to walk past it without noticing anything. Everyone remained motionless, petrified by a rarely experienced anguish, nerves stretched to the limit.

He continued on his way, stumbled past the bushes camouflaging the entrance, walked right past it and finally disappeared in a hollow in the ground. Immediately, our bodies relaxed; but instead of being relieved, happy that everything had gone off well, we remained weighed down by a heavy anxiety.

Horrible return to the world below! In the evening, instead of continuing to see ourselves as magnificently united, serene, all we did was argue in a futile way about the little subhuman.

Total incomprehension hovered over the camp of the Sparrowhawks as much as the Grey Falcons'. What danger could there be in the representations of sex on pieces of bark? Unless, at that moment, the migloo had been honouring a visual taboo which constituted a sexual taboo! In every way, whites have difficulties with sex! In the east, they have no women, which is absolutely contrary to the nature of men, even though they are subhuman. The little black-clad man lives without a companion but, more than that, he does not seem to be able to tolerate the representation of a penis, any more than that of a vagina, as it would appear from the destruction of all our bark paintings! That seems to suggest that the whites know nothing about ceremonies concerning reproduction, the ceremonies of fertility! That women play no part in their social organisation. We even suspected at a certain time that they did not exist. But if white women do exist, according to the news sent to us by the people of the east, they are extremely scarce, and the subhumans seem to consider them inferior beings. Some among them, we have heard tell, even treat them no better than their animals! Yes! We are convinced of this: we are dealing with human beings who have not found a way of breaking out of the constraints of animal life.

This evening, another topic crops up just as often in our discussion: the habit the little man has of raising his eyes and arms to the sky, without ceasing to pronounce the same formula with a rhythm and sonority resembling the sounds we make in the course of certain incantations; of always carrying that piece of wood around with him, according it the same respect as befits a sacred object, even though you do not drag sacred objects behind you the whole day!

The words of my people are still ringing in my ears. Wongu's voice, Mau's, as curious as I am about the little creature:

'When he lifts his arms and raises his eyes to the world in the sky, he seems to be speaking to someone that dwells in the beyond. Perhaps the whites have invaded the stars where our Heroes live. Would they have the means of communicating with those worlds, as we used to do in the old times, before the great catastrophe?'

'And among all those words he ceaselessly repeats with the rhythm of a magic formula, it is 'God' that comes back most often. I am beginning to think that it is the name of one of his Great Heroes. That could mean that the whites know some kind of religion. Such is my thinking,' Wongu says.

'You have spoken well. This is what I have been thinking. In effect, a rudimentary form of religion is likely. But then I ask myself why do the whites, with a religion so little evolved, possess the ability to transform substances, to make such objects, so much food? I do not know what to think, for nothing that I have learnt can make me face up to such a puzzle. Such are my thoughts.'

'Perhaps he commands the ability to see into the distance for, even though he is ignorant of the duty to share all his tools and supply of food, there is in him the glimmerings of a sense of mutual obligations. Which could prove that he has evolved further than the other whites we know. Perhaps he is one of their Men of High Degree, one that commands powers different from ours. So we should agree to listen to him, to accept what he calls 'God' so that one day he might offer to initiate us into his Instruction, the only way of getting to know his secrets. Such are the thoughts I wish to share with you.'

Sleep took a long time to arrive that evening. Too many unanswered questions were crowding in our heads, giving birth to an intolerable anguish concerning the coming celebrations in other sacred places, at a short distance from the actual camping ground. For close to two moons, it will be necessary for us to hoodwink the stocky little white creature.

Each ceremony lasted no more than two days, and did not involve all of us. Moreover, the elderly and the youngest were excused, or excluded. So they helped us confine the intruder to the camp. They kept him busy by asking questions about God, by pretending to be coughing, to have sore feet or toothache. Because our illnesses moved him greatly. He always tried to make our sick people drink some unknown beverage; or to rub them with a strange ointment with an unpleasant smell. Something I could not look on favourably.

A few days after all our bark paintings went up in flames, a dozen men are sitting around a small fire. We are chewing peacefully on a plug of tobacco, which we pass around. The air is dry, the heat extreme. The hot northerly wind stirs up the red dust, deposits it on the plants, giving them a tinge similar to the dark blue the sky takes on in a storm. Despite the wind, the flies are bothersome, and our hands are constantly flailing to chase them from our eyes, from our mouths. It has been three days now that I have been trying to influence the elements to make rain fall. This afternoon, my people can tell that I have succeeded because there's a storm in the air. We talk about the benefit the showers will bring to the site of the Woman Honey Ant, as much as to our supply of water, which is beginning to get dangerously low, and for the arrival of kangaroos which would then abandon the driest country to come into our region. Kangaroos can sense water from immense distances, and straight away bound off towards it. To drink, certainly, but also to breed, for, when there is water, the females allow the embryos held in suspension during a dry period to evolve.

'Yes, the ground will soon be much better supplied with game.'

We are all a little less troubled by the emotions we experienced at the end of the last ceremony. Despite the heat, despite the flies, we feel at ease.

But here he comes, clambering up the slope with much effort. He stands in front of us, swathed as always in his long black cape, impregnated with his unpleasant smell of sweat mixed with the emanations from an unknown vegetable powder. A powder with mysterious potency. We have often come upon him in the act of burning it in a small receptacle, which he swings from right to left, chanting all the while. Here he is behind us. Clumsily shoving one of us aside, he squeezes into our circle without asking permission, smiling his eternal smile, putting his backside down on the ground with considerable difficulty, fussing with the wings of his cape.

'It's going to rain,' he announces for our benefit, as if it were a revelation.

'We know,' Wongu replies in a hardly affable voice. 'Nari has made rain for us.'

'What kind of a story is that? Nari certainly hasn't the skill to make it rain,' he says, forgetting to smile for an instant. 'God alone knows how to make rain. When it seems good to him.'

Saying this, he raises his arms and eyes, as is his custom, to the sky, crosses himself, then looks at me severely.

'Who is God?' one of us asks.

'Very difficult to explain to you! And it would astonish me greatly if you would be able to understand!'

For some time now, I have been noticing that whenever he is loitering in our camp or is alone in his wiltja, fatigue, no doubt, playing a part, he starts speaking in a loud voice, and in our language besides. Also, I know that he thinks of us as mentally deficient! I was evidently not the only one to have noticed it. This amused us greatly. With common accord, we did nothing to dissuade him, convinced that such an attitude would quench his curiosity concerning anything that was other than our daily life. Moreover, we thought that he would be more inclined to share some of the secrets of his white powder with child-like beings than with True Men, men superior to him.

'God is in the sky. He sees everything, he hears everything. God created man, animals and plants. He is all-powerful!'

'I certainly do not believe that twaddle,' says a young man, who has just joined us, with a smile on his face. 'If God is a man, as you seem to be saying, he could not have given life!'

Straight away, in an aside, I tell him to watch what he is going to say, that in no way should the migloo be contradicted because – and this is a more persuasive argument, I am sure, than any advice – we would like him to continue giving us tobacco. Straight away, the young man drops his head to hide his laughing face, while the others assume an interested air.

'Who is God?' one of us asks again.

'God is our saviour. If you love him, he will rescue you from your miserable life.'

'You can see that I'm right,' Wongu whispers. '"God" is obviously the name of one of their Great Ancestors. They've got something of the beginnings of a religion, a smidgin of spiritual life. Something that would make us suppose that they possess some moral rules. Strange if they had none!'

That day, we caught a glimpse of a belief which has no impact on human behaviour! That day we stumbled, for the first time, on a religion ignorant of the two most important Commandments, the two Commandments on which depends the whole evolution out of human aggression, and from that, the whole of mankind's psychic evolution: to acknowledge the interdiction against leaving the territory granted by the Great Ancestors in order to invade that of others, and the interdiction against becoming attached to material things!

16

In the days that follow, a certain disquiet reigns over our two camps. Only the little subhuman shows any great contentment. He is certainly unaware of our preoccupied mood.

One morning, we see him clambering up the path to our camp. He arrives out of breath, slips into one of our groups and, squatting on his heels as he learned how to do some time ago, and without preliminaries, he talks to us about God, the Great Hero of the whites, about his son Jesus, a newcomer to his stories, and about Mary, his mother, who was impregnated by a spirit, sure enough, but whose foetus, according to what he said, had not been nourished by a man's sperm.

'All women are impregnated by a spirit,' a young man, who is still impulsive, answers him. 'But a spirit cannot recover its human form if it is not fed by a man's sperm!'

'What are you saying! Mary alone was impregnated by the Sacred Spirit. Other women cannot bear a child except after sexual intercourse. Don't blaspheme!'

And he berates us as ignorant fools.

'It's you who is ignorant. You believe, like us, that spirits impregnate women, but you know nothing about the part played by a man's sperm!'

Someone signals to the young man to be silent. The wiser ones try to distract the stranger from noticing the young man's clumsiness, ask questions, their faces assume a look of conviction when the little migloo answers: once again, the distribution of flour, sugar and, above all, tobacco is worth more than this small compromise!

In the evening, shortly before nightfall, the migloo returns and asks some of our young men to go with him to his camp. They agree, out of curiosity. For the same reason, I follow them. When we are all in front of his shelter, he takes us, one by one, by the shoulder and makes us line up in a row. We make a sign that we want to sit down, but he signals us to do nothing of the kind. So we are all standing there, feeling a bit foolish for obeying him, but too curious to find out what will happen next to leave.

He stands facing us, takes two steps to the left so as to be exactly at the middle of the line we have formed. We are not surprised to see him raising his arms and eyes to the sky, making the sign of a cross. Then, just as his strident voice strikes our ears, with his two arms held out in front of him, bent a little in front of his chest, fingers curled, except for the index finger, he traces some arcs in the air, at shoulder height. He sings. We hear an interval of notes and a rhythm which are both hurtful to our ears. A song so high-pitched that we have trouble stopping ourselves pulling a face, from feeling uncomfortable, then breaking into helpless laughter. But this lasts only a short time. The little black-clad man stops, looks at us intently; the palms of his hands, which he has turned towards the sky, are held out to us; he raises them and lets them fall as he shouts, more than sings, the word 'Alleluia' for the third time. We have understood! He wants us to repeat his words after him. For a laugh, we try to do it. A wave of hilarity breaks out over our group when we see him smiling broadly, with all his teeth showing, nodding his head up and down, clapping his hands to tell us how pleased he is. So we repeat a dozen unknown words, with the words 'God' and 'Alleluia' recurring endlessly, while in front of us the little migloo doesn't stop slapping his arms, shaking his head, jigging around. He comes to an end at last, and we with him. He makes the sign of the cross over our group.

From a concealed pocket in his cloak, he takes out three plugs of black tobacco, straight away breaking them into pieces to distribute among us. Two of my elderly fathers, who have joined us purely out of hope of this, take the piece he is holding out to each of us, and without a word, without a glance, turn their back abruptly on him and go away. Their hasty departure cuts short the gesture the migloo had just started to make. He stand with his arm half extended, forgetting to give the reward to the others, as if entranced by the shapes of the two old men as they are calmly walking away. I can make out great disappointment in his eyes. No anger, but a kind of sadness.

I stay where I am, curiously inspecting the faces of each of my people as they are receiving their miniscule portion of tobacco. Sure enough, the young men, whose faces betray greed, assume an ironic smile, somewhat contemptuous, as soon as they receive their 'due'; the True Men accept their portion without betraying any emotion. As I believe it good to do.

The time of our departure draws near. Soon we will be leaving the site of the Woman Honey Ant to take up once more our wanderers' path towards the site of the Woman Blue Tongue Lizard. And already our thoughts are taking wing towards that other sacred site, where other ceremonies will maintain our bodies and spirit in the state of grace we have recently acquired.

I remember. The dry season continues, not too troubling at present, but worrying in the light of our next long journey across extremely arid regions, poorly supplied with permanent watering places and, in consequence, with animals.

For several days, Nganamana, the oldest of my mothers, has been lying under her shelter of branches, unable to stand up, on account of the severe pain in her head and chest. At first, the old women attempted to cure her with poultices of mint-scented karingana. Without any success. Covering her with a paste made from another kind of plant, massages, fumigations, the beverages they forced her to swallow were no more effective. The old women had at first diagnosed an illness brought on by the malevolent powers of an alien medicine man.

In face of such an illness, there was nothing they could do. Only the power of a Man of High Degree could counter the negative forces that had been introduced into their sister's body. So they came to ask for my help, telling everyone they ran across about their diagnosis as they were making their way to my wiltja.

Straight away, the whole camp of the Grey Falcons is in turmoil. Its members make their way to a level piece of ground not far from their shelters. Men and women form into groups. A sharp, despairing note bursts out of one of the shelters, slashing the heavy afternoon air, soaring even higher, then sinking to a softer sound, to end in a dramatic, cavernous bass note; and before this final sound can fade, another group takes up the lament with the first high note. And so it goes on. The air is charged with our sorrow, plants, minerals seem all of a sudden to have turned grey, sad, heavy with our suffering.

The better to show her grief, her fear of malevolent forces, each woman strikes her skull with a stone or a sharp implement; as always the repeated blows slash the scalp, then make it bleed. All this time, the men inveigh against the evil forces, threatening them, some with a spear, others with a shield, a club. The children weep, the smallest howl. As soon as the turmoil reaches its peak, silence falls, all go back to their small fires and to their usual occupations.

I walk away, to be on my own and to reflect on what treatment I am going to choose. Equally, I have to relax in order to regenerate my Vital Energy, which must be at its highest pitch for it to be effective.

Nari must rid himself of all anxiety, above all of the sharp anxiety which has been provoked by their imminent departure: the idea of leaving his elderly mother to die all alone is intolerable. Such would be her fate since, the same morning, his partners have decided that if the healing power of their Man of High Degree fails, they would not take her with them on their travels, as their obligations of mutual aid demanded: they considered her too weak to endure such a trial; she would in any case die within a day or two, and the whole group would risk being delayed for a cause lost in advance.

Nari is even more concerned because the old women's cure should have been effective; but they have been frustrated by the mother herself who, he suspects, does not want to be healed. Now, he has assessed the strength of his Vital Energy, and he knows that its level remains highly satisfactory. Only, the old woman panics at the thought of not being able to go with the others. She cannot bear such anguish and is letting herself die.

His task turns out to be difficult. He must persuade her that the Great Ancestor is waiting for her over there, that he will make her capable of enduring this next stage of the journey, that she must not disappoint him.

The prisoner experiences once again the vigour of the waves he has succeeded in generating within his own body. He sees once more how he makes each of the slow passes with his hands over her body, from head to foot.

'How sure I was of myself that day!'

I place my hands on the back of her head, and on her temples, her face. Then with my lips, I suck from her throat the foreign substances responsible for her growing cold, substances I am going to spit out a little distance away. That action should have a pronounced effect on her state of mind.

Later, I make her drink some potions which are usually effective because they are extremely concentrated, far stronger than those used by the old women.

Then, I talk to her for a good while about her partners, who would be so happy to meet her again at the next assembly, about the respect she commands among the young.

Then I go to sit, all on my own, with the vast plain all around me. I light a small fire, and for a long time, without understanding their meaning, with my head lowered, letting the smoke envelope me, I recite the words charged with the healing power of the Great Ancestor who created them; words that engender beneficial vibrations in the human body, words whose power was reactivated by all of those after him who have employed them. The sound of my voice soars too, to the limit of its capabilities. Its waves should be able to annihilate the negative forces that have invaded Nganamana; my concentration should allow all of my flesh to transfer to her a little of my own Energy. A small amount of it would vanquish her suffering. Alas! After three days of treatment, I can detect no improvement.

I continue, concerned about my patient's condition. The subhuman is following me around, and I can do nothing to stop him. So we both come up to my elderly mother, whose fever has not abated. The little man takes her hand, places his thumb on the large vein in her wrist and waits for a few moments.

'Too much, too much of a fever! Why didn't you come to tell me about it?'

'We have been looking after her. But she does not want to be healed.'

'She doesn't want to be healed or you don't know how to take care of her? I'm going to get her on her feet again!'

'Sure, sure,' someone remarks with a mocking smile.

But the migloo has already turned his back on us and has returned to his shelter. He comes back quickly, holding by the handle a container with a white power suspended in water inside it. He shakes it vigorously before offering it to the patient.

'Go on! Drink this. You'll feel better in a short while. And I will give you something else again tomorrow. In two days, you'll be healed, you'll be a slip of a girl again!'

And she was cured. But very disappointed that the migloo's powder had not given her youth back to her.

How could I not remember that personal defeat! It was from that moment on that my reputation as a great healer began to be tarnished; it was from that moment on that my confidence in the superiority of my healing powers over the whites' skills was shaken. By aspirin tablets! The fact that it was my elderly mother, she whom I loved so much, who was the first to witness it rendered the trial even more painful.

From that day on, the great bird of my dream always superimposed itself on the little man clad in black. Yes! It was at that time that the insistent, disturbing dream revealed itself to have been, without any possibility of doubt, a warning dream. For I knew, as all the Men of High Degree knew, that the least interruption to the pattern of our way of life would bring with it our destruction. The little migloo, whom the children and some of the adults were beginning to address as 'Father', as he wanted them to do, only sought our good, I was sure of it. Perhaps he would make us a gift of some of his knowledge. But, despite everything, he was nevertheless the guardian of cows and calves, symbols, in our eyes, of white civilisation. Without his knowing it, without my people's being aware of it, he was our enemy.

However, from that day on, he was regarded with greater interest, and even with a little sympathy.

Day follows day, rich in food, without too much concern over water. We profit from all of this sweet life, to which our next journey would put an end. The displays, the evenings, discussions around one fire or another, combats between men in love with the same woman, the last bits of gossip running around the two moieties of our people, forbidden love games, games everyone knew about but pretended to ignore, all that renders the sedentary life much less dull. However, the air, becoming more and more dry, the flies which are more and more aggressive, and the flights of thousands of birds returning to the south unleash in our minds the desire to take to the path again. That evening I experience that desire with a painful sharpness.

To stop myself thinking about it, I go to sit at some distance from the group, facing the sun, which is sinking slowly behind the curved back of the mountain chain. The red sand is soft under my thighs and the breeze from the south begins to grow fresher, bringing with it the smell of eucalyptus mingled with that of burning wood. So I turn my recollections towards the Great Feats related to the Life of my Dreaming. Words and images unfurl in my mind, bringing me, as on every occasion, the same aesthetic pleasure, the same plenitude of ideas. I savour fully this contemplation. Then, abruptly, involuntarily, a question rises in my mind. What will the future be? And as soon as I experience the urge to know, I want to enter into the future.

I concentrate to the limit of my abilities, ignoring the rules of safety, risking unleashing serious physiological problems. My shoulders are shaking, I rock backwards and forwards and my heads sinks to my chest. Unendurable suffering spreads all over me, and with it, my body temperature rises and rises to the point of paroxysm. I lose awareness of the world down here. At last I attain the future.

An image comes to me from very far away: the far-reaching luminous rays of the future bring it to me without any great clarity. There I am on the path we will soon be following. The landscape reflects an unaccustomed dryness. Succulent plants are even scarcer than we had foreseen. There are one, two red kangaroos migrating east, something that is certainly not good news. And that cloud of red dust, what could it signify? It is not a willy-willy! It is making its way here, approaching in a straight line from the south. My body is doubled up on the ground, wanting to burst it seems. But I want to find out. I persist. I am there. I see exactly what is rising towards us. Three monstrous animals are making their way, one behind another, dragging huge wagons filled to the brim with goods, with two white men and four white women, all clad in black, sitting on top. Three camels, three huge pits inside which the water of our basin is going to disappear! Abruptly, my body disengages itself and, little by little, I recover my normal state. I stay stretched out on the ground for a good while to regain all the energy I had to expend to achieve that vision. And I go to the camp to announce the news. To my people, to that wretched Father, more of a black bird than ever! Who, sure enough, does not believe a word of it.

Eight days later, a caravan arrives, consisting of several wagons drawn by camels. And, very quickly, it sets up camp not far from our favourite site. A terrible anguish assails me day and night because I know that the 'tear' in the fabric of the world has just increased in size in a most disturbing manner. As for my people, they ignore my warnings; they don't want to do anything against the little migloo, anything against the new arrivals. They always live in hope of acquiring a little of the subhumans' power.

To our great relief, the Father did not allow those monstrous animals to drink from our waterhole. He carried a small quantity of water in round wooden barrels over to them. Then, after the next day, great agitation reigned in the camp. We took turns to be on the lookout, always invisible. No movement escaped our notice. In the evening, around the comforting night fires, people made all kinds of guesses concerning those white women. We were all rather excited by the thought of being finally able to let our gaze rest on one of them. We were very curious to find out why there were four of them, given that there were only three men and, according to what our trading partners from the far east had told us, the subhumans had the right to marry only one companion. And above all, once again, we could hardly believe that all these people had come without cows and calves.

For several days, the three migloos crisscrossed the surrounding countryside in search of young eucalyptus trunks. We saw them cutting down one, then two, then ten. To our great astonishment, and discontent! This region is sparsely timbered. Cutting down a part of what there was had just deprived of their habitat the marsupials, the birds, certain insects whose larvae represented an appreciable source of food for us. This kind of behaviour had severed the whole chain of the sacred Vital Energy, since all the forms of vegetation and animal life are directly linked one to another. As we are linked to them. The calamity that befell these different forms of life would inevitably rebound on us human beings. How was it possible to act in such a stupid way? Had there been a compelling enough reason for such destruction of vegetable life? I remember our relief when we noticed that they had not touched the few ironbark trees, the timber of which we employ for fashioning our weapons. Then they set about constructing a large wiltja with material taken from the huge crates the camels had brought.

That day, we forget the rules of politeness, we dare to show our curiosity. We approach the whites as they are at work. We are surprised, filled with admiration. Envious for a few moments. In order to see their implements better, to observe more easily the manner in which they use them, we dare to draw a little closer still. Working timber with plane and saw seems child's play. What kind of power made them discover such techniques?

The speed with which the migloos transformed tree

trunks into upright posts leaves us dumbfounded. Their tools are something special, sure enough. But also the unbelievable rapidity of their actions! Why are they in such a hurry? They certainly do not give the timber enough time to be impregnated with the beneficial waves their substance discharges, waves that would make their wiltja into a healthy shelter. Whites, we have been told, are always running, always hurrying, they do nothing calmly! The little man swathed in black was no exception. When the trunks were squared off, then cut into posts, they drove them into the ground down to a great depth. And we were astonished by the trouble to which both of them went. Why sink the posts in so deep? To think that they are making things hard for themselves!

Then the two men fastened these young tree trunks together with long poles, perfectly squared off in the same way, placed transversely on each of the four sides of the structure. All around this framework, they nailed large, absolutely even and smooth planks of wood. As we have never seen it done. Yes! We were very surprised, filled with admiration for so perfect a technique.

But quickly enough, sadness and a sense of depression overcame all of us! What huge trees the subhumans must have cut down to obtain such large posts! What fine old trees, which harboured, perhaps, the valour of our Great Ancestors, had been sacrificed for a construction so little needed in a country where rain falls, in reality, only once in every ten or twenty Great Assemblies! What would we find on our way next journey along our southern route, where the new migloos had come?

We return to the camp with our hearts so heavy, the news we bring back so impossible to accept, that this prompts the elderly, who stayed behind in the camp for the sake of discretion, to flout just once the rules of politeness: they go off to verify what we had said. I go back there with them.

As they are looking on, they shake their heads from left to right, clicking their tongues against their palates. We take the news back to the women who, when the strangers arrived, took their smallest children away with them, to protect them from possible danger. Like us, they react with sadness to what we tell them has happened. I can still hear their 'Ah!' of consternation! And their surprised laughter when we tell them that the white women were carrying extremely heavy loads, despite their long, flowing black garments, which impeded their movements, as much of the legs as of the arms, and despite their large, tall white headpieces, resembling the wings of the brolga, which hid their hair and prevented them from looking sideways.

When the work is finished, the two new migloos go away again, taking the three camels with them, but leaving the women behind. Four lubras for a solitary white man!

17

So the four black-clad white women, who also resembled great birds, came and went around the camp of the Sparrowhawks, as well as the Grey Falcons', to which our lubras and their children had not yet returned. They seemed to be indifferent to the sun, the heat, fatigue. They were mild-mannered, busied themselves only with the elderly who, without them, would have suffered from the absence of their spouses and fellow spouses. They went about their business so well that one by one the mothers rejoined the camp.

I recall the happy face of one of these migloos when Yarald came back with her little girl Kerema. The face of the tall, strong woman with blue eyes, whom we would come to call Sister Mary, took on a tender look, as if she had never seen a baby before; then one of sadness when, in front of her eyes, the child buried her head between her mother's breasts and started kneading them, crying all along. It took several days for the child to grow used to her clothes, her pale face, her pointed nose, her eyes the colour of the sky. And her smell.

We had learnt a short time before that this little girl would later on become the wife of Lingal, a Man a little older than me, who, despite his training, was barely heeded in the Assembly of Wise Men, for he had little intelligence, he was incapable of controlling the way he reacted to things, incapable of rapidly coming to a good decision when he needed to do so. When, a few days later, Sister Mary found out about this marriage, her face took on a look of disbelief, she seemed horrified, and let out a flood of words in her own language, which, judging by the intonation of her voice, expressed true indignation without any ambiguity! We could not understand her reaction. The same evening, the story ran around the two camps.

'I'm myself sure that she thought that the marriage would be consummated very soon!' Lamanga said between two bursts of laughter.

'You say well. I am of your mind,' the old Nganamana, who has got over feeling cold all the time, replied.

And laughter rang out around all the fires.

Sister Mary must have shared her sense of horror with the little migloo that very same evening, because the Woman Sun had hardly left the land of the dead when, like a whirlwind, he rushed into the camp looking for the mother and her child. The families awoke slowly, each sitting up around their hearth, gazing at the coals of the night fire, which had set alight the twigs the women were absentmindedly throwing on it as they talked in hushed voices. Our naked bodies rejoiced at the caress of the morning air, charged with the exhilarating smell of the burning wood, which quickly warmed everything. No one wanted to disrupt this privileged moment between the oblivion of sleep and the life of activity to come; even the usual little squabbles had not yet broken out. Also, no one paid any attention to the questions of the subhuman. One after the other, our faces took on a foolish look when he stopped in front of our hearths to ask where Yarald and her child could be found. But sure enough, the first time he asked the question, all unbeknownst to him, an adult signalled to one of the young women to go to warn the woman he was looking for. And the news spread from fire to fire without his suspecting anything. What did he want with that woman? Making a detour so as to walk past him unnoticed, I went to sit not far from her so that I might hear what the migloo would ask of her.

The Father, who had peered at all the lubras he passed, finds at last the woman he has been looking for. I see him hesitating, for he is never able to distinguish our faces very well. The presence of the little girl puts an end to his hesitation. So he abandons his concerned look and assumes his habitual smile again. Here he is standing in front of them, his black cape brushing the naked backs of the two women sitting by the same little fire, which is smoking more than it burns; no one gives him a glance; a man continues chewing on a yam, another rubs his hands with sand, a woman scrapes away the ashes, others cough, their eyes vacant. I can still hear him.

'The night is freezing. Aren't you too cold?'

No reply, no head is raised or turns towards the intruder. Then he leans down and puts out his hand to stroke the cheek of the little girl; she runs off in terror to seek refuge in the flanks of her oldest mother.

'Come on, come on!' he says. 'Don't be afraid!'

He rummages for a moment under his cape and pulls out a titbit much favoured by children, a small amount of salt wrapped in an unknown fibre, which crumbles at the slightest touch. He holds the packet out to the old woman, who takes it while continuing to gaze at the fire; she puts it immediately into Kerema's hands. But the little fair head remains obstinately buried between her two breasts. Then the Father talks about everything and nothing, asks news of the woman he had cured, whose name, it goes without saying, he has forgotten. Curiosity gets the better of the little girl's stubbornness. At last her head emerges from the opulent breasts. She looks for a moment at the packet held out to her. The old woman takes it from her and opens it with care; the child laps a little of the salt inside. When her little pink tongue has licked all of it up, she consents at last to raise her eyes to the migloo, still not wholly reassured. He smiles at her and, rummaging around in his cape once more, he pulls out another little packet, giving it to her. Without hesitation, and with a lively gesture, Kerema grabs it, clenches her fist over it and hides it very quickly behind her back, letting her head drop. As if to say, you won't get any of this! The Father smiles and manages, this time, to stroke her cheek gently.

'Is it true that you've given this little girl in marriage to Lingal?' he says, addressing Yarald.

'I am the one that arranged the marriage,' replies one of the child's uncles. 'It is a good marriage.'

A long silence. The migloo's gaze comes to rest on the man who has just spoken, his face sceptical, apparently waiting for a better explanation; then, with a questioning look, he walks around the members of the family who have assembled there. No one replies, all are stubbornly looking in a different direction. Then, in the language of the whites, a flood of words sweeps over the impassive group. And, even though no one can understand a word, all know that these are not friendly words. No one reacts.

'But,' says the Father, turning to Yarald, 'you are the mother. You cannot agree to the marriage of this little girl to an old man!'

'This doesn't concern you,' Yarald starts to reply, as she turns a grub over in the hot ash. Then, recalling that it is necessary to treat him with caution, she explains:

'Lingal belongs to the moiety of the Sparrowhawks, my daughter to that of the Grey Falcons. For that reason, this marriage is proper! What is more, the three wives of this man are good women; they will be kind to my daughter. So, you see, it is a good marriage! Such is my thinking.'

The migloo scratches his head, seems to reflect for a long time as he stares at the ground, then raises his arms and eyes to the sky, makes the sign of the cross and, clearing his throat several times, tells the company at large that he would very much like to see Lingal, that someone should ask him to come to him at the 'mission'. With a laugh, a young man repeats the word 'mission' several times in a questioning way. The Father has to explain that, from now on, that is what his wiltja must be called.

His explanation over, he turns his back on us and goes down to his own domain.

From one fire to another, discussion is in full flow. What will Lingal do? Here he is coming from the camping ground of the Sparrowhawks, where the news of the Father's new demand has already spread.

'What does he want from me, that smelly migloo? If it's to sing an alleluia again, I'm not going anywhere without tobacco. Yesterday he gave us nothing. No tobacco, no alleluias.'

'He wants to see you about your new wife.'

'My marriage to Kerema! Are you joking or what?'

'He thinks you're going to sleep with your baby wife!' a woman says with a laugh. 'You know very well that he takes us for witless savages!'

Lingal scratches his head, his gaze is vacant. Then he goes over to the circle of men, which has just formed at a little distance from the other fires. I hand him my plug, which he takes with an absent air; his mind is obviously elsewhere. He is a rogue and there is no doubt that he will know how to profit from the situation, whatever it might be. We advise him to ignore the little subhuman's wishes, since we are going to leave the site of the Woman Honey Ant in a few days, and it will not be difficult to stay out of his way until then. He listens to what we say, makes no reply and stands up to go back to his own people.

At the end of the evening, one of my partners from the Sparrowhawks comes to warn me that Lingal is making his way to the 'mission' – seeing that there is a 'mission'. He suggests that both of us should try to overhear what he is about to say. So we go down quickly, to be the first to get there. There we are, then, sitting cross-legged, leaning against a little mound of stones, the colour of our bodies mingling with that of the mineral, at a distance from which it is possible to see and hear without being noticed by the white; as for Lingal, we know that he will not betray us. Once again, we are astonished by the size of the Father's new wiltja. Even though he has four wives, why is it so large? All around, there's a heap of half-opened crates, unused stakes, various containers, peculiar looking sticks, to the ends of which the Father had fastened armfuls of twigs, which he uses to push the rubbish lying on the ground into a large heap that sends out a sickening smell! The favourite place of the hens, which cackle as they scatter around the dirt they feed on.

We see the little migloo coming out backwards, carrying a large plank, which he sets on four posts. The Father goes back inside again when one of the 'sisters' comes out to wipe the surface. He returns with a container, which he puts on the ground. Kneeling, he lifts the lid, seems to be lost in thought as he inspects what is inside, and decides to remove an iron axe, the most desired object for most of us, then several knives of different sizes. From another large box, which Sister Mary has just brought over to him, he takes out four fine rounds of black tobacco, the stuff he distributes among us in so measly a fashion.

'Ah,' whispers one of my Sparrowhawk relations,

without taking his eyes off the scene. 'What is he going to do with all that?!'

The women disappear inside, in a hurry, it seems to us, to get out of the air and the sunlight. The migloo stays there on his own, busying himself without our being able to see any purpose to what he is doing. And here is Lingal now, close to us, muttering a hoarse 'Fuck the camp!' without slackening his pace.

He goes over to the Father who is still absorbed in his work at the left of his wiltja. Catching sight of him, the migloo calls out, taps him on the shoulder as a sign of welcome, and leads him over to the fabulous array. Then we see Lingal coming to an abrupt halt, his eyes nailed to all that treasure. His look, as flabbergasted as it is astonished, provokes a great burst of laughter from the Father. I am furious, for I am thinking that the subhuman is going to believe that we are all like that good-for-nothing, incapable of hiding our feelings! What an idiot! What clumsiness! What other deplorable attitude is he going to reveal in the course of this interview? I'm shuddering in advance!

The Father picks up the objects one by one, turns them around and around in front of Lingal's eyes, makes him smell the tobacco, remarking for his benefit that since it is fresh, having arrived with the sisters, it smells strongly of honey. Lingal has not budged at all. The Father places the axe in his hands. We see him stroking its head with the same gentleness with which he must caress his wives, he tests the edge with his fingers, taps it lightly on his palm to ascertain the size of the blade, raises and lowers the implement to see how it handles. He puts it down at last. Without waiting to be asked, he picks up the knives one by one, runs his index finger along each blade and, regretfully, puts them back in their place. I am wondering where this performance is going to lead us! I guess that the second part of this show is about to commence when the Father asks him news of his three wives.

'They're well,' our Lingal replies foolishly. 'Very well, they are good women.'

'Then why have you taken a fourth? What good would such a small child be to you?'

'When my first three wives grow old, I'll have no one to find food for me. And my first three wives would need a young person to look after them in their old age. They agree with this new marriage.'

'But you'll be dead before your new wife will be able to find food for you! She's still hardly an adolescent!'

'Perhaps, but it's like it is. Kerema is my fourth wife! Her relations have become mine, that means that I have still more partners to help me out.'

'But you yourself have obligations too towards all those people.'

'Bah! I'm old! They won't ask very much of me!'

We see the Father raising his arms to the sky, making the sign of the cross and straightening his back as if to give himself confidence. He speaks some words so quickly that we think at first that we have not heard them properly. Lingal obviously also needs confirmation, for we see him raising his eyebrows in a questioning manner. So the migloo, in a louder voice, separating each of his syllables clearly, says again:

'I am offering to exchange your baby wife with you.'

Astonishment disfigures Lingal's face, probably as it is also disfiguring ours!

'Exchange my fourth wife!'

'Yes. You give me Kerema, and all these implements are yours. Also the tobacco. The tools and the tobacco.'

Lingal says nothing, scratches the end of his nose, then his dishevelled hair.

'You, you have four wives! Why do you want a fifth?'

'The sisters are not my wives! They are the wives of God! And Kerema will not become my wife! I hope that she will become the wife of God as well!'

'The sisters are God's wives?'

All this is far above Lingal's head. And ours too, besides! To be able to think things over better, he sits down not far away. The Father goes over to him, sits beside him and waits. And we others, the two spies, wonder what we should be doing. Go over to them to put an end to the transaction? Run off to warn Yarald? Sadly, we can no longer understand what the two companions are saying. Before we are able to reach a decision, we see Lingal standing up and walking abruptly away from the migloo saying; 'No, no,' over and over again. When he comes over to us, he confirms that he has not sealed the bargain. He wants more tobacco! And he will have more tobacco.

Some days before our departure, nothing is able to stop him from taking his baby wife to the mission, not Yarald's pleas, nor the reproaches of all his people, nor the exhortations of the Wise Men. According to our laws, Kerema belongs to him, and he is free to do whatever he likes with her. As would all those men who are more concerned about their own gain than their old age have the right to do! The rent in the Dreamtime has turned into a chasm!

As soon as the other mothers get to know that Lingal had swapped his fourth wife for implements and tobacco, they will have no other thought but to flee from the migloo. They will snatch up their platters, their digging sticks, place them on their heads, put their babies on their hips, take the bigger ones by the hand and urge to the older ones to follow them quickly. In a short instant, the two camps will be empty of all their lubras and their piccaninnies. They will hide in a cave, a good day's journey from the little black-clad man and his four 'wives'. There he will not be able to see their little girls, and the urge to buy them will not afflict him. In that secure place, each of the women will wait for their group to pass and rejoin it for the new wandering.

So, on the same day, alone or in little groups of two or three, the Sparrowhawks and the Grey Falcons also set out with a nonchalant air from the site of the Woman Honey Ant. Without any bustle to alert the migloo to our definite departure. The poor man will be very surprised when he finds the two camps with their fires extinguished, without a solitary human being. Then he will find himself alone with his four 'bird-wives' and … with the little Kerema inside his vast wiltja.

So here we are on the path again, making our way with more or less haste, as our mood dictates, scattered throughout the day, meeting up again, joyfully, at the evening camp. Some get there with their stomachs well filled with the surplus of their hunting for the benefit of less fortunate relations. The many things we managed to accomplish throughout the day enliven our conversations during the night watch. The best storytellers, who have been idle for some time now, give free rein to their skills in lengthy explanations of their observations and the events of the journey. We experience these first days as a marvellous homecoming, revel in the life of the eternal wanderers that we are, with the path stretching to infinity before of us; the sung, beloved path, this umbilical cord which connects all of us to all the great centres of the sacred ceremonial grounds.

Yes! For several days, once again alone on the immense and endless red plain, the men and women of my group will rediscover the sense of becoming one with the earth, the sky, the plant and animal life all around us; they will experience the sensation of finding themselves again in the sacred cocoon of the eternal Dreamtime. And after the departure of the Woman Sun for the land of the dead, when no tree, no feature of the landscape slashes the horizon, then the pure light of a myriad stars in the endless deep blue of the night sets all our being ablaze with true rejoicing.

But food grows much more scarce very soon, the watering places less dependable. Drought sets in well in advance of the season, takes hold where we are not yet expecting it. Happily, we still have ample reserves of fat in our bodies, acquired during the three moons' camping, when we were settled at the site of the Woman Honey Ant! So we stay in good health and high spirits. But not for long!

I remember. Since morning, Wongu and I have been searching for large game. As my dream had forewarned me, kangaroos, both large and small, have deserted the region; emus and geese seem to have done the same. The heat is so intense that, in an instant, we make for a clump of water shrubs. At their roots, we scrape the earth away with our woomeras, over a considerable surface. And straight away, we lie down on this cleared ground, in the coolness of the slight moisture sent out by the roots. Above us, glinting leaves keep themselves upright to evade Okerka's vertical rays; they nevertheless protect us from the old woman's fiery darts; and the sweet liquid oozing from the elongated, cylindrical milky flowers, in which we are bathing, enhances our temporary sense of well-being.

Thirst becomes difficult to endure. At the moment when I am getting ready to dig beneath the tree in search of one of its water-gorged roots, my gaze lights on a fissure in the ground, rising to the base of the clump of bushes, which was caused when one of the roots broke free of the ground. With a sharpened flint, I detach a part of the root, the length of two hands; I cut it into two lengthwise. After extracting the long segment, I chop it into small pieces, placing them in the hollow of my shooting stick. We wait patiently for the moisture to trickle out. Then, so as not to lose a drop, we lick, each in turn, the slightly sweet, almost cool liquid. After recovering a little of our strength, we pull out other fragments of root, we cut them up, place them in our woomeras and wait once more for the water to trickle out and to sprinkle it on our faces and necks. What a marvellous sense of well-being in that time of scarce water!

We travel throughout the afternoon. Our shadows move in front of us, growing longer and longer, without our coming across any living thing. We reach the camping place at the precise moment when Okerka begins to sink towards the dead.

The women rejoin us a little later. Their containers are overflowing with food. Thanks to them, the evening meal will be abundant. A latecomer arrives, all excited. She has discovered a field of desert pukara.

'Ah! It's full of it, full! And it's there, just over there!'

The children leap with joy.

'Come on, don't get yourself worked up like that, we must wait till the morning!' Gauera tells them.

Anticipation of the feast to come raises our spirits throughout the whole evening. We decide that everyone should set out at dawn. And everyone sleeps soundly.

We are walking quickly, illuminated by the Man Moon, who is slowly travelling towards his daytime death. The cold drives its spikes into our naked skin and we feel the heat regulation of our bodies working at its highest pitch. We clamber over a succession of dunes covered with large, round patches of spinifex grass. Far ahead of us, the day star slowly rises on the horizon. Soon, light from its cape floods the landscape with coppery reflections. Our bodies bathe with delight in its soft restorative warmth. The vegetation trembles under the caress of the first morning breeze. We continue walking, always in high spirits. Suddenly, the smell of the pukara, with its distinctive scent, pulls us up short.

At our feet, stretching as if to infinity, thousands of flowering shrubs, pink or white, a little shorter than a man in height, barely separated by a few patches of deep red soil, sparkle with the myriad pearls of the morning dew.

We rush down the last of the dunes more quickly than before, and, straight away, we do nothing to resist the pleasure of stuffing all this pinkness into our bowls and platters. And into our mouths. We shake the bushes, we sing, we joke, we praise our generous land!

'Ah! Ah! The pinkness falls from the leaves, the pinkness fills our pitis, fills our wiris! Ah! Ah! The nectar is flowing for us!' the women sing.

'Ah! Ah!' the men reply.

Now and then, straight out of the wooden receptacles, everyone takes a mouthful of syrupy liquid! The Woman Sun appears in all her round beauty; she makes the last lingering cold of the night flee. Our stomachs are clamouring for some solid food, but we go on harvesting the wonderful nectar. We go from one bush to another, tap carefully on all the foliage, now calling out joyfully 'Pau! Pau! Pau!' We go on, quickly scaling another dune before the heat makes the gift from the sky disappear.

Our containers are all filled. So we go quickly back to the camp to drink, and to continue drinking together, almost lying on top of the cinders of our fire to give some warmth back to our bodies, which are still feeling the effects of the morning cold. Then, content, we continue on the path once more, trying only to think about the present.

18

The next day arrives, heavy for me with the cares of yesterday and of the days to come. Leaving far behind the delight of the previous day's nectar. But the others seem quite content, eager to meet our trading partners from the south-west. We set out early enough, for it will take half a day's journey along the path to reach them. We all make our way with good cheer, imagining no doubt the bountiful exchanges we will be able to make with the two rounds of tobacco Lingal gave our group.

A good while before we arrive at the meeting place, light grey plumes in the crystalline sky announce that our associates have arrived. They have got there before us.

'How imprudent to send up signals!' my old father mutters. 'To think that the news has not reached them!'

They are waiting for us where our respective paths cross, sitting around some embers, kept alive by a light breeze. Good manners oblige us to chat for a certain time before getting down to business. Normally, we enjoy these conversations, in the course of which snippets of news are exchanged. This time, we would like to cut it short, for we have just noticed, next to their spears and other possessions, some ititikas, large pieces of cloth, deep brown in colour, similar to those owned by the little migloo at the site of the Woman Honey Ant. Certainly, as politeness demands, we do not show our interest, we barely cast a glance at them.

However, we forget about them quickly enough in the light of what our bartering partners are telling us. According to them, large numbers of migloos from the south are making for the interior, planting enormous tree trunks in the ground, which had been made perfectly rectilinear; they place them at the distance of several spear's throw from one another in a dead straight line; they then connect them with curious thick vines made out of an unknown substance. Men and goods have arrived on the backs of monstrous animals, led by subhumans who belong, in all probability, to another species of lesser beings, for their skin is a little less white than the others'. And they conceal their bodies beneath billowing clothes, allowing air to circulate around their skin; they reek less than the migloos. They seem, in addition, more even-tempered than the latter. Nevertheless, the whites evidently hold them in contempt.

'To my mind,' says one of us, 'the worrying thing is those vines in the air.'

We all agree.

What could the migloos want with all those high-slung vines? Our partners' disquiet seizes us too. Little groups are formed, each around a few dried-out roots, which begin to burn quickly. Our partners indulge in guesses, which we all discuss; they share with us their fear of the malevolent power those symbolic phalluses driven deep into the ground, growing more numerous each day, advancing inexorably towards the interior regions, could command! And how many trees has all that cost? How many of them gave shelter to an Ancestor?

The old men shake their heads sadly. I look at the younger ones: once more they seem fascinated by the invaders' schemes.

Later, we recount our experiences of the little black-clad man, of his four wives, who arrived on similar monstrous animals; and the way in which one of them had practically drained our billabong in an instant or two! Our partners know the danger these monsters represent. We all agree that one solitary beast of this kind can swallow in one go a greater quantity of water than a mob of kangaroos! More than many cows and calves!

'But,' they say, 'some of the whites, who arrived on the backs of these animals, had been generous. They wanted to give us a large number of ititikas, wonderfully warm coverings. Warm but heavy, alas! They wanted to give us 'plenty'! What would we do with so many coverings! Before reaching a decision we held a long discussion to work out whether having them would be good for our group; our dingo or kangaroo skins have always protected us well; moreover, they are skins impregnated with the virtues of the Great Dreaming, which we honour each evening by putting them under our heads or over our bodies. So, why should we burden ourselves with new possessions, made from who-knows-what animal or plant, and not knowing with what kind of virtue they may be impregnated. And why did the migloos ask for nothing in exchange? Were these malevolent objects? A True Man from a tribe in the far south, the trading partner of one of our own, assured us that his group has owned several of these for a number of moons and no deadly waves seemed to flow out of them, because, since that time, nothing out of the ordinary has happened to his people. After much hesitation, we ended up accepting two for our group,' Wongu's partner explains, 'and as we were due to meet you in a short while, we agreed to bring a third with us to trade with you.'

Someone holds up the thick cloth, large enough to protect the weakest of us against the cold of the night. Hardly have I looked at the covering than I experience the warning shock of a premonition. I withdraw a few paces to isolate myself in order to capture the message better. I do not manage to receive it very well. I understand only that something evil awaits us. But why would that be because of the whites' ititika? So many other difficulties are going to assail us as soon as we approach the regions which have been taken over by the migloos and their animals. This blanket? Strange objects have been penetrating our trading circuits for some time now, what harm could this piece of cloth bring us? Wongu's voice puts an end to my reflections:

'It's too heavy, in fact!' he says, to lower the value of this new object for barter.

From the tone of his voice, from the look on the others' faces, entirely different from mine, I understand that everyone would like us to take away this blanket. So, unsure of the source of the evil I can sense as a terrible presence around us, I dare not interfere. Like the others, in order to reduce its value, I turn my back on the desired object, to concentrate on two honey-coloured moleskins stacked a little farther away.

After prolonged chitchat, we obtained the two furs and the whites' blanket for two plugs of tobacco. A good bargain!

We continue travelling a little further before setting up the evening camp. My mood is not in harmony with my people's, who are rather pleased with their barter. I continue to sense the evil that has come to stand before us. A muted anguish rises in my heart, grows, slithers into my whole self without my being able to work out what provokes it. So great is my apprehension that I do not want to drag the truth out of the back of my mind. But, all the same, entirely unbidden, a truth floods into my consciousness. I see foreign goods replacing, more and more often, our traditional objects, as much as the natural products of our land; I see them slowing down the circulation of the latter, overburdening the trading networks connecting the paths of all the people of our immense land. I see ourselves deprived of objects and materials which, since the dawn of Time, have made their way to us from the most remote corners of the east, the west, the north and the south. Essential objects and material, far more indispensable for our lives as Guardians of Creation than an ititika of the subhumans, an iron axe or a plug of black tobacco, which none among us had either the pleasure or the skill to make. Yes! That is without doubt what my perception of a future, which I never managed to capture, wanted to say to me. So, I sense with all my flesh the renting of the Dreamtime. Alas! The evil that I would come to feel hovering over our group for days and nights emerged from a far less distant future.

The drought grows more and more fierce. However, this morning we are making our way along the path of the Woman Blue Tongue Lizard under a low swelling sky adorned with the all the shades of greys, even more luminous and joyful when darker and more menacing. The clouds are rushing by, buffeting each other, repelling one another, merging, suddenly drawing apart to don once more the dark blue colour of the night, while the wind howls, battering our naked bodies.

We make our way in single file, not dispersed, as is our custom, to gather food or to hunt, for we must reach the nearest shelter before the tempest breaks. We are walking with long strides, with the red immensity in front of us clashing against the dark masses in the sky. The elderly find it difficult to keep up, they are out of breath, lagging far behind, little black shapes over which, from time to time, one of us keeps watch. We haven't really eaten properly for three days and, despite our determination not to take that into account, our strength is not at its peak. I sometimes put a little distance between them and myself to observe their faces. Their drawn features reflect fatigue, but their eyes shine with the hope of good rain; in the arms of their mothers, sitting astride their hips, the little faces of the youngest frown under the cloudbursts; they laugh, they whine, they cry, they shout with expectation; the youngsters aged from four to six Great Assemblies manage to tag along as well as they can; sometimes one of them grabs hold of a passing thigh to try to get someone to pick them up. The older children, in between two gusts of wind, play, run to test their resistance against the wind, enjoy that kind of battle with the elements; among the adults, the most elderly grumble, their shortness of breath signalling the beginnings of great fatigue. As for me, with greater and greater clarity, I perceive the evil pursuing us, constraining us all, above the storm.

Suddenly, thunder shakes the air and the earth. Thunder, the father of Okerka, the Woman Sun! The most powerful of all the cosmic forces streaks the sky with long waves of fire, followed by a violent rolling, then by a deafening clap overhead. The wind redoubles in violence, raising clouds of sand that sting our skin, get into our eyes, stick to our bodies, which it covers with a fine coating of red dust, the blood of the women Ancestors. To struggle against the whirlwind, we bend our backs as we run towards a small heap of stones, the one likely place of shelter nearby.

We lie on the ground behind the rocks, which block a little of the battering of the searing air. At a little distance from us, a clump of dry grasses and twigs whirls, for an instant above the sand, then, constantly increasing its circular motion, it soars violently, swathed in red earth, blown by a willy-willy. On the horizon, clouds, transformed into a gigantic mountain chain darker than the blackest night, are speeding towards us, menacing, terrifying. In a few seconds, they are floating above our group, and, as if to give us a sign, without stopping in their career, send out a spout of water, stinging our bodies with a rarely experienced force. The children, terrified, are weeping, others, laughing, raise their little faces to the sky; the elderly cough, groan, sigh with relief; several adults show their astonishment, then their satisfaction with repeated 'Ahs'; others, under the protection of the Rain Dreaming, discern a good omen in this violent downpour. Not only for the life it will give back to us for several days on the path, but equally as a happy presage for our coming sojourn on the edge of the vegetable world.

For a few moments, the sky pours down cataracts of water. Then, just as abruptly as it came, the rain stops, the raging clouds vanish and the blue of the sky is resplendent, purer, more crystalline than in the morning; the Woman Sun quickly dries our bodies. Lively once more, we take up the path again.

A light silvery veil of warm vapour slowly rises at our feet. In front of us, the gold of the sun and the ultramarine of the sky play on this moving, evanescent mist, embellishing it with the colours of the rainbow. Our bodies bathe with delight in this bath of steam to warm themselves properly again and, just as quickly, to be exhausted by it. So we walk more slowly. On the ground, little plants are sparkling with the thousand coloured fires of the droplets trembling at the tips of their leaves or stalks.

In the sky, the soft and vapoury arc of the seven colours of the Rainbow Serpent bestrides the infinity of the plain, adorns the crystalline sky with its magnificence.

'Look!' one of the little boys calls out, 'the Ancestor has left the places where he makes water to go to another.'

'Speak with greater respect,' one of the women tells him.

'He will protect us,' whispers another.

Each greets it in his own way, admires its exultant beauty, reassured that it will render the end of this day sweet.

Some time later, we stop near a clump of wattle, not far from a stream, a gift of the downpour. The water has stirred into life the seeds of plants which have been dormant on its banks until now. Their tips have already sprouted; in a few moments they are covered with small buds; others, in front of our eyes, push through the soil, as swift as lightning; the buds burst open to set free their soft-coloured petals drunk on sunlight. Soon, various kinds of creeping plants display their myriad reproductive organs, fully open, rivalling each other in beauty, each hoping that its shape and individual scent, patiently transformed in the course of time to augment their chances of reproducing themselves, will be the first to seduce an insect or a pollinating bird. Greedily, the leaves gorge themselves on water; under the pressure of the liquid, their shapes swell, until the reserve reaches its limit – the limit that will allow the plants to withstand drought, give them time to propagate, to increase their territory. And the flowery carpet, woven in a few hours, makes the deserts vanish quickly under its assault, as if it were intoxicated with its own rebirth. In a few days it will be the only sign left of the fugitive resurrection of the creek.

Birds arrive in their thousands, eager to breed in the short time afforded by the fleeting wet season of the region. Straight away, each species sends out a signal that it has taken possession of its realm. The fresh evening breeze carries their calls, piercing or low, their chirping, their squawking, their warbling. Until sunset, their joyous music will accompany the joy of human beings.

The children splash around laughing, transforming the crystalline water into a coppery liquid, where the light of the setting sun is at play. Voluptuous scent rises from the ground; pleasing to our sense of smell, spreading like a savour in our throats, rousing our desire for men or women. Discreetly, couples withdraw, and very soon their two bodies are fused, their pleasure magnified by the sweet embrace of the clammy warmth of the great body of Mother Earth, in which their movements bury them. Later, the balmy air is charged with the smell of our wood fires, sharpening our sense of communion with all other forms of life. The women tip out from their wiris the bush tomatoes, the yams and the grasses they had gathered during the day. Once more, thanks to them, the evening meal satisfies us. Nevertheless, I still cannot find peace of mind again. Evil, I know, is always lurking nearby. What is more, I am worried about my elderly mother. Despite the mild evening, she seems to be feeling the cold. I see her two fellow wives wrapping her for the night in the migloos' ititika. And I am disturbed by that.

We set out early the following morning. The rain has also brought back the kangaroos and lizards, which are warming themselves in the sun, in greater numbers than usual. The path of the Woman Blue Tongue Lizard turns bountiful again; it teems with game as much as with religious sites. Life returns to what it had always been, easy, rich in time for leisure. For how long?

Forgetting for the moment the tribulations which will be our lot as soon as the path enters the despoiled land again, the elderly recount the exploits of the Hero Creator of every feature of the landscape: the young listen, ask questions. Everyone returns to their proper role in life. If it were not for Yarald who, each evening, weeps for the little daughter who had been sold, the strange migloo and his four wives would have been soon forgotten.

The benefit of the rain was certainly short-lived. The game started migrating. Women scoured the landscape for the last remaining patches of water beneath crusts of heavy earth. Yabbies, hatched a few days after the rain, were scurrying around in it. With the return of the dry, the wind dispersed their eggs, which are able to stay alive for many moons, for years in clay that has grown as hard as rock; they would wait patiently for the return of rain before hatching. That day, Wongu, Mau and I set out in search of a kangaroo, hoping that it will have been unaware enough not to have smelt the return of the great drought.

Since sunrise, we are on the lookout, downwind, close to a patch of grass favoured by these animals. At last, when the Woman Sun is barely a quarter of a way through her course, we see a wallaby coming towards us with relaxed little bounds. With the first thrust of his spear, Wongu strikes it in the heart. The kangaroo leaps twice, then falls; its limbs twitch for an instant before the stillness of death.

We think of the Kangaroo Ancestor, neither entirely human, nor an animal, who has allowed us to feed ourselves thanks to one of his creatures.

Straight away, using my flint knife, I cut open its belly to extract the intestines, a source of rapid putrefaction. With one hand, Wongu grabs hold of one end, and presses on the gut with the other to force out the excrement. Emptied in such a way, dry and supple at the same time, it will make excellent rope for various purposes. To prevent the cavity of the animal's belly from bleeding too much and to protect it from the sun and insects, I sprinkle sand over it. The pleasure of these gestures!

Our return to the camp. Men and women greet us with joyful cries of satisfaction and welcome. Immediately, a wairbi in his hand, Mau goes off to dig a cooking pit in the most propitious place. Two old men light a generous fire to singe off the kangaroo's fur and to make its skin go hard, in order to keep the blood in the meat. For his part, Wongu gathers roots and dry branches, which he places at the bottom of the hole where, very quickly, the fire strikes, takes strength, and is soon able to heat the stones we place over it.

As soon as they are hot, we throw the animal on top, cover the ditch with grass, branches and sand. Then, passing a plug of tobacco around, we wait for the cooking to finish.

When it is done, the pit is opened and the meat taken out. The hunter cuts up the animal, offering each of us the portion to which we are entitled. As tradition demands, Wongu, who was the one to kill the kangaroo, gets the poorest portion.

That was the last evening we spent in the image of our former life, the image of our life in the Dreamtime, which we believed to be eternal. Because the next day, while I was still aware of the omnipresence of evil, there arrived what I took to be the greatest and most fatal setback for our world. Alas! It only announced the prolongation of our extended agony!

19

The night is in mourning for the death of Bahloo, the Man Moon. For all their sparkle, our little fires cannot manage to repel the thick shades of night.

Under a makeshift shelter constructed by her fellow wives, and wrapped in the migloos' blanket, with a kangaroo skin thrown over her, Nganamana is shivering. The heat her body sends out alarms her sisters, whom I can hear discussing how they should care for her. Soon, the patient turns delirious again, vomits more and more frequently; in her brief moments of lucidity, she complains of aches in the head, of pain all over her spine. Throughout the night, two elderly women try in vain to make her more comfortable. In the morning, they come looking for me. Alas! Despite all my efforts of concentration, despite the power of my hands, which is particularly strong that day, despite repeatedly sucking on her body to draw off the evil, despite the chants I have been intoning for a day and a night, the illness resists all my efforts.

After this fresh defeat, with an intensity even greater than the previous days', I can sense the furious evil assailing my people. The evil, as I realise today, carried by the ititika, the invaders' gift. I want to burn this malevolent possession straight away. But, with surprising unanimity, Nganamana's fellow wives resist it vehemently.

'You want to make your old mother die of cold!' Woonawalla cries.

I look at them in disbelief, seeking support from the faces of the two elderly healers. But they lower their eyes. I feel that they are ashamed at not contradicting the young women, ashamed at the lack of respect, at the lack of politeness towards a Man of High Degree. However, they do not contradict their young sisters, and busy themselves around the patient, making up new broths for her; without giving me even a glance, the two young women have just sat down at the entrance of the shelter, near the little fire which was lit to chase evil spirits away.

I am shattered by their reaction. In healing Nganamana, the little migloo at the site of Honey Ant had certainly got the better of me. But I never imagined that my influence and superiority would be called into question again so soon, and that I would so quickly lose the trust of my own people!

In despair at not being able to make this evil blanket disappear, fearing the worst for our group, I go away to meditate on what is happening to us, to me and to my people.

I seek solace from the sacred words engraved in my memory. All in vain. At the very moment when I am making ready for a voyage into the future, Mau crouches down beside me, irradiating me with his anguish.

He rubs his hands on his thighs, spits into the fire, removes the plug of tobacco he carries behind his ear and holds it out to me.

'This evil affects more than Nganamana. The whole group is afraid of the manifestation of other people's malevolent powers, which are obviously very potent. They think that you have lost a great deal of your skill as a healer. They want to try the little migloo's again. It's certainly impossible to go back there! We will not be able to break camp tomorrow.'

'We could wait here for a few more days, since we

are ahead of our schedule; and the women have not exhausted the foodstuff lying around; they caught a python yesterday and managed to discover several nests full of eggs. Nothing is really pressing.'

'Yes. You are right. We could delay our departure by several nights. I think they will agree.'

After a long silence, during which I read his thoughts, I reply to the question he has not uttered!

'Why did I want to burn the ititika? Because I think it is responsible for Nganamana's illness. It sends out deadly waves. I became aware of it when I first caught sight of it during our meeting with our partners. The whites' malevolent powers are immense. Besides, can you believe that they would all of a sudden turn so generous towards us? So then! They are trying to get rid of us just as they are getting rid of the kangaroos, never forget that!'

'Yes, you are right,' he replies in the language of gestures.

We remain silent. The night draws on. The Woman-Sun is now trailing her long golden cloak, to take it back to the land of the dead. The beauty of the end of day entrances us. For a short instant, our bodies and spirits melt into this unreal splendour.

Four days later, peculiar red spots appear on Nganamana's skull, on her face, then on her hands, arms, trunk and finally on her long limbs. Very soon, they swell up. A few days later, they are gorged with liquid and turn hard to the touch. Our eyes avoid the patient, for her appearance is nauseating. None of us has ever seen anything like it.

One morning, loud cries of distress, of sorrow, then prolonged sobbing, slash the tranquil air. They warn us of the death throes of my elderly mother.

Impossible to send out signals to alert her many relations, for we are too close to the ravaged lands.

I see the women crowding into the shelter. One of the old women gently places the unrecognisable head of the dying woman on her knees, pushes the flaccid breasts against her lips to transmit, symbolically, a little of her own vital flux. Others, crouching, sobbing loudly, bend their heads over this repugnant, nauseating body.

At times, a great cry of despair freezes their tears and gasps of sorrow. The nails of the closest relatives began to claw the skin on their cheeks, their faces, their nose, until their blood, an impulse from their souls, starts oozing from the scratches, and prove to the dying woman that their true selves, their intangible selves, are also sharing the great sorrow which has been unleashed over her final moments. Soon the others are imitating them.

Intermittently, the clamour of these displays of sorrow grows less pronounced, they are transformed into hoarse sounds of infinite sadness. A chant soon rises, slow, calm, monotonous. It is the song of the Dreaming of the dying woman, which one of her fellow wives is humming in her ear; this song, for ever associated with her origins, should give her the courage she needs to be reconciled to the idea that the body of flesh she acquired at the time of her rebirth is about to vanish, to inspire her with the strength needed for the return of her yowie to the intangible world of the Invisibles.

The Men mime a combat against the forces of evil assailing their sister. Their movements are jerky, their feet stamp on the ground and their arms are extended, ready to hurl a weapon, as they do in real warfare. Then they draw close to the shelter and remain outside, at a short distance from it. From time to time they embrace each other, hugging longest the body of the elderly husband who is soon to be a widower; so that their sorrow might merge, grow greater, strong enough to convince Nganamana of their suffering, and perhaps to repel the malevolent forces tormenting her.

Here is Tumenti gashing his thigh with a knife. Straight away the others do the same. Then the men, as they are watching the blood flow, set up a long, hoarse plaint. At this signal, Kabbarti, one of the other wives, emerges from the shelter of branches. Her body bent, she stands up quickly, runs over to Tumenti. When she is in front of him, she seizes both his thighs, quickly leans down to place her lips against each of her elderly husband's wounds, sobbing without restraint between two kisses.

Barely has she embarked on this show of communion in sorrow than loud piercing cries of terror and despair emerge with unprecedented violence from the shelter, spreading far beyond the camp, carried by a growing anguish. They announce Nganamana's last breath.

Woonawalla, the second wife, lost in terror and rage, comes out, hurling curses against whoever in the alien people's tribe was responsible for letting loose the forces of evil that have just killed her sister; she begins to tear away some of the branches out of which the shelter had been constructed. In a few moments, the fragile hut of foliage is demolished; the dead woman and the sisters around her find themselves fully exposed to the wind. A much more violent wind that mingles, for a good while, the cries, the tears and the curses of the living, distraught with sorrow and fear.

And I, I am thinking of the ititika, of the whites' blanket. Standing a little to one side, my gaze lost in the unfathomable depth of the sky, I am considering how I would be able to get rid of it. I am sure that it alone must be responsible for that prolonged illness, for that long agony, for that death. I do not follow the train of my thoughts for very long because a faint smoke signal rises in the twilight sky. The Sparrowhawks, the first to arrive at the site, are telling us how the territories of the

Woman Blue Tongue Lizard have been laid waste again! Faces grow even more sombre.

Like they, we resolve to infringe the safety measures we have put in place: I reply to them, and tell them about the death of Nganamana. The smoke bearing the message is light and of short duration.

To remedy that, in part, one of the men takes to the path to warn other groups which, in their turn, will try to warn still others.

Fear of the whites, fear of Nganamana's spirit! Which is the stronger?

We wait for many days without seeing anyone arriving. Neither our messenger nor other groups of our people. We would so much like to send more signals! But we cannot run that risk one more time! No more than we can stay for very long or in great numbers in the one place. After lengthy discussions, we decide that it would be too dangerous to go on waiting, all the more so because we would risk compromising the coming ceremonies by arriving too late. The help of the appropriate Ancestor, the Man Gecko, was more indispensable for us than ever. With death in our souls, drunk on sorrow and fear, we decide to carry out the first funeral ceremonies without waiting any longer for all our people to be present around the 'empty' body.

In the days that follow, our anguish grows without cease. In our more optimistic moments, we think that, despite our diminished numbers, our displays of tormented sorrow were sufficient to help our relative's spirit return to its Dreaming place, where it dwelt before it was reborn. We hope that it knew how to find again, without difficulty, the parallel world which was formerly its own; and that, satisfied, it will have no reason to avenge itself on those close to Nganamana who are still alive. Then uncertainty seizes us. A terrifying fear of

Nganamana's all-powerful spirit conquers us, it increases because we are approaching the edge of the plant world, the realm of the subhumans and their accursed animals!

We take to the path again. We have enough trouble merging ourselves into its memory. Nevertheless, it takes possession of us slowly, dulls the impact of our troubles and anguish and, for long intervals, we forget the changes that overcame our lives, we forget that the Eternal Dreamtime has been altered.

So the landscape sings again the glorious deeds of the Great Ancestors who ranged there in times immemorial. As we are making our way, each of us recalls once again the sacred songs corresponding to each of their exploits. Songs which we interpret according to the degree of Knowledge each of us possesses. Slowly, in the course of time, what we see, what our spirit sings, what our naked skin perceives, all merge together. And we enter into the great timeless river of Knowledge.

Marvellous intercessor in the life here blow, which we are all surprised to be able to continue experiencing, despite our failings in what its sacred Commandments demand.

I can still hear my mother Waela's voice.

'Listen,' she says to the young Imiala. 'We are entering the land of the Unthippa Women, mischievous women from the far west. Wonderful performers who arrived dancing in our land a long time ago and taught Men how to make young boys suffer less during their circumcision. They showed them how to cut the foreskin instead of burning it. Men owe a great deal to them.

'At that time, these women were not entirely male nor entirely female, but a little of both. They met by chance people belonging to the group of the Carpet Snake as they were busily engaged in the circumcision ceremony. They danced and danced in front of them. Much better than

I do nowadays,' Waela said, sending rapid, rhythmical movements all over her body. Movements which Imiala immediately copied, laughing.

'And while they were dancing, they chose adolescents whom the laws of marriage permitted them to marry. They led them into their frenzied dancing, abandoning them here and there along the way. They kept on dancing, with an ever increasing rhythm, more and more violently. To such an extent and with such effect that their sexual organs fell off. Their blood flowed for a long time, a long time. In the course of time, it turned into the red ochre of our beautiful land. Then the Unthippa Women vanished underground to settle forever in the Great Land of Women. And the mountain chain, which we have just entered, these fabulous outcrops, sparkling with flashes of pink quartz, commemorate their passage through our land.

'Remember my story, you are perhaps one of the Unthippa Women! Unless you are another of the Great Ancestors who has returned to earth. You will find out about that later on. Dance back to where your other mothers are, I can see them on our right, digging to trap a monitor lizard.'

We had stopped at one of the sites mentioned in the story of the mischievous women. Suddenly, Woonawalla herself started shivering. The first symptoms of the disease of my elderly mother, which rekindled our fear straight away.

The manifestations of evil arrived in the same order. And when the swellings were filled with pus, we knew that it was announcing that her death was close. To our surprise, the pustules continued to evolve. Soon they formed into small pits and became even more repulsive. The old women diagnosed a worsening of the disease. But, to our surprise, the evil swellings dried up. Very quickly, Woonawalla was covered all over with nauseating black scabs. The women prevented the children from going near her, terrified by this new manifestation of the forces of evil.

However, the sick woman was feeling better and the journey went on without her people having to carry her any longer or help her walk. Then, gradually, the scabs fell off, and her whole body was riddled with innumerable white depressions, scars which the sun did not seem to want to turn dark. Her skin, formerly smooth and soft, looked at the time like a lizard's. Her elderly husband was not troubled by that, only too happy not to have lost a second wife: sorrow had aged him much more. More than ever, he needed the tenderness of his two young wives. And their material help.

One more time, evil struck. It chose one of the young people, renowned for strength and endurance. Then, the following day, another member of the group, and yet another. Their determination to participate in the ceremony honouring the Woman Blue Tongue Lizard was such that they continued travelling well beyond their strength. For a time, able bodied men and women helped them, half carrying them. We left the least afflicted to look after themselves as well as they could, only to see them abruptly falling down at times, lifeless. It was necessary therefore to make a detour to search for their bodies and, the same evening, to improvise funerals, observing the rites even less thoroughly this time. They died within a short time of one another, felled by heat and dehydration. For we could no longer manage to cover the traditional stages in our journey, which would assure us of coming upon a permanent supply of water perhaps, some underground water, or the presence of kurrajongs, water trees. My wife held out for a long time. Her spirit was the last to leave us.

So the survivors dwelt in constant terror of the vengeance of the spirits of our ever-present dead. Because we had neglected the rites, they could not leave us easily; they resented that, and had their revenge.

The halts increased, what we managed to gather and hunt diminished. Nevertheless, we, the ones who were spared, always hoped to reach the ceremonial site in time.

But the great evil attacked again, sparing only Wongu and myself. The last to suffer, even though they still retained some strength, understood that all was lost, that they had to give up, to stop for good at the nearest underground source of water. For most of the day, with the evil more and more present among us, depriving us of our strength and the regular rhythm of our footsteps, the path was no more than a mere thoroughfare, a way leading us from one point to another. Ours senses drew information from it, but it reached us like faint shadows cast on the sand. Truth remained hidden from us: we found ourselves reduced to the state of subhumans, conscious only of the world here below, treacherous and constricting.

We needed two days to accomplish a half-day's journey.

Two days of tribulations the likes of which we had never known.

When the Man Moon revived into the fullness of his strength and beauty, Wongu and I were the two sole survivors.

Smallpox, with which the blankets distributed among my people had been deliberately impregnated, had just started to work as a gravedigger.

20

Go on with the journey! Take up once more what had been in times past the path of song! Just the two of us!

We are walking, silent, afflicted by the horror of our fate, incapable, most often, of communicating with or even thinking about the invisible world. At these moments, our senses, which can perceive nothing except the temporal world, force us to discover an environment we do not know: a red immensity, dry, empty, baked and then baked again by relentless heat. An agonising world. So our courage abandons us, for the path never seems to want to end and our journey never to stop.

At the end of the morning, the hard, trivial imperatives of earthly life overwhelm everything else: we are hungry. To hasten the moment when we will meet our people again, we make do with a little fruit, a few roots and some lizards. Considerably weaker, we are less able to endure the heat which, each day, seems to us more searing. We set out early in the morning, and as soon as the Woman Sun is high in the sky, we stop in the flimsy shade of the first clump of bushes we come upon, to wait for the semblance of coolness which will arrive with Okerka's journey towards the west. Then we continue on the path and walk until the earth wraps itself in the great mysterious serenity of evening.

Days pass. Well before we reach the edge of the plant world, emus and kangaroos become scarce, then vanish, a sign that the invaders have penetrated even further west since our last journey. From then on, we must once again make our way, concealing ourselves as much as possible all the time, in case horsemen should have ventured this far; we must make do without fires, the smoke of which, in daytime, could betray our presence. Nevertheless, despite the absence of that protective and benevolent companion during our halts, despite the detours made necessary by the fact that we must ceaselessly conceal ourselves, despite the disappearance of large game, despite the polluted waterholes, we walk on, impatient to find our people again, impatient to be with our own kind. Food becomes even more of a secondary consideration, so great is our haste to meet them, to tell them about the terrible calamity about which, we suspect, they know nothing; for the messengers who had set out at different times with the news never returned, and the news conveyed by the smoke of our feeble little fires never received a reply.

For the death of our own people affected them as much as it was affecting us; with them, many links in the chain of mutual obligations, of planned marriages, of barter among partners, our whole way of life has been damaged. A true upheaval will emerge from it. Not to speak of the sorrows, the fears, the anguish which this news is to provoke when we confess to them that the funeral rites had not been fully respected.

Lost in these sad thoughts, we walk on. At nightfall we go to sleep. And at first light we set out again. Such a regular repetition of our actions, free of our customary spiritual thoughts, transforms our concept of Time, reducing it to an implacable and enervating presence, into a calamity for material world. We become increasingly aware of how much its passing delays our meeting up with our people. From henceforth, the past and the future no longer exist for us, and our constricted present circumstances never cease to torment us.

At last, rising above the straight line of the horizon, here is the solitary rocky peak we have been anticipating so eagerly, the last resting place of the Woman Ancestor before she reached the sacred High Place where we will soon be honouring her. We quicken our pace. Imperceptibly, the image of that mineral formation increases in size in step with our progress; it shimmers in the overheated air. Through the purple veil in which it is sheathed, its sparkling seems to us like the kindly glance of her who was one of our Great Civilisers. It gives us the energy we need to keep walking for a few days longer, before reaching her, before being able to rest properly in the huge cave situated near the nanja where we are sure to be safe. So, slowly, the path becomes the Path again.

One morning, when there is only a night left before reaching it, the silence reigning over the surroundings alarms us. I read Wongu's thoughts and I know that he is anxious, as I am. Our fingers tighten around our spears, we prick up our ears, sniff the air, look for human footprints in the sand. But it is impossible to discern a sound, a smell, a trace left by any of our people on the sand. Even the birds have vanished from the sky. What is happening?

'I know that the site is still far away, but we should, all the same, have found traces a long time ago to tell us that several groups have passed through here! Generally, all our people rest in the nearby nanja. It's from there that they rejoin our path. They can't surely all be dead, they too!' Wongu thinks without saying it.

We continue on our way, all our senses alert. Right over there, to the west of the rocky outcrop, hundreds of black cockatoos with red tail feathers are flying around, sending out their noisy danger signals. Their alarm has not yet been quelled when the neighing of a horse from the same direction pulls us up abruptly. A horse: migloos!

We immediately throw ourselves flat to the ground and, despite the stony surface, slither behind a heap of rocks. Motionless, we wait for a long while, our throwing sticks and spears parallel to our bodies. Okerka climbs higher in the sky, flooding the landscape with the orange-coloured fire of her cape; her light interferes with our vision, bleaching the spot we are watching.

We are still waiting. Without exchanging a word. Alone. With fear embedded deep within us.

When the Woman Sun embarks on the fourth part of her journey, five or six horsemen spill out from behind the rocky outcrop, manes and clothing flapping in the wind. They fly like spears in front of the glowing orb, terrifying black silhouettes from a hated world. Where they are probably returning for the night. Before they disappear in the east, we seem to hear women crying.

Without a word, we sit down to reflect on what we should be doing. At the moment when the Man Moon rises above the huge solitary peak, we take large leaps towards the tiny entrance to the cave, sliding down, dropping the height of a man into the interior. Some twenty Sparrowhawks, heads raised, look on as we crash to the ground. Our eyes take in their mournful faces. Standing upright, in small groups, the men are silent while the women, crouching in the darkest recesses, weep soundlessly.

Mashubi, the Sparrowhawks' Man of High Degree, looks at me for a long time, then launches into his account of what came to pass:

'We could not follow the usual path because, since the last journey, the whites have taken over a large part of the territory it crosses. We were forced to go on a long detour to the north-east, making us very late.'

'That's why we've seen no trace of your journey.'

'Of our journey. But you should have seen those of other groups. Now, we are the only ones at this resting place, one, moreover, that is very busy as a rule. What could have happened to them?'

'But you yourselves, why are you hiding in this cave? Who were those horsemen? Did you see them? Where is Natati?'

'She has been taken from us. A short time before we arrived here, despite the spies scattered in a semicircle, who went ahead of the main part of our group, some whites came by surprise on the women who were lagging behind, picking berries. Natati was one of them.'

Hearing the name of his wife, my one true love's old husband groans, rolling his sad eyes at me.

'So? What happened? Tell us quickly.'

'Turning around to make sure that everything was going well, I saw a cloud of dust announcing the arrival of the subhumans on horseback. Since we found ourselves close to the secret entrance at the south of the cave, someone had the presence of mind to push away the rock concealing the entrance and to get the women and children to slip inside. Flat to the ground, the men waited, ready to intervene if they could. They soon realised that they were powerless to do whatever might be necessary, for the women were too far away for help if something happened to them. They resigned themselves to going inside the cave. I was the only one to stay outside, perfectly still behind a thorny hillock, telling them that I would imitate the cry of the curlew three times to signal that the danger was over. I thought that if the migloos noticed me – I doubted that they would from such a distance – they would mistake me for a half-dead bush.'

Mashubi folds his legs to squat on his haunches, looks vacantly in front of him without saying a word. I wait politely, and Wongu does the same. Then unable to wait any longer, in a voice that I would like to sound less agitated, I beg him to go on with his story.

'Well, as soon as they caught sight of them, the horsemen made for them. They had a chance to escape, for they got as far as the northern entrance, easy to get through, that one, if you know your way across the tangle of scrub leading to it. They would have had time to slip inside before getting caught and I guess they'd thought they had taken that direction. But when their pursuers were still a few spear's throws from them, with one hand, one of them raised an armful of rope above his head, he twirled it several times before casting it in front of himself. The end of the rope curled around Natati's chest as the horseman pulled up his mount. Brought to an abrupt halt in that way, our sister fell. Another horseman did the same with Gunur. And I, I was there, aware that the best spear thrower, armed with the best spear, would have been unable to reach the attackers. Powerless therefore, beside myself, sick with anguish and shame, I could do nothing but to go on being a foolish onlooker.

'I looked over towards Kabbarti and Unkara. The other horsemen had managed to capture them. I saw the two of them leap at the same time on both of them, rolling around in the sand. A struggle followed. The women must have dug their nails into their faces for the wind carried the whites' shouts of pain and anger to us; then I saw the men straightening up, getting to their feet, each grasping his victim with one hand and striking her brutally with the other; they managed to lift them up and throw them across their horses, then quickly leap astride, behind the women. I did not see any of the women moving, and I thought they were dead. Hardly had they got into the saddle when the migloos dug their heels into their mounts' flanks to set off at a gallop, with shouts of victory, making for the creek.

'They then made a half-turn and set off towards the nanja, the resting place of our Ancestor, the Woman Lizard. The two other kidnappers were waiting for them there, Natati and Gunur also lying motionless across the beasts.

'One after the other, the four horsemen galloped around the outcrop several times, then they took off towards the east, where they vanished.'

'But,' says Wongu, 'we heard women's cries. They must have recovered from the blows and started fighting for their lives again. Perhaps they managed to escape.'

Only sobs, growing ever more searing, answer him. Sobs that increase when Wongu and I recount the disaster that befell our own group. For a long while, we remain motionless, speechless, overcome by a hitherto unknown despair.

The subhumans would surely not come back at night. We are all relieved at that for, despite the terror that is still making the women tremble, we cannot resolve to stay in the cave; we have to sleep surrounded the beneficial waves of our friends, the stars in the sky, and those that the mineral world transmits to our bodies with its soft warmth. We leave the cave in small groups, and each settles around a tiny protective fire. Despite our despair, we are able to sleep better than we feared.

At daybreak, we obliterate every trace of our fires. And we go back under the protection of the earth to wait, in case the stolen women might turn up.

A slight noise of scratching above our heads, followed by the song of the night parrot, brings our rest to an end: there is someone is standing on top of our southern hearth. Someone in the cave takes up the same note to signal our presence. Our eyes travel to the faint light seeping through the opening overhead. Two legs appear, then Unkara's body. She lands more easily than we would have thought. She stays there, crouching, her head on her knees, which she clasps with her arms, revealing her sorrow, her terror, her despair in a long, lugubrious lament. Women crowd around her to mingle their lamentations with hers. Then, little by little, the sobbing grows less frequent, the sighs, the outcries cease. We are waiting for Unkara to speak.

She rubs her eyes with one hand, her mouth with the other, takes a deep breath, clears her throat, and with a supreme effort of will, fights back the sob welling up in her.

'I lost consciousness because of the blow on the head. When I came to, I was lying across the horse, in front of the rider. The animal was carrying us at a terrifying speed. A sensation that made me shut my eyes in anguish. It stopped abruptly, and I was pitched mercilessly to the stones on the ground. Ever since, my side has hurt terribly. My sisters were also thrown brutally to the ground, where they stayed, half spread out over tufts of spinifex, completely in a daze. But very quickly, the subhumans, indifferent to the blood flowing from many parts of our bodies, pulled us up and dragged us violently into the shade of a bush. We had no more strength to resist them, as much through fear as exhaustion. Okerka had run three quarters of her journey and the approach of night increased our terror. I was on the ground again, next to a thicket. Before I could get up, the migloo threw his whole body on top of me.

'How much he smelled of death! You cannot imagine! I felt that he had thrown a corpse on top of me. A corpse squashing all of my flesh. Ever since, that smell has been pursuing me, making me ill! Every bit of my skin stinks of death!'

Unkara stops, leans her head on her knees once more, sets about lamenting again.

I see the women next to her taking little sniffs at her.

'You don't smell of death,' one of the old women says to her. 'Go on with your story.'

Unkara also sniffs herself, waits, then continues at last.

'Well, the smell of death made me unable to react for an instant. He took advantage of it to put me on the ground flat on my back. When I saw him take his penis out of his stinking clothes, I turned aggressive again. I bit him, my nails made deep scratches on his face, I tried to kick his genitals with my knees. That made him swear, whistle, and sometimes laugh in a sardonic, terrifying way. I had a lot of trouble fighting him off; he managed to get on top of me again. The metal on his belt injured my stomach, the rough cloth of his shirt rubbed against my breasts. He pulled my thighs apart with such force that I felt that they would be torn away from my trunk.

'And he managed to penetrate me.

'He had barely finished enjoying himself when another of them threw himself on top of me to exploit my body too. Cries of anger, of sexual pleasure, malevolent laughs drowned out my howls of rage, of suffering, mingled with those of my raped sisters, who were themselves not far away.

'When they were replete with pleasure, night enveloped us. We were all lying on the ground, motionless. My physical body dead, my astral body vanished. Then a feeling of disgust, a disgust so great that it was palpable, overwhelmed me, bringing me back to reality. Disgust at myself, Unkara, raped by a subhuman reeking of death! Disgust at the thought of a 'long' penis, an uncircumcised penis, a filthy penis being thrust into me!'

Finishing these terrible words, Unkara could not hold back a long cry of desolation. She went on straight away.

'Night had come. One of the migloos lit a fire. The flickering of the flames brought me a little comfort.

'A little later, our violators suddenly turned their heads towards a thicket from which a muted sound had emerged. Natati, whom I had seen throwing a large pebble in that direction, immediately sped off in the opposite direction and disappeared. I had time to do the same, because Gunur, probably to help her, had just thrown another stone at the same spot and the migloos turned their heads once more without having enough time to cast a glance at their captives. It was lucky that my eyes were turned to Gunur at that moment, for, as soon as she started throwing the stone, understanding at the same instant what she was doing, I pulled myself together without any abrupt movement and, taking off with less noise than a snake makes, I managed to vanish into the black of the night a few paces away. I almost tripped over Natati who, like me, had leapt into the middle of a clump of bushes thick with apara, not far from the fire. As still as hunters, holding back our breath, we waited. We heard the subhumans swearing, shouting, questioning each other. The noise they were making told us that they were going to look for us in the other direction; they then returned to their campfire, which was now sputtering dangerously. Then I saw Natati standing half erect, ready to hurl the stone she had the presence of mind to pick up before she leapt. The stone hadn't yet stopped bouncing as we rushed away in the opposite direction. Without consulting one another, we separated, neither knowing which direction to take. Finally, after running around for a long time, it occurred to me to look up at the stars. I asked the Maludaianini men, who were strolling around up there, to come to my aid. Which they did, seeing that I am here.

'After I had been wandering around aimlessly for a long time, my strength left me, I had to stop. Fear had made me ignore the malevolent forces of the night. Still shaking, I lay down in the middle of large patch of tall spinifex, difficult for a horse to cross. The smell of death sticking to my body tormented me, made me live through the rape again. I bit my lips to stop myself sobbing, for I did not know how far I had got from the migloos. At last, fatigue got the better of me, and I fell asleep. I woke to the morning bird's cry. I did not dare move; I was waiting for goodness knows what. Just as well, for a few moments after the last veils of the night were lifted, I heard, from the south, the lowing of several cows and noticed a horseman, far away, near the horizon, driving them in front of him, toward the east. I thought this probably had to do with the stray beasts the migloos had been looking for since the day before. Which would explain their presence so far to the west. Then I followed the path to the cave. I don't know what became of my sisters. So there. That is all I can tell you.'

Muted 'Ahs' of distress break out here and there.

'Perhaps our sisters also managed to save themselves,' someone says at last.

'Let's hope so. But what should we do now?'

'We must discuss it,' Mashubi answers. 'Let us hold a meeting.'

The Wise Men of the Sparrowhawks assemble in the shaft of sunlight penetrating the cave through the airhole above our heads. With the preciously guarded night cinder, one of the Wise Men lights a piece of wood that had been blown there by a violent storm. Someone, using a shield, prevents the smoke from getting sucked through the airhole. Very quickly, joyous little tongues of flame are leaping around. The men sit cross-legged around it, and, together with Wongu, I find a place in their circle. We huddle against each other a little more closely than usual, so important is it for our waves to intermingle, so that we may better understand each other.

Slowly, relaxing our bodies, and emptying our minds for an instant, we obtain a climate favourable for reflecting on things.

Mashubi starts speaking:

'Here is the fruit of my reflections. What would be necessary to find out before anything else is why the migloos have strayed so far from their station. For, according to our partners from the east we met recently, their last wiltja must be quite a distance from here. A distance that represents all the evening camps, one after the other, corresponding to one whole life of the Man Moon. The incursion of the rapists as far as this may only be an accident. Perhaps they were, in fact, only searching for their animals. In that case, they will not come back very soon. This is the fruit of my reflecting on the first problem we should consider.'

'You are probably right. But can we take that risk? Go on with our journey as if nothing had happened? That is the question I ask myself.'

A long silence follows my intervention. Each of the Wise Men hesitates accepting the responsibility, without having considered all the eventualities, which a yes or a no could entail. All are probably experiencing the same anguish as I am at the thought that the subhumans could have robbed us of the sacred site of the Woman Blue Tongue Lizard.

The air in the cave is heavy with the smoke of the fire. It makes the silence all the more perceptible. A silence punctuated now and then by a cough, a sigh, the whispering of the women. Even the children stay silent.

Each in his turn, the Wise Men begin to speak. Then, with the agreement of our sisters, we take the risk of going on with our journey. Sure enough, we decree the total banning of all fires, we decide to break up into groups, reduced to two or three people. Then, with an anxiety that grows more and more acute with the passage of time, we wait so that our violated women would have time to return.

Okerka has already run a third of her course and Natati, Kabbarti and Gunur have still not come back. Another decision must be taken.

We delegate three young men of the Sparrowhawks, newly enrolled among the Wise Men, to follow in the tracks of the kidnappers. Tracks which should lead them to their 'station'. Certainly, they will have to be equally on the look-out for the footprints of our sisters, in case one of them had managed to escape.

The three trackers set out straight away, one following the trail of the horses, the others on either side of him, a good spear's throw away.

For a long moment, we watch them as they vanish, incapable of moving on to the next action, that is to say to decide who should leave with whom. At last, after much hesitation, and much heartbreak, groups of two or three people are formed. With death in their souls, they leave the safety of the cave to merge into the landscape, each taking a different direction to reach the sacred site by way of various detours.

I find myself alone with Wongu again. Once more, the path is transformed into a common thoroughfare. And we, Guardians of Creation, entering newly or recently ravaged lands, are turning into common fugitives.

21

The site of the Woman Blue Tongue Lizard.

No smell of burning wood, not a child cries, no laughter, or men and women shouting signals the presence of our people at the sacred place. None of the usual high spirits after we have reached the final stage of our wandering! Rather, I detect their presence, for their waves of despair rush into my head, seep into all the fibres of my body.

After slipping through a narrow cleft in the rock, we find ourselves in the middle of a rocky hillock, a small perfectly round space created by the Ancestor, the pink earthen steps of which rise well above our heads. At its base, the men embrace each other in twos and threes; the women, crouching, do the same. All are wearing mourning garb, often made from white clay, distempered over their bodies. This light colouring, dull, lacklustre, which gives them the appearance of the dead from whom the first layer of skin has been removed, emphasises the dramatic appearance of the scene. Their stifled laments rise to strike the walls, which send them back to the centre of the space.

I recognise many of my relatives from the Grey Falcons and new members of the various groups of the Sparrowhawks. But it is in vain that I look for Natati.

As we arrive, men and women come towards us. They have been waiting for us for such a long time! They call out all together; words, sobs, cries of despair mingle for an eternity. All the same, we manage to understand them. And we are shattered. Entire groups have all but disappeared. Groups of the Sparrowhawks, but equally several of the Grey Falcons', as they had learnt. And their people have seen their number reduced by a half! Since then the spirits of the dead are like a cowl over their heads, stopping them from sleeping, thinking.

I ask if they had any news of the abducted women. During a long silence, filled with consternation, their faces take on a questioning look. Our last small hope vanishes: they know nothing.

Wongu begins the tale of the misfortunes of our group and of Mashubi's. Then tears, laments, cries of rage mingle, clash once more against the unchanging serenity of the surroundings of our sacred place.

When everyone has calmed down again, I recount the long illness of my paternal relatives, their death, I own up to the shortcomings of our funeral rites.

A long silence reigns once more, broken by muffled plaints.

We all share the same hopelessness, the same oppressive anguish.

Wongu is the first to find the courage to break it.

'Is it likewise the great disease that caused your people to die?'

'I do not know what you mean by the great disease. Some had their bodies covered with black pustules, others died of a strange catarrh after days of high fever, in the face of which the healers and even the Men of High Degree remained powerless. At first we held the malevolent forces of some of our neighbouring people responsible. Then, certain of our partners from the far east assured us that these diseases came from the invaders. Do they really have the power to kill at such a distance? For the greater part of our dead had never seen a subhuman!

Most of our paths are moons away from the devastated regions! We were hard put to credit such notions, all the more because no sign of the use of the Death Bone had been found. Their power to harm surpasses ours!'

A glimpse of the ititikas lying on the ground tells me, however, that that is far from the truth. But I am too exhausted to face up to a discussion. I am content to let out a sigh. And, I must confess, the theft of our women agitates my mind too much for me to be able to consider another problem, even if it were of far greater importance. However, what does the disappearance of three of our relatives represent when all our people are dying? But it is like that.

'You haven't really had any news of our three sisters? No news of the men who set out in search of them?'

'Nari! Why ask these questions again?'

I do not answer. We lose ourselves in our thoughts.

All around us, the rocky surroundings adorn themselves with the soft ochre of evening, we recall that night is approaching. Where are we going to set up the night camp?

One of the Sparrowhawks informs us that teams of six men are taking turns to watch all around the site. We can sleep outside the nanja, without lighting protective fires, since the first of the migloos' wiltjas is several night-camps from here.

Dragging our feet, as if in regret, we leave the semicircular space in little groups of two or three. We go back to the place where we have always set up camp, the Sparrowhawks to the east of the site, the Grey Falcons to the west. This evening, once more, only the women ensure with the produce of their gathering that there is to be a meal. Food passes from the better provisioned families to those that have the least.

I go to sit at some distance from my people. Overhead,

the stars, indifferent to my distress, unchanging, Canopus, as migloos call it, the most brilliant, and behind it the star they call Sirius and so many others, spill their energy over the tangible world of the night. I allow my gaze to lose itself in the sparkle of these other worlds. Slowly, I recover my calm. So I experience the desire to enter into the future, to find out what is waiting for us.

I put myself into a receptive state. I am burning up a dangerous amount of my energy. My head drops to my chest. Time passes without my being aware of it. I leave my human condition behind.

Here I am outside of time, making my way along the stream of the Sacred Energy, where our future is inscribed. I impregnate myself with this knowledge, and, more quickly than I would have wished, come down to earth again.

Now, I know that our suffering will increase, and what is more, over many long generations. Our tribulation will be terrible. But despite all the scars that the subhumans will inflict on it, despite all the indications of an approaching agony, our World of the Eternal Dreamtime, momentarily vanished, will slowly revive itself to recover in all its beauty. For it is Time within Time. It is Eternity.

Early the next morning, we decide to hold an exceptional meeting of the Council to consider the best decision to take concerning the celebration of the Woman Lizard Ancestor, the purpose of this journey.

I set off immediately with Mashubi to establish a circular 'force field', around which the members of the Council would be seated.

By dusk, no group that might have been delayed has reached us. And we hope for no more. So we are far less numerous as we sit, legs folded, knees spread, around the circle which reacts to our presence with its invisible forces.

Before the meeting, Nari must steel himself to banish the image of Natati from his mind. Then he listens as each participant gives his advice. All agree that they recognise that they are far too crushed by personal grief, by the problems brought on by the disappearance of so many of their partners for them to be able to make decisions necessary for re-establishing the chain of their alliances. Those alliances, the nerves of their economy and affective attachments. What is more, they confess that they are completely crippled because, losing their trading brothers, their blood relations, their Dreaming relatives, the survivors have lost the identity of their group. They now find themselves face-to-face with their individual selves, up to that time complementary to the first, and less important.

How to go on living without the great chain of mutual obligations, economic as much as affective, the source of emulation at each moment? Which among them could endure the thought of being reduced to their insignificant personal selves? When the others are this living, severe reflection, which alone permits each of them to improve himself in order to approach as close as possible to his exemplary model of Alcheringa Time?

Certainly, not all their partners have died; but the umbilical cord connecting one to another, transforming them in the course of ceremonies into the one great entity, this cord has just been torn apart, casting them into terror and despair. For they have the presentiment that once deprived of this insertion into the collective, the centre of their joint consciousness, which alone allows them to find their place in the cosmic pattern, they would not know how to recover the divine spark partially hidden within them. And without this spark, revived during each wandering, they would fall into ignorance once again; they would become mere human animals, subhumans.

All these cares, Nari thinks, immerse us completely in temporal life; I suddenly see them as potential murderers of our spiritual life, the only life worth enduring.

The night's veil thickens as we reach an agreement to acknowledge that only the glorification of the Woman Blue Tongue Lizard will permit us to achieve the calm and the wisdom indispensable for dealing with such serious problems. So, despite our reduced number, and the absence of certain of our members who usually play important roles in the course of this ceremony, we determine to hold the religious service the following day.

To obtain benefit from the rite, as always, but more than ever, harmony must reign among all of us. So, before the ceremony, it is with great candour that we empty our hearts, speaking in turn to explain the reasons behind our anger, our bitterness, our jealousies, our desire for revenge against one or another. Words mingle, a few blows are exchanged, more symbolic than real. At the end comes the dance, the rhythm of which, punctuated by songs of propitiation, manages at length to render us serene, each of us towards everyone else.

At last we are ready, the officiating men, standing at the centre of the space, each 'clothed' in the appropriate symbols traced on his body with a layer of the plant world, nose ornaments and armlets; not far from them, groups of dancers, similarly adorned. The women squat on their heels, in a semicircle around them. Eyes downcast, they are waiting for the huge churinga to be raised, that representation of the Dreaming shared by our two families, symbol of the Eternal Dreamtime, unchangeable reality, at the base of Time, which expresses itself through it. A receptacle of such powerful forces that only the initiates can look at it and touch it without peril.

The master of ceremonies makes his appearance, holding aloft the adored object, the sacred passage, oh how narrow, between the tangible world and the invisible. Catching sight of it, all our minds, all our hearts concentrate with fervour on the acts of the Ancestor, growing taut with piety towards her through whom the bountifulness of this region is maintained. More dancing, new rhythms, new songs slowly put us into a trance, into a state to receive what is otherwise invisible.

Imperceptibly, I leave behind the world down here, I raise myself towards the gentle light of the upper spheres. At length I enter into the parallel world of Alcheringa. A fleeting moment of communion with the great stream of the Sacred Energy. Alas! Too fleeting to find there the revelation capable of saving our people from a death which had already been announced long ago.

For many a long day, we worship the Great Ancestor, we dance for days, we sing her praises, we execute designs to glorify her.

Then, while the air is still thrumming with the rhythm of the dance praising her perfection, I am obliged to sit down. I am trembling, my body is thrown backwards, my eyes turn in on themselves: I have just captured the waves sent out by one of our people, who is hurrying towards the site.

The following morning, Inoa appears among us.

Before he has spoken a word, I know that he has found Natati. Our eyes cross and his message reaches me: yes, he has found her, but we are all in great danger.

'Leave quickly,' he says to the women, who straight away grab a baby with one arm, haul them on their hips and go away very quickly, followed by the older children, whose large black eyes send out terrified glances.

We hurry to the ritual objects.

But they cannot be handled except with respect, slowly. And we would need many moments to put them back in their secret hiding place. Wongu, the master of ceremonies for the day, has just finished wrapping up the great churinga when the call of the morning bird rings out: a warning signal, seeing that the day is coming to an end. With too rapid an action, a truly sacrilegeous act, Wongu clasps the cult object, taller than he is, against his body to take it to the secret hiding place. A horse neighs. The sound of a subhuman's footsteps is approaching.

With horror, I see a very young migloo coming into the rocky enclosure, looking at us in surprise, and, fearlessly, stepping towards us. He sends out no negative waves. His eyes cross mine and I can find only honesty there. My two companions have turned to stone, Wongu, who is about to step towards our reliquary, the great churinga clasped against his chest, and Mashubi still bending down to pick up a smaller one. Those that I am responsible for lie at my feet, and I force myself not to glance at them, to prevent the migloo noticing them.

Yes, I can see that moment again: talking all the time, the migloo approaches Wongu, and with the inevitably patronising gesture the whites use, taps him on the shoulder. With his impure hands, he seizes our cult object, tries to get it away from my friend's chest. We all shiver as we see a subhuman letting his impure gaze come to rest on one of the most precious but also dangerous of our creations. Wongu recoils, clasping the venerated wooden object even more closely to his chest. I catch his intention of throwing the sacrilegious white man to the ground. In a flash, my eyes weigh up the scene: the killing-stick slung over the migloo's shoulder; my unarmed companions; and I understand that he must be allowed to take it. At the moment when he is concentrating all his strength in his right fist to strike the migloo on the head, I stop him with a glance. Wongu, astonished and puzzled throughout, trusts me; he holds the large wooden image away from his body. The migloo inspects the work. It seems to interest him. He takes it in both hands, holding it away from his body to look at it at arm's length. His face reflects his appreciation. And his astonishment. Astonishment that makes him inspect us from head to toe, one after the other, as if to say: 'Is this really your work?' For an instant, we feel proud.

He gives the churinga back to Wongu and signals that we should stay where we are. And we stay there! Indecisive, incapable of acting. Kill him?, one of us is thinking. Our weapons are not far away, another replies. Break his neck?

But he has already come back, a smile on his lips, an axe held at arm's length. Even before he has embarked on his mimicry, we have realised that he wants to exchange it for the object imprinted with our immutable Reality, with our means of communication between the past, the present and the future, the all-powerful object, the force which allow us to live in this place of wandering; we have understood his desire to exchange our guarantee of life for a common iron axe. Wongu clasps our most precious possession a little closer to himself and begins to walk away with it.

At that moment, laughter, shouts ring out at the other side of the space, flooding into the narrow passage leading to it, to fade as the noise strikes its walls. Voices call out a name, surely the name of the man talking to us, as the tone of his reply indicates; he turns to look at the newcomers. And we see them too. Three tall, red headed migloos. I capture their harmful waves. So disturbed are we that our telepathic waves get confused. Motionless, we wait, casting despairing looks, in spite of ourselves, at the object which is as essential to our temporal life as to the spiritual.

The whites are talking among themselves. It is not difficult for me to understand that the first intruder is explaining the barter he wants to make with us. The other three let out a loud peal of laughter, apparently to mock him. Two of them approach Wongu. One punches him while the other grabs the churinga to give it to the first intruder. With an instinctive movement, we hurl ourselves at him, trying to recover our property. But already, the rock-face sends back the deafening noise of a gunshot sent off course by the youngest of the whites, which has missed its target. The three migloos aim their rifles at us while our protector seems to be pleading on our behalf.

'OK, OK,' the eldest of the three calls out.

They move off backwards, their rifles still pointed at us. When they have disappeared, our eyes look down; the iron axe which the first white had thrown down, before following the others, is lying there. Overwhelmed, in despair, we fall to the rocky ground to wait for the signal announcing the departure of the sacrilegious thieves; a signal which the women who are hiding in a place where they can see everything yet not be seen, we are sure, will not fail to give.

What happened then? Too many emotions have muddled my mind for me to register the facts accurately.

On returning to the others, I see Inoa again, who is still shaking, giving me information about where the migloos are holding Natati captive. I see again the families, or what is left of them, vanishing one after the other into the landscape straight after the disaster. Without consultation, in blind panic. Once again I find myself all alone with Wongu.

The last to set out, we leave the site of the Woman Blue Tongue Lizard. We are going to hide some distance away. Crouching in the middle of an abundant wattle bush nourished by an underground source of water, we wait for the time to come when we may return to our normal state. Night falls. We sleep without a protective fire, waking a hundred times to listen, to assure ourselves that no spirit of our dead is going to come to torment us, to scream that they are in league with the subhumans.

The next day, we reach a decision. Our first objective: setting out in search of the three stolen women has become utterly important for the survivors. We know more or less exactly where to find Natati. She would tell us, no doubt, where the others had been taken.

So, for an entire moon, we have been making our way, doing our best to merge into the landscape. For an entire moon, we walked the whole day, practically without stopping, frugally feeding on berries and seeds. During an entire moon, we deprived ourselves of our evening fire. We felt cold. I saw Wongu lose the fine curve of his shoulders, his features are caving in. I read in his eyes that he saw the same in me. Nevertheless, we were lucky to be swallowed up by a country rich in water trees, succulent plants and the spouts of subterranean springs.

In the morning, following Inoa's instructions, we took an easterly direction, walking in the straight line between the exact point on the horizon where Okerka emerged and that of the Southern Cross. Our only thoughts turned on the necessity of moving as quickly as possible, without being seen, on the necessity to eat, to drink, the nagging question of whether we were following the correct route always at the back of our minds. Such was our anxiety that no memory or yearning for our transcendental journeys of the past surged within us: we had regressed to the condition of subhumans, solely preoccupied with sordid material difficulties.

The Man Moon had grown perfectly round again when, at long last, the prints of cows and calves sang of our coming success. At the same time, we became aware of the characteristic smells of a cattle station. From there, finding the wiltja where they were holding captive the one I loved proved child's play. As we were drawing nearer, the dogs barked. Prudently, we approached in a roundabout way.

Concealed behind the vegetation, we rested. Wongu handed me a plug, not of tobacco but of wild leaves hastily plucked the previous day and dried during our journey. Chewing them calmed us down. We returned to our normal state. I am concentrating, therefore, on sending a message to the prisoner straight away, hoping that the successive shocks she has just endured would not have deprived her of her power to know what others are thinking. Then we are lost in our thoughts.

This time we know nothing about the owners of the place. When do they sleep? When do they get up? We decide to risk attributing to them the same customs as the whites of the far west, and, during the night, to warn Natati in a much more ordinary way, in case our waves had not reached her. As we had done so many times, we will make use of the morning bird's call at the beginning of the night.

Having reached a decision, we wait. We think that we are safe. Only a dog would be able to discover us. But the whites rarely let their dogs loose.

Nevertheless, the storm continues to rage in my head. The waves of a thousand simultaneous thoughts collide, without any of them contriving to find a passage to my understanding. I breathe slowly, I relax my muscles, which have been tense for such a long time now. In the calm of the evening, my body and my mind become friends once more.

The dogs were stunned before they were able to bark a second time. Backs flattened against the timber sides of the whites' shelter, we whistle the joyous song of the morning bird. And we wait patiently for the migloos to go back to sleep at last. I take up the song again, on a lower note. In the distance, a cow lows and this stupid, unusual noise fills me with apprehension. The icy cold of the night gets the better of the way our bodies regulate their heat. Strangely, I seek no comfort from the sky studded with all its sparkling ornaments, I expect nothing of the Man Moon. Anguish robs me of all initiative. Wongu huddles against me so that the combined warmth of our bodies might overcome the cold better. Our eyes are nailed to the entrance.

That is when I capture the waves of my beloved. Slowly, I can feel them coming nearer. I see the door taking an eternity to swing, then open at last. Natati comes out. Why isn't she already next to me? What is going on? But here she is, her usual odour transformed by her sojourn in the world of the whites.

'I've shut them inside, just in case they wake up,' she says to me. 'Come over here. If there is an emergency, I know where we can hide.'

Silently, we vanish into the black night, the jewels in the sky have become our friends again.

22

With all our senses alert, we ran as fast as we could, ears straining to catch any sound of pursuit in the silence enveloping the night. Only the love call of a dingo, the screech of an owl, the air overhead agitated by the laborious flight of a bird of prey, and the cries of the curlew disturb, from time to time, the profound calm of the darkness.

When we had put a safe enough distance between us and the cattle station, we slackened our pace a little, changed direction and continued walking briskly.

It was not until the first pink glimmering of the imminent return of Okerka that we stopped at last, in a dry creek bed. We slid under a tangle of dead branches and tree trunks, which had been swept down by turbulent water during the last storm, coming to rest against a clump of dwarf wattle. Concealed in the scented tunnel of the flowering plant, I watched how Natati fell asleep straight away. I had trouble recognising her in her migloo clothes. Her smell made me uneasy. Why hadn't she tried to escape? For the first time, I experienced real jealousy; her sexual dealings with her husband, a man imposed on her by our people, had never caused me much irritation. That was what the laws of marriage demand, for the benefit of all. But with a subhuman! An inferior being, uncircumcised! Lost in my thoughts, I let Wongu go to sleep first for, naturally, we had decided to keep watch in turn.

I opened my eyes when the familiar, strident cries of a colony of thousands of pink cockatoos could be heard. The vapoury cloud of feathers flew past overhead. Glimpsed through the foliage, their soft pink breast feathers disappeared, suddenly replaced by the shiny grey of their backs as they started to wheel. As soon as they settled on the highest branches of three eucalypts, the silky white trunks growing in the red soil of the bank, the noise of their pecking increased. So much so that it roused Natati.

As soon as she came to her senses, she tore off the whites' clothes with enraged hands!

After burying them, she breathed more easily. And at last started to tell her story:

'One of the men who raped us, the youngest, came on me by surprise the following morning, as he had just rounded up his cows and calves. I can't remember arriving at the station, I was in too much shock. I only remember my astonishment at not being mistreated by the migloo who had taken me back to his place. He is a bachelor. Little by little, I got to know him. And I didn't understand how he could have acted so despicably. In fact, throughout the following days, he turned out to be quite a kind boy, even showing me a little respect. I agreed to perform sexual services for him; then, because I was bored to death, I helped him with his daily tasks. I looked after his birds, hens as they call them, which lay eggs regularly; I swept the ground outside the dwelling. None of that was unpleasant. And I ate well. Coming out of my shock, I thought things over for a long time. I came to the conclusion that no amount of resisting would help me, that it would serve me better to gain the trust of my abductor, to benefit from it one day. So I accepted my fate, one definitely less atrocious than I had feared. Except when his two accomplices on that accursed day came to visit him. Both arrived with a bottle in hand. Laughing, they put it down on the table, very proud of the gift they had brought. My migloo called out to me to bring glasses and, until evening, they kept drinking their strange-smelling brew. My gaoler quickly lost his mind. And his kindness! The more he drank, the more aggressive, the more ignoble he became. On the first visit, he forced me to drink with him. Very quickly, after a few mouthfuls of the horrible liquid, everything started spinning around me. I could not walk in a straight line. I couldn't even stand upright. I couldn't stop myself from bursting out with laughter. Suddenly, I was stunned, stupefied, panicking: I was seeing all the subhumans double! No matter how much I shut my eyes, opened them again, pinched myself, the image stayed the same: two heads, two bodies for one white. What was happening to me? Then nothing more, not one recollection of what happened after that. I woke the next morning with an unfamiliar ache in my head, a kind I'd never had.'

'And the other two?'

'The visitors were no longer there. And my subhuman did not seem too proud of what had happened the previous day. He even offered to let me go. Some time later, when his friends came back, I ran away, to hide far away in what they call the bush.'

'You must have become his friend, he must have been very fond of you if he offered to let you go.'

'Yes, I think he liked me very much. But for me he remained a rapist and a thief. But, as I told you, I had thought about it a good deal. Where could I go? I had no idea where I was! And the fear of being kidnapped by a white for the second time, by one less honourable than that one, robbed me of all initiative, all courage. Besides, I was certain that one day or another one of my own people would come to rescue me. So, I waited patiently. That's it. That is all I can say.'

'And our other sisters, what became of them?'

'I think they were taken much further east. I heard the two visitors saying the names Gunur and Kabbarti several times. I fancied I understood that they were working at the same cattle station. That's what makes me think that both live under the same roof.'

'Those two, did they often come to visit your migloo?'

'I saw them twice. They brought him provisions and what they called letters. They are very thin flexible pieces of white bark covered in symbols, which they interpret to find out what was happening to their people far from here.'

'I am going to go back to the station to wait for them,' Wongu says straight away. 'I'll follow their tracks as they are making their way home. I'll arrange for Kabbarti and Gunur to escape. I must. Our people need all their womenfolk.'

Our first impulse is to go with him. We discuss it for a long time. We reach the conclusion that it would be better for him to go by himself. In case of a mishap, he would be the only one to be captured. If all goes well, Gunur and Kabbarti, once set free, would catch up with us at the site of the Woman Blue Tongue Lizard. I would also go straight back there, with Natati, to wait for them and also to make sure that no group of the Grey Falcons or Sparrowhawks, who came by later on, have left behind any trace of their passing through. It is essential that we find out if our people have been reduced to the twenty or so people of the last meeting. We will wait for them at the site for two moons. Afterwards, on our own or with them, we will make for the nearest sacred place which, in normal times, should be the object of our next journey, in the hope of finding some of our people there.

So I set out with Natati. Without too much difficulty, we had been able to find food while we were waiting for our companions, who never came. When the Man Moon revived himself for the second time, we decided to take to the path again.

Throughout many other moons, we went from one sacred place to another, always hoping to find some of our brothers and sisters there. Alas! Each new stage of our journey brought us disappointment. Were we disenchanted? We were experiencing such passion!

A passion that called into play our physical strength, annihilating our powers of reflection, making us forget our fervent devotions. All the more because, on our own, it was impossible for us to worship the Ancestor of the sacred place as the rites demanded. Because for that you needed dances, songs, symbols and represenations, the gaze of others, everything that gives everyone access to the perfection of the model. By themselves, two people could not soar to the higher spheres.

Throughout this time, the path seemed to me like a long ribbon of mineral and fragrant vegetation, strewn with marvellous resting places for sexual frolicking. Forgotten, the superiority of the world of the Invisibles. Forgotten, meditation, transcendental communion with all that lives, my endeavours to reach the Universal, and, sometimes, to make a timid incursion into it. Forgotten, the hope of gaining a victory over myself each day. The tangible world fulfilled me. I no longer saw it as either treacherous or constricting.

Everything about my companion – her glances, her words, her actions – brought back to me a wonderful image of myself. In a truly earthly euphoria, unknown until then, I felt myself to be perfect.

Every evening, after the games of love, entwined next to our small fire under the vault of the myriad sparkling flames in the sky, caressed by the breath of Mother Earth, exulting in the immense plain of the desert, of which we were the centre, we tasted delicious repose. We felt so small, so lonely and yet so wonderfully powerful.

Then came the day when I began to ask myself how I could account for the emergence of my new outlook on life. How the sole presence of my companion came to translate me into such celestial spheres! Our love, by itself, seemed to make us recover the sacred nature of the two beings we were at Alcheringa Time. Was that possible?

A great sense of disarray overwhelmed me from time to time. Then it became more and more frequent. The breath of passion grew less violent. I started wanting to understand the reason for our love. What could I have really found in this woman who made me so forgetful of the essentials of what had always been my life?

Came the day when I asked myself whether I loved her for herself or if I loved her in order to love myself through loving her. What she confided in me made me understand that she was asking the same questions. She realised that a certain self-love had invaded her because of me. But she refused to accept such reductive notions. To make her happy, I insisted for her sake that it was nothing, that in each of us there was a better part, and that our two parts had been created so that we might fuse into one invincible force. We were alone in the world and, dare I say it, for a time that would suffice. Yes! We adored ourselves. But in some part of my mind, there was embedded the knowledge that only the Sacred Beings can support being adored.

One day, that knowledge broke free, to strike me

like a whip. I then realised that our love had fused our two spirits; that we made up only one and the same person. And that we had lost, in consequence, the 'you', the mirror image of what made us persist. I had become an 'I' without a 'you'! I could progress no further in my quest for the Ideal Being I had always been. So, Natati, with her body and soul, no longer satisfied me.

Our behaviour towards one another remained the same nevertheless, and our journey went on, wandering followed wandering without ever allowing us to meet one of our own people. We hoped then to find some of our foreign partners again, in places where trading usually took place. In vain. Were we the two sole survivors on the face of Mother Earth?

The rainy season took us back to the desert. Passion no longer exalted our daily life and we realised that it was growing more and more crude and joyless. Looking for food each day, isolated, apart, became enervating. Natati yearned for the time when laughter, jests and even occasional quarrels with her companions prevented boredom or lassitude from taking hold; and for my part, I yearned for my companions, hunting with whom had seemed like a game, now nothing but agonising uncertainty.

Our solitude became harder and harder to bear. Our mood more and more sombre. We started quarrelling. When we made up, it momentarily brought back the ecstasy of passion. Then we regressed.

A strange time! Days pass, monotonously, with difficulty. More than ever, the path is merely a common thoroughfare we were forced to follow. We are in haste to arrive at the site of the Woman Honey Ant, our last hope of finding our people again. The heat is overpowering, and we should stop to wait for cooler air. We can't make up our minds. We keep walking over the searing rocky ground of the mountain chain we must cross. Suddenly, without my anticipating it, the vision arrives, clear and precise. I cannot believe my eyes. But I see my own people, I catch their waves, such tranquil waves, and that is all I am able to retain.

'Natati, they are over there. I can see them. Sparrowhawks and Grey Falcons. They haven't all died. I can also see the little black-clad migloo.'

Without replying, Natati increases her pace. We are almost running. And I realise that I had lost my fine self-mastery, and that I have become just as thin-skinned as a subhuman.

However, after an instant, we must really stop if we do not want to become entirely dehydrated. In the half-light of the Monitor Lizard's cave, lying down on the the cool sand, we recover our strength, overcome by the optimism that rekindles our tenderness, if not our passion.

We reach the site the next evening.

A terrible memory.

Mashubi, the Sparrowhawks' Man of High Degree, is coming towards me. At first I do not recognise him. He is wearing a migloo jacket, which hides his body as well as the magnificent decorations scored on his chest and back. The clothing stops short at his waist, leaving his penis fully exposed; it flaps pathetically, at the least movement, against the cloth. Naked below this rig, his long legs seem too thin and ridiculous. I look at him in disbelief!

'Wait, you will understand: when we got here, we were safe at last. Alas! Too weak to find proper food. The little migloo was still living at the site – if you had seen how happy he was when he caught sight of us. With the help of his wives, he looked after the sickest, saved several babies from death. Then he offered us a deal: sing alleluias several times a day, stop going around naked, all that in exchange for his looking after us, giving us flour, sugar, salt, tobacco. What else could we do but accept? Straight away he handed out things to cover our bodies, these old 'skins'.

'You have to understand that he likes to see our bodies covered. You know well enough that the whites have a problem with their bodies! He wanted me to cover the rest, but my sex will not endure being enclosed. It gets irritated and has an unpleasant smell.'

I did not tell him that the jacket was enough to suffocate me with an unendurable stink!

We were soon surrounded by all the survivors, anxious for news; all of them looking so sadly ridiculous in their clothes: the women concealed their stomachs and sex under long, faded, half-tattered skirts or peculiar drawers reaching to mid thigh; some of the men covered their whole body, others their legs. All stank of stale sweat. This vision of horror left me speechless.

I can see again the day when, all alone, after long months of compromise, I abandoned my people, who had become poor wretches lacking all pride, physical or moral dignity: the price of their survival. Natati did not go with me. I did not ask her to.

I took up the path again, linking one journey to another, as was proper. My solitary wandering brought me back to the spiritual life. As before, I could identify myself with the Path, live out again the myths it was singing. In front of each nanja, intoxicated with solitude, I tried to sanctify myself with my songs, my dancing, by placing my hands on the sacred rock. From these short sojourns, I set out again, my soul at peace. Only for a little time, however.

In the dry season, I found myself again at the edge of the plant world, practically denuded of all of its animal life. I knew hunger, thirst. My body's weakness enhanced my ability to see faraway things. But I caught only visions of cows and calves. Also, I imagined that my obsession and hatred for those animals, added to my physical deterioration, disturbed the mechanism of being able to see into the distance. I attached little importance to it.

I was no more than half a day's journey from the site of the Woman Blue Tongue Lizard; the joy of being able soon to sanctify myself, of regaining strength through contact with the rock! Yes! I was almost happy at that moment. But not for long.

The breeze brings to my ears the lowing of bulls and cows. I think I am hallucinating. But that is what my eyes make out in the distance: their numberless shapes. I stop, petrified. A wave of despair hurls me to the ground. For a long while my mind is blank, it rolls around in nothingness in an attempt to refuse to acknowledge reality.

I get up again. I make my way, as if in a bad dream, to the middle of the plain strewn with those accursed animals. Suddenly, for the second time in a short while, my mind refuses to acknowledge what my eyes are seeing: a new cattle station rises a spear's throw from our sacred site.

For days, unseen, famished, miserable, I roam around the new despoilers. One night, I decide to steal a calf. A suicidal thing to do because I know well enough that migloos are keeping watch. But no reasoning can stop me. I must steal that damned animal, as much through hatred as from hunger. No matter that they might shoot me as if I were a kangaroo.

They did not fire at me. I am still surprised by that. Apparently, the whites do not shoot blacks as easily as all that. They caught me, treated me harshly, put clothes on me, then imprisoned me in the hollow trunk of a sacred old baobab. One of our ancient trees impregnated with the virtues of the Man Bandicoot Ancestor.

In the Sacred Place turned into a prison, I remained standing upright, without anything to eat or drink for two long days, chained by the neck to three other blacks of unknown origin. The subhumans did not know that we, True Men, and I the Great Initiate, who have acquired various degrees of Knowledge, did not fear physical hardships. Our civilisation had exploited that skill during our formation as True Men, preventing us, at the same time, from employing it against our own people. In truth, what interest is there in making someone else suffer when he knows how to overcome that suffering? When suffering is not a humiliation but, on the contrary, proof of courage? Thanks to that, my people have always been ignorant of the sadistic pleasure of torture. Torture, the most shameful act there is, actions dictated by the malevolent forces within humankind, until Knowledge neutralises them.

I ignored the metal encircling my neck, ignored the alien blacks against whom my body had to press, ignored the calls of nature that soiled my carnal sheath. In the course of those days, I allowed myself to be impregnated by the virtues deposited by the Ancestor in the fibres of that hollow trunk. During this confinement, I took up again the study of legends, which my memory sang effortlessly, at my beck and call. I recovered my moral strength as a Man of High Degree. Thanks to that, I slowly returned to the spiritual world.

As did my companions in misfortune.

Then one day, the subhumans made us all get into a

cart, bringing us here. To this tiny airless, sunless place where the beneficial waves of the world find it difficult to penetrate. Where I cannot breathe. This must be a dream, an evil dream!

23

Darkness falls on the little township in the back of beyond. Straight away, the cold of the night replaces the life-giving heat of day. The Man Moon slowly rises over the mountain range, hoping that the peculiar barracks, built of sturdy planks, with corrugated iron roofs, which he has to illuminate from now on, would have vanished. The faint light cast by a pub on the wide roadway which has been cut through the stony ground and the sand makes him smile, for he finds this strip of yellowish light pretty ridiculous; he alone has the power to illuminate the immensity of the night.

Laughter, quarrelling, the voices of drunkards rise towards him. And he is yearning for the serenity of former times, when brown men, the sole masters of this place, used to address him with respect. These new humans with white skin doubtless fail to recognise his importance! His beams flood through the high, narrow window of the gaol and caress the face of the elderly black man lying on the icy floor. They bring him back to reality.

In a daze, the prisoner stares at his surroundings. A flash of panic crosses his eyes. Suddenly, he is out of breath. His eyes are bulging; he is panting. He sits up, looks around him, gets to his feet. He stretches his arms, as if to push the walls away, breathes heavily, agitates the air in the cell, makes his back crash with all his might against one of the walls. He is suffocating. He cannot bear being shut in. With superhuman effort, he makes himself calm down. He breathes in deeply, slowly, exhales for a long time, starts all over again. His eyes grow alert once more. He has just reached a decision.

He takes off his cotton shirt, twisting it carefully into a cord. He takes off his trousers and does the same with it; then ties the two lengths end to end. Holding them in his hands, he goes over to the bench, pushes it to the middle of the cell, climbs on it, still holding on to the bulky cord. Without much difficulty, he throws it around a beam and fashions it into a dangling noose. Then he falls silent, perfectly still. Naked in the middle of the cell, he can feel again how the warm air hugs his brown skin. He delights in this for a brief instant before he begins to put his head in the noose.

'No! Not yet. Before leaving, I want to know. I have to know. Despite my degradation, I am still capable of leaping into the future.'

He sits on the table, banishes everything from his mind, all the sensations reaching him from the physical world. Through force of will, he even manages to forget his claustrophobia. Slowly, he channels the Cosmic Energy, and at last achieves total relaxation. His head drops to his chest. He is completely still. A few moments later, after the usual signs, he makes contact with the influx flowing down from the sky to the earth, bearing Knowledge, the primordial wisdom, that impalpable phenomenon which Men call the source of all that lives, that is to say the Mother or the Supreme Being. Then, as he had desired, images of things to come unfold behind his eyes.

He sees the streets of the little settlement turning into a small town. Some time ago, the invaders had lifted the ban on alcohol for Aborigines. Numerous young blacks, decked out as stockmen, each with a bottle of beer in his hand, stroll aimlessly on the black asphalt paving, a veritable rape of the subtle ochres of the landscape that the Ancestors had created. Several of these youths are staggering, talking in loud voices, without any restraint. They lean against a wall, throw their heads back to let that degrading brew flow down their throat more easily. Two whites are walking towards them. When they reach the young men, one spits at them while the other kicks and punches them to force them to go away. The young men endure the blows without protest. Staggering, a black woman rushes at them, babbling insanely. Her filthy, tattered, foul smelling clothes give her a pitiful look. Policemen arrive and, egged on by the two aggressive white men, drive the men and the woman with brutal force towards the gaol. The gaol which has become the largest building in the place!

In another large building, he sees the children of his people who have been taken away from their parents being brought up by missionaries, and held in ignorance of the wonders of their civilisation.

Without looking at them, the man forces the next images to unroll faster. Then, far in the distant future, he experiences the feelings of one of his own people who has become a person of mixed blood. He notices the exertions of this black brother, who is dedicated to forgetting the memory that had been passed onto him by his white father, to keep intact solely that of his black mother and experiences the ardent desire to become a descendant of the Guardians of Creation. He sees the man failing in his quest. Failing because the Instruction has been corrupted, and because the two memories, one inherited from the white world, the other from the black, are in conflict. The prisoner feels the anguish of his half-brother's distress. He can do nothing. Then he steps a little further into the future.

Here are his people trying to adapt to the invaders' ways. Sitting impassively at desks in bush schools, they receive sporadic instruction. They cannot see any purpose whatever behind this. How could these subjects, which shove them ceaselessly towards the material world, the world their people have struggled against since the dawn of Time, arouse their interest? But they are determined. They manage to assimilate some rudiments of the whites' knowledge, something of their behaviour, indispensable for entering into the new world. Some are able, therefore, to perform repetitive daily tasks for a short time; work that transforms a man little by little into a merely rational creature, letting all the gifts of the creator slumber; depriving him of time to meditate, without which his spirit cannot soar.

Between two alleluias, they hear the missionaries telling them and telling them again that the money people earn belongs to those that work; that such people have no obligation whatever to help all of their people, but only those who form a part of a man's blood family, his one true family!

So the young people try to persuade themselves that the Elders knew nothing, that individualism is by no means the most abject form of behaviour, that perhaps it carries some moral value. They try to forget age-old ethical imperatives. But, very swiftly, in spite of themselves, those imperatives worm their way into them, they return. Once again, they resume the immemorial customs of their people. It makes them happy: they share everything they own, all that they earn with all the members of their far-flung relationships, whatever merit these people might have. 'So did the Ancestor wish it,' their atavism whispers to them. The Ancestors, about whom they've heard a few vague things during the initial stages of an initiation that was never completed. And the whites come to the conclusion that these people are good for nothing.

The prisoner sees them trying to find something uplifting in the religious ceremonies of the Christians. They've tried Protestant services, Catholic masses, Baptist meetings. And all the others. Here or there, they look at the 'master of ceremonies', listen to bad music, stand, sit down, kneel, all on command, their gaze wandering, as do their thoughts, incapable of concentrating. No ceremony gives them what they are waiting for.

How could this merely passive presence lead to transcendence? To achieve that, they would need to participate physically, with their bodies, dancing to the appropriate rhythms. They would need songs, with the cadence and sonority inherited from the Knowledge of the beginning of Time. These alone have the power of allowing human beings to escape the evils of the temporal world, rather than prostrating themselves in front of images they had not 'created', the field of forces which no one has reactivated. They would need to make depictions for themselves of the image of Jesus Christ and of the others; to paint them with gestures through which all the waves of their faith would flow. They would need to be in the open air once more, and not with a roof over their heads, for roofs contain none of the virtues or powers of the Dreamtime. Nor should they have those completely 'empty', useless planks under their feet, or all the other barriers around them. How could the Sacred Energy penetrate all this to sanctify them, when everything is done to isolate them from it?

In truth, they have always known that the Supreme Being could not be enclosed in a human construction, whatever the name of that structure might be. Besides, was there not a white man once who was wise enough to say that nature is the finest place for prayer? Why was he not heeded?

Yes! They need active participation, as much as communion with their environment, communion with the infinite cosmos above their heads. They need the sanctuary of Mother Earth which alone can help them soar to the higher spheres.

Then the black man see the efforts his people make to live in dwellings. He sees them suffering from claustrophobia, and, after a certain time, they abandon living in enclosed places, give up being deprived of the beneficial influx of the sky and earth when they are asleep. He sees what contempt the conquerors have for such behaviour.

Here are his people trying to adapt themselves to money, those slips of paper or pieces of metal which give prestige and notoriety to those who know how to accumulate them. Without intrinsic human values ever coming into play in any way at all.

His people do not know how to manage money. The missionary teaches them how to do it. He teaches them to respect money. Money, the real God of the whites. Their only religion. Like the subhumans, they allow themselves to be corrupted by it. And by alcohol, in order to forget their aimless life on earth.

In despair, the man wants to find comfort once more in images of the wonders of his Mother Earth before he embarks on his voyage to the beyond. He transports himself to the site of the Man Kangaroo. There, the 'great man', the splendid red kangaroo, is still hunted. The population, preserved with so much care and respect since the dawn of Time, is in peril.

Further to the east, whites amuse themselves by

shooting the lazy koala, the little bear that does not drink: he sees hundreds of small bodies rotting in gumtrees, without anyone profiting from it.

At the site of the Woman Blue Tongue Lizard, a hellish plant has just arrived: blackberries. It spreads all over the rocky site, over the body of the Woman Ancestor, concealing it, holding captive the virtues irradiating the minerals. He sees the canes, enraged by the immense territory still to be conquered, making great strides, from east to west, killing on the way most of the plant-life of the Dreamtime. The thorny tangle injures some of the marsupials, deprives them of their usual shelter, chases away the bower bird that can no longer build its tunnel where it used to construct it in the past.

He sees thousand-year-old forests, all regarded as enemies by the white man, felled without hesitation. Millions of eucalypts are chopped down without a second thought in a fury of demented destruction. Splendid trees, indispensable for the reign of harmony among all living beings, including the mineral world; for, without forests, the mineral realm becomes unstable, slides and disappears for ever. And the memory of the Dreamtime impregnated within it.

In these vast denuded spaces, the old man sees millions of cattle and sheep making the flora of the Dreamtime disappear inside their stomachs. He sees koalas and all the little marsupials of the forest dying out as their habitat is transformed.

Here are the whites, longing to see animals that are considered pests in their own country, introducing rabbits into the land of the eternal Dreamtime. An animal just as diabolic as blackberries in its effect on the land. In a few years, they will conquer the entire continent, squatting in the holes of the shy platypus, reducing the habitats of small marsupials, eating up, almost to the last morsel, the plant life of the great arid plain of the Centre, as much as of the coastal regions. Very quickly, the rabbit becomes a dangerous rival to kangaroos, which have trouble enough contending with cows and calves. And the sheep. Rabbits breed at an unimaginable pace.

Without the benefit of any sacred ceremony! Little by little, the blacks adapt to eating rabbits. Here they are, now satisfied with rabbits, now disgusted by them. They dream of a fine roasted kangaroo tail. They are not hungry, but they are not happy. How could they be, since they know nothing about the origins of this animal, nothing about its Ancestor, having no affective connections with it. How to respect it, to thank it as they trap rabbits coming out of their burrows, for being prepared to die in order for them to live?

Other images of the future make him see groups of white men, yellow-skinned men, simultaneously spreading all over his land. All the dregs of humanity converge on the one place. Some of his own people mingle with these new invaders. He sees blacks, whites, yellow people stealing and fighting and killing each other. He sees famine hovering over their camp and, a little time later, blacks, whites, yellow skinned people eating each other's flesh. The old man does not understand the reasons behind such a frenzy of violence and blood, the reason for such collective insanity. But here are lumps of gold extracted from the red ochre, from the blood of the sacred Women of Alcheringa Time. He sighs when he come to understand that all this evil is unleashed because of the whites' lust for a 'nugget' or a little bit of yellow dust! For gold! Greed which no social structure can constrain, which only the derided sacred Commandments, overlooked or forgotten long ago, vainly attempt to neutralise.

The images that follow teach him that, in the new world

established in his land, gold serves as a means of barter. It is transformed into money. And only money opens the doors of respectability and power. He shudders with horror, but wants to know whether anyone among the whites wants better things. Then he sees the Wise Men of this degraded world, people lacking all ambition who most often live in solitude, preoccupied with discovering their ideal selves. Without the mirror of other people, alone, self-absorbed, as individualists. Without any great chance of success. He also sees communities of white men living in ivory towers, without sharing their skill, or only feigning to do so.

Implacably, the future projects images of mechanical monsters which, in a din of hellish torment, tear out the entrails of the paths at precisely the most sacred places. The double rape of Mother Earth! A Mother Earth so rich that she does not end up entirely raped, torn, fractured, riddled with gigantic cavities. Violated in the deepest of her entrails, in her specificity, so that the whites can seize for themselves all the minerals slumbering within her, those supports of memory, of the powers and virtues of the Mother which these minerals have been diffusing since the dawn of Time.

Once more, the man thinks that unfamiliarity with Instruction and, along with that, ignorance of the peril of interfering with Creation, could have allowed the insane evolution of these triumphant techniques, then the folly of playing fast and loose with them.

He sighs, but wants to go even further. He casts himself into the south-west of his beautiful land, there where he used to meditate so well, there where his communion with the Universe became most intense.

Here is a blinding flash of light spreading over his beloved plain. He becomes aware of a shock wave, then of the fury of a tempest like those at the beginning of

Creation. A huge pink mushroom with red highlights rises to the sky. In the places around it, the heat scorches rare plants, transforms them into cinders, brutally incinerating the animals and the Dreamtime brothers which happened to be there.

The old man would like to make the vision stop, but the images of the future continue to unfold. Later, he sees his own people making their way along the sacred path where Life can no longer exist where healthy men are irradiated through contact. He sees stillborn infants, or deformed ones, deaths by contamination increasing. The most secret of myths, those which he was not able to understand fully until he had studied them for many years before he could untangle all the symbols concealed behind other symbols, come into his mind. 'They have done it!'

The prisoner shudders, them murmurs:

'No, I want to know no more. I want to believe that some will survive. That they will understand. And will no longer have any choice. They will realise that they are merely one cog among the myriad cogs of the mechanism of Life. And not the masters in charge of making it work. Like us, with us, they will become the Guardians of Creation.'

The black man gets to his feet with great care. He puts his head in the swaying noose, and kicks the table away with force. His last thought plunges him into the eternal Dreamtime which, he is sure, will one day revive again.

Without regret, his yowie takes flight towards the world of the Invisibles, guided by Bahloo, the Man Moon, who is smiling on him from high.

Translator's Note

In this English translation of *Alcheringa*, I have attempted to reproduce as faithfully as possible the characteristic flavour of the original. Because it was intended in the first place for a French reading public, the novel seeks to render the social organisation, religious beliefs and customs of a distant, perhaps exotic world comprehensible to those readers, and also to indicate affinities with European modes of thought and religious and philosophical speculation. As the translator of *Alcheringa*, I have tried to preserve, as far as practicable, those elements of Betty Villeminot's book.

Andrew Riemer

Acknowledgements

I would like to thank my husband Jacques Villeminot, my daughter Patricia and all those friends who knew how to encourage me with their advice, and their criticism wherever necessary, as I was finishing this novel.

I would express my gratitude to the late Professor AP Elkin of the University of Sydney who advised us in 1955, and thanks to whom we were able to spend some time with a group of Central Australian Aborigines.

I owe a debt of gratitude to the work of two pioneer Australian anthropologists, Spencer and Gillen, to Alain Testart for his analysis of their work; equally to Arnold van Gennep for his book *Mythes et Légendes australiennes*. Extracts from this study and paraphrases of them have proved indispensable in my attempts to glimpse the richness of the poetic imagination of Aboriginal people and of their knowledge and beliefs. I am equally indebted to Roland and Catherine Berndt, Mircea Eliade, WEH Stanner and the other writers whose work I have consulted.

I wish to express my particular gratitude to Henry Reynolds, whose remarkable research into Aboriginal resistance against British invaders enriched this novel with certain then little-known historical facts concerning the first Australians.

I have fond memories of our friend the late Milton Liddle, an Arunda-Australian from Alice Springs, who, thanks to his knowledge, made us discover the red heart of his country at the time when Uluru had just been discovered by a handful of white people.